SHADOW GAMES

Half of winning a battle is showmanship.

The pink point grew up fast and shed light on the river. There must have been forty boats sneaking towards us. They had extended their croc hide protection in hopes of shedding fire bombs.

I was glowing and breathing fire. Bet I made a hell of a sight from over there.

The nearest boats were ten feet away. I saw the ladder boxes and grinned behind my croc teeth. I had guessed right.

I threw my hands up, then down. A single bomb arced out to shatter the nearest boat.

The trap was almost too good. Fire sucked most of the air away and heated what was left till it was almost unbearable. The survivors had no stomach left for combat. That was the first wave, a distant rattle announced the second wave. I was laying for these guys, too.

GLEN COOK

THE FOURTH CHRONICLE OF THE BLACK COMPANY

SHADOW GAMES

FIRST BOOK
OF THE SOUTH

TOR
fantasy

A TOM DOHERTY ASSOCIATES BOOK
NEW YORK

SHADOW GAMES

Copyright © 1989 by Glen Cook

A TOR Book
Published by Tom Doherty Associates, Inc.
49 West 24 Street
New York, NY 10010

Cover art by Keith Berdak

ISBN: 0-812-53382-8   Can. ISBN: 0-812-53381-X

Library of Congress Catalog Card Number: 88-51639

First edition: June 1989

Printed in the United States of America

0 9 8 7 6 5 4 3

Got to be for Harriet McDougal,
whose gentle hands
guided Croaker and the Company
out of the darkness

With Special Thanks to
Lee Childs of North Hollywood,
for historical research
and valued suggestions

Chapter One:
THE CROSSROADS

We seven remained at the crossroads, watching the dust from the eastern way. Even irrepressible One-Eye and Goblin were stricken by the finality of the hour. Otto's horse whickered. He closed her nostrils with one hand, patted her neck with the other, quieting her. It was a time for contemplation, the final emotional milemark of an era.

Then there was no more dust. They were gone. Birds began to sing, so still did we remain. I took an old notebook from my saddlebag, settled in the road. In a shaky hand I wrote: *The end has come. The parting is done. Silent, Darling, and the Torque brothers have taken the road to Lords. The Black Company is no more.*

Yet I will continue to keep the Annals, if only because a habit of twenty-five years is so hard to break. And, who knows? Those to whom I am obliged to carry them may find the account interesting. The heart is stilled but the corpse stumbles on. The Company is dead in fact but not in name.

And we, O merciless gods, stand witness to the power of names.

I replaced the book in my saddlebag. "Well, that's that." I swatted the dust off the back of my lap, peered down our own road into tomorrow. A low line of greening hills formed a fencerow over which sheeplike tufts began to bound. "The quest begins. We have time to cover the first dozen miles."

That would leave only seven or eight thousand more. I surveyed my companions.

One-Eye was the oldest by a century, a wizard, wrinkled and black as a dusty prune. He wore an eyepatch and a floppy, battered black felt hat. That hat seemed to suffer every conceivable misfortune, yet survived every indignity.

Likewise Otto, a very ordinary man. He had been wounded a hundred times and had survived. He almost believed himself favored of the gods.

Otto's sidekick was Hagop, another man with no special color. But another survivor. My glance surprised a tear.

Then there was Goblin. What is there to say of Goblin? The name says it all, and yet nothing? He was another wizard, small, feisty, forever at odds with One-Eye, without whose enmity he would curl up and die. He was the inventor of the frog-faced grin.

We five have been together twenty-some years. We have grown old together. Perhaps we know one another too well. We form limbs of a dying organism. Last of a mighty, magnificent, storied line. I fear we, who look more like bandits than the best soldiers in the world, denigrate the memory of the Black Company.

Two more. Murgen, whom One-Eye sometimes calls Pup, was twenty-eight. The youngest. He joined the Company after our defection from the empire. He was a quiet man of many sorrows, unspoken, with no one and nothing but the Company to call his own, yet an outside and lonely man even here.

As are we all. As are we all.

Lastly, there was Lady, who used to be the Lady. Lost Lady, beautiful Lady, my fantasy, my terror, more silent than Murgen, but from a different cause: despair. Once she had it all. She gave it up. Now she has nothing.

Nothing she knows to be of value.

That dust on the Lords road was gone, scattered by a chilly breeze. Some of my beloved had departed my life forever.

No sense staying around. "Cinch them up," I said, and set an example. I tested the ties on the pack animals. "Mount up. One-Eye, you take the point."

Finally, a hint of spirit as Goblin carped, "I have to eat *his* dust?" If One-Eye had point that meant Goblin had rearguard. As wizards they were no mountain movers, but they were useful. One fore and one aft left me feeling far more comfortable.

"About his turn, don't you think?"

"Things like that don't deserve a turn," Goblin said. He tried to giggle but only managed a smile that was a ghost of his usual toadlike grin.

One-Eye's answering glower was not much pumpkin, either. He rode out without comment.

Murgen followed fifty yards behind, a twelve-foot lance rigidly upright. Once that lance had flaunted our standard. Now it trailed four feet of tattered black cloth. The symbolism lay on several levels.

We knew who we were. It was best that others did not. The Company had too many enemies.

Hagop and Otto followed Murgen, leading pack animals. Then came Lady and I, also with tethers behind. Goblin trailed us by seventy yards. And thus we always traveled for we were at war with the world. Or maybe it was the other way around.

I might have wished for outriders and scouts, but there was a limit to what seven could accomplish. Two wizards were the next best thing.

We bristled with weaponry. I hoped we looked as easy as a hedgehog does to a fox.

The eastbound road dropped out of sight. I was the only one to look back in hopes Silent had found a vacancy in his heart. But that was a vain fantasy. And I knew it.

In emotional terms we had parted ways with Silent

and Darling months ago, on the blood-sodden, hate-drenched battleground of the Barrowland.

A world was saved there, and so much else lost. We will live out our lives wondering about the cost.

Different hearts, different roads.

"Looks like rain, Croaker," Lady said.

Her remark startled me. Not that what she said was not true. It did look like rain. But it was the first observation she had volunteered since that dire day in the north.

Maybe she was going to come around.

Chapter Two:
THE ROAD SOUTH

"The farther we come, the more it looks like spring,"
One-Eye observed. He was in a good mood.

I caught the occasional glint of mischief brewing in
Goblin's eyes too, lately. Before long those two would
find some excuse to revive their ancient feud. The
magical sparks would fly. If nothing else, the rest of us
would be entertained.

Even Lady's mood improved, though she spoke little
more than before.

"Break's over," I said. "Otto, kill the fire. Goblin.
Your point." I stared down the road. Another two weeks
and we would be near Charm. I had not yet revealed
what we had to do there.

I noticed buzzards circling. Something dead ahead,
near the road.

I do not like omens. They make me uncomfortable.
Those birds made me uncomfortable.

I gestured. Goblin nodded. "I'll go now," he said.
"Stretch it out a bit."

"Right."

Murgen gave him an extra fifty yards. Otto and Hagop
gave Murgen additional room. But One-Eye kept pressing up behind Lady and I, rising in his stirrups, trying to
keep an eye on Goblin. "Got a bad feeling about that,
Croaker," he said. "A bad feeling."

Though Goblin raised no alarm, One-Eye was right. Those doombirds did mark a bad thing.

A fancy coach lay overturned beside the road. Two of its team of four had been killed in the traces, probably because of injuries. Two animals were missing.

Around the coach lay the bodies of six uniformed guards and the driver, and that of one riding horse. Within the coach were a man, a woman, and two small children. All murdered.

"Hagop," I said, "see what you can read from the signs. Lady. Do you know these people? Do you recognize their crest?" I indicated fancywork on the coach door.

"The Falcon of Rail. Proconsul of the empire. But he isn't one of those. He's older, and fat. They might be family."

Hagop told us, "They were headed north. The brigands overtook them." He held up a scrap of dirty cloth. "They didn't get off easy themselves." When I did not respond he drew my attention to the scrap.

"Grey boys," I mused. Grey boys were imperial troops of the northern armies. "Bit out of their territory."

"Deserters," Lady said. "The dissolution has begun."

"Likely." I frowned. I had hoped decay would hold off till we got a running start.

Lady mused, "Three months ago travelling the empire was safe for a virgin alone."

She exaggerated. But not much. Before the struggle in the Barrowland consumed them, great powers called the Taken watched over the provinces and requited unlicensed wickedness swiftly and ferociously. Still, in any land or time, there are those brave or fool enough to test the limits, and others eager to follow their example. That process was accelerating in an empire bereft of its cementing horrors.

I hoped their passing had not yet become a general suspicion. My plans depended on the assumption of old guises.

"Shall we start digging?" Otto asked.

"In a minute," I said. "How long ago did it happen, Hagop?"

"Couple of hours."

"And nobody's been along?"

"Oh, yeah. But they just went around."

"Must be a nice bunch of bandits," One-Eye mused. "If they can get away with leaving bodies laying around."

"Maybe they're supposed to be seen," I said. "Could be they're trying to carve out their own barony."

"Likely," Lady said. "Ride carefully, Croaker."

I raised an eyebrow.

"I don't want to lose you."

One-Eye cackled. I reddened. But it was good to see some life in her.

We buried the bodies but left the coach. Civilized obligation fulfilled, we resumed our journey.

Two hours later Goblin came riding back. Murgen stationed himself where he could be seen on a curve. We were in a forest now, but the road was in good repair, with the woods cleared back from its sides. It was a road upgraded for military traffic.

Goblin said, "There's an inn up ahead. I don't like its feel."

Night would be along soon. We had spent the afternoon planting the dead. "It look alive?" The countryside had gotten strange after the burying. We met no one on the road. The farms near the woods were abandoned.

"Teeming. Twenty people in the inn. Five more in the stables. Thirty horses. Another twenty people out in the woods. Forty more horses penned there. A lot of other livestock, too."

The implications seemed obvious enough. Pass by, or meet trouble head-on?

The debate was brisk. Otto and Hagop said straight in. We had One-Eye and Goblin if it got hairy.

One-Eye and Goblin did not like being put on the spot.

I demanded an advisory vote. Murgen and Lady abstained. Otto and Hagop were for stopping. One-Eye and Goblin eyeballed one another, each waiting for the other to jump so he could come down on the opposite side.

"We go straight at it, then," I said. "These clowns are going to split but still make a majority for . . ." Whereupon the wizards ganged up and voted to jump in just to make a liar out of me.

Three minutes later I caught my first glimpse of the ramshackle inn. A hardcase stood in the doorway, studying Goblin. Another sat in a rickety chair, tilted against the wall, chewing a stick or piece of straw. The man in the doorway withdrew.

Grey boys Hagop had called the bandits whose handiwork we encountered on the road. But grey was the color of uniforms in the territories whence we came. In Forsberger, the most common language in the northern forces, I asked the man in the chair, "Place open for business?"

"Yeah." Chair-sitter's eyes narrowed. He wondered.

"One-Eye. Otto. Hagop. See to the animals." Softly, I asked, "You catching anything, Goblin?"

"Somebody just went out the back. They're on their feet inside. But it don't look like trouble right away."

Chair-sitter did not like us whispering. "How long you reckon on staying?" he asked. I noted a tatoo on one wrist, another giveaway betraying him as an immigrant from the north.

"Just tonight."

"We're crowded, but we'll fit you in somehow." He was a cool one.

Trapdoor spiders, these deserters. The inn was their base, the place where they marked out their victims. But they did their dirt on the road.

Silence reigned inside the inn. We examined the men there as we entered, and a few women who looked badly used. They did not ring true. Wayside inns usually are family-run establishments, infested with kids and old folks and all the oddities in between. None of those were evident. Just hard men and bad women.

There was a large table available near the kitchen door. I seated myself with my back to a wall. Lady plopped down beside me. I sensed her anger. She was not accustomed to being looked at the way these men were looking at her.

She remained beautiful despite road dirt and rags.

I rested a hand upon one of hers, a gesture of restraint rather than of possession.

A plump girl of sixteen with haunted bovine eyes came to ask how many we were, our needs in food and quarters, whether bath water should be heated, how long we meant to tarry, what was the color of our coin. She did it listlessly but right, as though beyond hope, filled only with dread of the cost of doing it wrong.

I intuited her as belonging to the family who rightfully operated the inn.

I tossed her a gold piece. We had plenty, having looted certain imperial treasures before departing the Barrowland. The flicker of the spinning coin sparked a sudden glitter in the eyes of men pretending not to be watching.

One-Eye and the others clumped in, dragged up chairs. The little black man whispered, "There's a big stir out in the woods. They have plans for us." A froggish grin yanked at the left corner of his mouth. I gathered he might have plans of his own. He likes to let the bad guys ambush themselves.

"There's plans and plans," I said. "If they are bandits, we'll let them hang themselves."

He wanted to know what I meant. My schemes sometimes got more nasty than his. That is because I lose my sense of humor and just go for maximum dirt.

We rose before dawn. One-Eye and Goblin used a favorite spell to put everyone in the inn into a deep sleep.

Then they slipped out to repeat their performance in the
woods. The rest of us readied our animals and gear. I had
a small skirmish with Lady. She wanted me to do
something for the women kept captive by the brigands.

"If I try to right every wrong I run into, I'll never get to
Khatovar."

She did not respond. We rode out minutes later.

One-Eye said we were near the end of the forest. "This
looks as good a place as any," I said. Murgen, Lady, and I
turned into the woods west of the road. Hagop, Otto, and
Goblin turned east. One-Eye just turned around and
waited.

He was doing nothing apparent. Goblin was busy, too.

"What if they don't come?" Murgen asked.

"Then we guessed wrong. They're not bandits. I'll
send them an apology on the wind."

Nothing got said for a while. When next I moved
forward to check the road One-Eye was no longer alone.
A half-dozen horsemen backed him. My heart twisted.
His phantoms were all men I had known, old comrades,
long dead.

I retreated, more shaken than I had expected. My
emotional state did not improve. Sunlight dropped
through the forest canopy to dapple the doubles of more
dead friends. They waited with shields and weapons
ready, silently, as befit ghosts.

They were not ghosts, really, except in my mind. They
were illusions crafted by One-Eye. Across the road
Goblin was raising his own shadow legion.

Given time to work, those two were quite the artists.
There was no doubt, now, even who Lady was.

"Hoofbeats," I said, needlessly. "They're coming."

My stomach turned over. Had I bet to an inside
straight? Taken too long a shot? If they chose to fight . . .
If Goblin or One-Eye faltered . . .

"Too late for debate, Croaker."

I looked at Lady, a glowing memory of what she had been. She was smiling. She knew my mind. How many times had she been there herself, albeit on a grander game board?

The brigands pounded down the aisle formed by the road. And reined in in confusion when they saw One-Eye awaiting them.

I started forward. All through the woods ghost horses moved with me. There was harness noise, brush noise. Nice touch, One-Eye. What you call verisimilitude.

There were twenty-five bandits. They wore ghastly expressions. Their faces went paler still when they spied Lady, when they saw the specter-banner on Murgen's lance.

The Black Company was pretty well known.

Two hundred ghost bows bent. Fifty hands tried to find some sky-belly to grab. "I suggest you dismount and disarm," I told their captain. He gulped air a few times, considered the odds, did as directed. "Now clear away from the horses. You naughty boys."

They moved. Lady made a gesture. The horses all turned and trotted toward Goblin, who was their real motivator. He let the animals pass. They would return to the inn, to proclaim the terror ended.

Slick. Oh, slick. Not even a hangnail. That was the way we did it in the old days. Maneuver and trickery. Why get yourself hurt if you can whip them with a shuffle and con?

We got the prisoners into a rope coffle where they could be adequately controlled, then headed south. The brigands were greatly exercised when Goblin and One-Eye relaxed. They didn't think it was fair of us.

Two days later we reached Vest. With One-Eye and Goblin again supporting her grand illusion, Lady remanded the deserters to the justice of the garrison commander. We only had to kill two of them to get them there.

Something of a distraction along the road. Now there was none, and Charm drew closer by the hour. I had to face the fact that trouble beckoned.

The bulk of the Annals, which my companions believed to be in my possession, remained in Imperial hands. They had been captured at Queen's Bridge, an old defeat that still stings. I was promised their return shortly before the crisis in the Barrowland. But that crisis prevented their delivery. Afterward, there was nothing to do but go fetch them myself.

Chapter Three:
A TAVERN IN TAGLIOS

Willow scrunched a little more comfortably into his chair. The girls giggled and dared one another to touch his cornsilk hair. The one with the most promising eyes reached, ran her fingers down its length. Willow looked across the room, winked at Cordy Mather.

This was the life—till their fathers and brothers got wise. This was every man's dream—with the same old lethal risks a-sneaking. If it kept on, and did not catch up, he'd soon weigh four hundred pounds and be the happiest slug in Taglios.

Who would have thought it? A simple tavern in a straitlaced burg like this. A hole in the wall like those that graced every other street corner back home, here such a novelty they couldn't help getting rich. If the priests didn't get over their inertia and shove a stick into the spokes.

Of course, it helped them being exotic outlanders that the whole city wanted to see. Even those priests. And their little chickies. Especially their little brown daughters.

A long, insane journey getting here, but worth every dreadful step now.

He folded his hands upon his chest and let the girls take what liberties they wanted. He could handle it. He could put up with it.

He watched Cordy tap another barrel of the bitter, third-rate green beer he'd brewed. These Taglian fools paid three times what it was worth. What kind of a place never ran into beer before? Hell. The kind of place guys with no special talents and itchy feet dream of finding.

Cordy brought a mug over. He said, "Swan, this keeps on, we're going to have to hire somebody to help me brew. We're going to be tapped out in a couple days."

"Why worry? How long can it last? Those priest characters are starting to smolder now. They're going to start looking for some excuse to shut us down. Worry about finding another racket as sweet, not about making more beer faster. What?"

"What do you mean, what?"

"You got a grim look all of a sudden."

"The blackbird of doom just walked in the front door."

Willow twisted so he could see that end of the room. Sure enough, Blade had come home. Tall, lean, ebony, head shaved to a polish, muscles rippling with the slightest movement, he looked like some kind of gleaming statue. He looked around without approval. Then he strode to Willow's table, took a seat. The girls gave him the eye. He was as exotic as Willow Swan.

"Come to collect your share and tell us how lousy we are, corrupting these children?" Willow asked.

Blade shook his head. "That old spook Smoke's having dreams again. The Woman wants you."

"Shit." Swan dropped his feet to the floor. Here was the fly in the ointment. The Woman wouldn't leave them alone. "What is it this time? What's he doing? Hemp?"

"He's a wizard. He don't need to do nothing to get obnoxious."

"Shit," Swan said again. "What do you think, we just do a fade-out here? Sell the rest of Cordy's rat piss and head back up the river?"

A big, slow grin spread across Blade's face. "Too late, boy. You been chosen. You can't run fast enough. That

Smoke, he might be a joke if he was to open shop up where you came from, but around here he's the bad boss spook pusher. You try to head out, you're going to find your toes tied in knots."

"That the official word?"

"They didn't say it that way. That's what they meant."

"So what did he dream this time? Why drag us in?"

"Shadowmasters. More Shadowmasters. Been a big meet at Shadowcatch, he says. They're going to stop talking and start doing. He says Moonshadow got the call. Says we'll be seeing them in Taglian territory real soon now."

"Big deal. Been trying to sell us that since the day we got here, practically."

Blade's face lost all its humor. "It was different this time, man. There's scared and scared, you know what I mean? And Smoke and the Woman was the second kind this time. And it ain't just Shadowmasters they got on the brain now. Said to tell you the Black Company is coming. Said you'd know what that means."

Swan grunted as if hit in the stomach. He stood, drained the beer Cordy had brought, looked around as if unable to believe what he saw. "Damned-foolest thing I ever heard, Blade. The Black Company? Coming here?"

"Said that's what's got the Shadowmasters riled, Willow. Said they're rattled good. This's the last free country north of them, under the river. And you know what's on the other side of Shadowcatch."

"I don't believe it. You know how far they'd have to come?"

"About as far as you and Cordy." Blade had joined Willow and Cordwood Mather two thousand miles into their journey south.

"Yeah. You tell me, Blade. Who in the hell besides you and me and Cordy would be crazy enough to travel that far without any reason?"

"They got a reason. According to Smoke."

"Like what?"

"I don't know. You go up there like the Woman says. Maybe she'll tell you."

"I'll go. We'll all go. Just to stall. And first chance we get we're going to get the hell out of Taglios. If they got the Shadowmasters stirred up down there, and the Black Company coming in, I don't want to be anywhere around."

Blade leaned back so one of the girls could wiggle in closer. His expression was questioning.

Swan said, "I seen what those bastards could do back home. I saw Roses caught between them and . . . Hell. Just take my word for it, Blade. Big mojo, and all bad. If they're coming for real, and we're still around when they show, you might end up wishing we'd let those crocs go ahead and snack on you."

Blade never had been too clear on why he had been thrown to the crocodiles. And Willow was none too clear on why he had talked Cordy into dragging him out and taking him along. Though Blade had been a right enough guy since. He'd paid back the debt.

"I think you ought to help them, Swan," Blade said. "I like this town. I like the people. Only thing wrong with them is they don't have sense enough to burn all the temples down."

"Damnit, Blade, I ain't the guy can help."

"You and Cordy are the only ones around who know anything about soldiering."

"I was in the army for two months. I never even learned how to keep in step. And Cordy don't have the stomach for it anymore. All he wants is to forget that part of his life."

Cordy had overheard most of what had been said. He came over. "I'm not that bad off, Willow. I don't object to soldiering when the cause is right. I just was with the wrong bunch up there. I'm with Blade. I like Taglios. I like the people. I'm willing to do what I can to see they don't get worked over by the Shadowmasters."

"You heard what he said? The Black Company?"

"I heard. I also heard him say they want to talk about it. I think we ought to go find out what's going on before we run our mouths and say what we're not going to do."

"All right. I'm going to change. Hold the fort, and all that, Blade. Keep your mitts off the one in the red. I got first dibs." He stalked off.

Cordy Mather grinned. "You're catching on how to handle Willow, Blade."

"If this's going down the way I think, he don't need handling. He'll be the guy out front when they try to stop the Shadowmasters. You could roast him in coals and he'd never admit it, but he's got a thing for Taglios."

Cordy Mather chuckled. "You're right. He's finally found him a home. And no one is going to move him out. Not the Shadowmasters *or* the Black Company."

"They as bad as he lets on?"

"Worse. Lots worse. You take all the legends you ever heard back home, and everything you heard tell around here, and anything you can imagine, and double it, and maybe you're getting close. They're mean and they're tough and they're good. And maybe the worst thing about them is that they're tricky like you can't imagine tricky. They've been around four, five hundred years, and no outfit lasts that long without being so damned nasty even the gods don't screw with them."

"Mothers, hide your babies," Blade said. "Smoke had him a dream."

Cordy's face darkened. "Yeah. I've heard tell wizards maybe make things come true by dreaming them first. Maybe we ought to cut Smoke's throat."

Willow was back. He said, "Maybe we ought to find out what's going on before we do anything."

Cordy chuckled. Blade grinned. Then they began shooing the marks out of the tavern—each making sure an appointment was understood by one or more of the young ladies.

Chapter Four:
THE DARK TOWER

I piddled around another five days before working myself up to a little after-breakfast skull session. I introduced the subject in a golden-tongued blurt: "Our next stop-over will be the Tower."

"What?"

"Are you crazy, Croaker?"

"Knew we should have kept an eye on him after the sun went down." Knowing glances Lady's way. She stayed out of it.

"I thought *she* was going with *us*. Not the other way around."

Only Murgen did not snap up a membership in the bitch-of-the-minute club. Good lad, that Murgen.

Lady, of course, already knew a stopover was needed.

"I'm serious, guys," I said.

If I wanted to be serious, One-Eye would be, too. "Why?" he asked.

I sort of shrank. "To pick up the Annals I left behind at Queen's Bridge." We got caught good, there. Only because we were the best, and desperate, and sneaky, had we been able to crack the imperial encirclement. At the cost of half the Company. There were more important concerns at the time than books.

"I thought you already got them."

"I asked for them and was told I could have them. But

18

we were busy at the time. Remember? The Dominator?
The Limper? Toadkiller Dog? All that lot? There wasn't
any chance to actually lay hands on them."

Lady supported me with a nod. Getting really into the
spirit, there.

Goblin pasted on his most ferocious face. Made him
look like a saber-toothed toad. "Then you knew about
this clean back before we ever left the Barrowland."

I admitted that that was true.

"You goatfu—Lover. I bet you've spent all this time
concocting some half-assed off-the-wall plan that's guar-
anteed to get us all killed."

I confessed that that was mostly true, too. "We're
going to ride up there like we own the Tower. You're
going to make the garrison think Lady is still number
one."

One-Eye snorted, stomped off to the horses. Goblin
got up and stared down at me. And stared some more.
And sneered. "We're just going to strut in and snatch
them, eh? Like the Old Man used to say, audacity and
more audacity." He did not ask his real question.

Lady answered it for him, anyway. "I gave my word."

Goblin did not mouth the next question, either. No
one did. And Lady left it hanging.

It would be easy for her to job us. She could keep her
word and have us for breakfast afterward. If she wanted.

My plan (sic), boiled down, depended entirely on my
trust in her. It was a trust my comrades did not share.

But they do, however foolishly, trust *me*.

The Tower at Charm is the largest single construction
in the world, a featureless black cube five hundred feet to
the dimension. It was the first project undertaken by the
Lady and the Taken after their return from the grave, so
many lifetimes ago. From the Tower the Taken had
marched forth, and raised their armies, and conquered
half the world. Its shadow still fell upon half the earth,
for few knew that the heart and blood of the empire had

been sacrificed to buy victory over a power older and darker still.

There is but one ground-level entrance to the Tower. The road leading to it runs as straight as a geometrician's dream. It passes through parklike grounds that only someone who had been there could believe was the site of history's bloodiest battle.

I had been there. I remembered.

Goblin and One-Eye and Hagop and Otto remembered, too. Most of all, One-Eye remembered. It was on this plain that he destroyed the monster that had murdered his brother.

I recalled the crash and tumult, the screams and terrors, the horrors wrought by wizards at war, and not for the first time I wondered, "Did they really all die here? They went so easily."

"Who you talking about?" One-Eye demanded. He did not need to concentrate on keeping Lady englamored.

"The Taken. Sometimes I think about how hard it was to get rid of the Limper. Then I wonder how so many Taken could have gone down so easy, a whole bunch in a couple days, almost never where I could see it. So sometimes I get to suspecting there was maybe some faking and two or three are still around somewhere."

Goblin squeaked, "But they had six different plots going, Croaker. They was all backstabbing each other."

"But I only *saw* a couple of them check out. None of you guys *saw* the others go. You heard about it. Maybe there was one more plot behind all the other plots. Maybe . . ."

Lady gave me an odd, almost speculative look, like maybe she had not thought much about it herself and did not like the ideas I stirred now.

"They died dead enough for me, Croaker," One-Eye said. "I saw plenty of bodies. Look over there. Their graves are marked."

"That don't mean there's anybody in them. Raven died on us twice. Turn around and there he was again. On the hoof."

Lady said, "You have my permission to dig them up if you like, Croaker."

A glance showed me she was chiding me gently. Maybe even teasing. "That's all right. Maybe someday when I'm good and bored and got nothing better to do than look at rotten corpses."

"Gah!" Murgen said. "Can't you guys talk about something else?" Which was a mistake.

Otto laughed. Hagop started humming. To his tune Otto sang, "The worms crawl in, the worms crawl out, the ants play the bagpipes on your snout." Goblin and One-Eye joined in. Murgen threatened to ride over and puke on somebody.

We were distracting ourselves from the dark promise looming ahead.

One-Eye stopped singing to say, "None of the Taken were the sort who could lie low all these years, Croaker. If any survived we would have seen the fireworks. Me and Goblin would have heard something, anyway."

"I guess you're right." But I did not feel reassured. Maybe some part of me just did not want the Taken to be all dead.

We were approaching the incline that led up to the doorway into the Tower. For the first time the structure betrayed signs of life. Men clad as brightly as peacocks appeared on the high battlements. A handful came out of the gateway, hastily preparing a ceremonial in greeting to their mistress. One-Eye hooted derisively when he saw their apparel.

He would not have dared last time he was there.

I leaned over and whispered, "Be careful. She designed the uniforms on them guys."

I hoped they wanted to greet the Lady, hoped they had nothing more sinister in mind. That depended on what news they had had from the north. Sometimes evil rumors travel swifter than the wind.

"Audacity, guys," I said. "Always audacity. Be bold. Be arrogant. Keep them reeling." I looked at that dark entrance and reflected aloud, "They know me here."

"That's what scares me," Goblin squeaked. Then he cackled.

The Tower filled more and more of the world. Murgen, who'd never seen it before, surrendered to openmouthed awe. Otto and Hagop pretended that that stone pile did not impress them. Goblin and One-Eye became too busy to pay much attention. Lady could not be impressed. She had built the place when she was someone both greater and smaller than the person she was now.

I became totally involved in creating the persona I wanted to project. I recognized the colonel in charge of the welcoming party. We had crossed paths when my fortunes had led me into the Tower before. Our feelings toward one another were ambiguous at best.

He recognized me, too. And he was baffled. The Lady and I had left the Tower together, most of a year ago.

"How you doing, Colonel?" I asked, putting on a big, friendly grin. "We finally made it back. Mission successful."

He glanced at Lady. I did the same, from the edge of my eye. Now was her chance.

She had on her most arrogant face. *I* could have sworn she was the devil who haunted this Tower—Well, she was. Once. That person did not die when she lost her powers. Did she?

It looked like she would play my game. I sighed, closed my eyes momentarily, while the Tower Guard welcomed their liege.

I trusted her. But always there are reservations. You cannot predict other people. Especially not the hopeless.

Always there was the chance she might reassume the empire, hiding in her secret part of the Tower, letting her minions believe she was unchanged. There was nothing to stop her trying.

She could go that route even after keeping her promise to return the Annals.

That, my companions believed, was what she would do. And they dreaded her first order as empress of shadow restored.

Chapter Five:
CHAINS OF EMPIRE

Lady kept her promise. I had the Annals in hand within hours of entering the Tower, while its denizens were still overawed by her return. But . . .

"I want to go on with you, Croaker." This while we watched the sun set from the Tower's battlements the second evening after our arrival.

I, of course, replied with the golden tongue of a horse seller. "Uh . . . Uh . . . But . . ." Like that. Master of the glib and facile remark. Why the hell did she want to do that? She had it all, there in the Tower. A little careful faking and she could spend the rest of her natural life as the most powerful being in the world. Why go riding off with a band of tired old men, who did not know where they were going or why, only that they had to keep moving lest something—their consciences, maybe— caught them up?

"There's nothing here for me anymore," she said. As if that explained anything. "I want . . . I just want to find out what it's like to be ordinary people."

"You wouldn't like it. Not near as much as you like being the Lady."

"But I never liked that very much. Not after I had it and found out what I really had. You won't tell me I can't go, will you?"

Was she kidding? No. I would not. It had been the surface understanding, anyway. But it was an under-

24

standing I expected to perish once she reestablished herself in the Tower.

I was disconcerted by the implications.

"Can I go?"

"If that's what you want."

"There's a problem."

Isn't there always if there's a woman involved?

"I can't leave right now. Things have gotten confused here. I need a few days to straighten them out. So I can leave with a clear conscience."

We had not encountered any of the troubles I expected. None of her people dared scrutinize her closely. All the labors of One-Eye and Goblin were wasted effort with that audience. The word was out: the Lady was at the helm again. The Black Company was in the fold once more, under her protection. And that was enough for her people.

Wonderful. But Opal was only a few weeks away. From Opal it was a short passage over the Sea of Torments to ports outside the empire. I thought. I wanted to get out while our luck was holding.

"You understand, don't you, Croaker? It'll only be a few days. Honest. Just long enough to shape things up. The empire is a good machine that works smooth as long as the proconsuls are sure someone is in charge."

"All right. All right. We can last a couple days. As long as you keep people away. And you keep out of the way yourself, most of the time. Don't let them get too good a look at you."

"I don't intend to. Croaker?"

"Yeah?"

"Go teach your grandmother to suck eggs."

Startled, I laughed. She kept getting more human all the time. And more able to laugh at herself.

She had good intentions. But he—or she—who would rule an empire becomes slave to its administrative detail. A few days came and went. And a few more. And a few more still.

* * *

I could entertain myself skulking around the Tower's libraries, digging into rare texts from the Domination or before, unravelling the snarled threads of northern history, but for the rest of the guys it was rough. There was nothing for them to do but try to keep out of sight and worry. And bait Goblin and One-Eye, though they did not have much luck with that. To those of us without talent the Tower was just a big dark pile of rock, but to those two it was a great throbbing engine of sorcery, still peopled by numerous practitioners of the dark arts. They lived every moment in dread.

One-Eye handled it better than Goblin. He managed to escape occasionally, going out to the old battlefield to prowl among his memories. Sometimes I joined him, halfway tempted to take up Lady's invitation to open a few old graves.

"Still not comfortable about what happened?" One-Eye asked one afternoon, as I stood leaning on a bowstave over a marker bearing the name and sigil of the Taken who had been called the Faceless Man. One-Eye's tone was as serious as it ever gets.

"Not entirely," I admitted. "I can't pin it down, and it don't matter much now, but when you reflect on what happened here, it don't add up. I mean, it did at the time. It all looked like it was inevitable. A great kill-off that rid the world of a skillion Rebels and most of the Taken, leaving the Lady a free hand and setting her up for the Dominator at the same time. But in the context of later events . . ."

One-Eye had started to stroll, pulling me along in his wake. He came to a place that was not marked at all, except in his memory. A thing called a forvalaka had perished there. A thing that had slaughtered his brother —maybe—way back in the days when we first became involved with Soulcatcher, the Lady's legate to Beryl. The forvalaka was a sort of vampirous wereleopard originally native to One-Eye's own home jungle, somewhere way down south. It had taken One-Eye a year to catch up with and have his revenge upon this one.

"You're thinking about how hard it was to get rid of the Limper," he said. His voice was thoughtful. I knew he was recalling something I thought he had put out of mind.

We were never certain that the forvalaka which killed Tom-Tom was the forvalaka that paid the price. Because in those days the Taken Soulcatcher worked closely with another Taken called Shapeshifter and there was evidence to suggest Shifter might have been in Beryl that night. And using the forvalaka shape to assure the destruction of the ruling family so the empire could take over on the cheap.

If One-Eye had not avenged Tom-Tom on the right creature it was far too late for tears. Shifter was another of the victims of the Battle at Charm.

"I'm thinking about Limper," I admitted. "I killed him at that inn, One-Eye. I killed him good. And if he hadn't turned up again, I'd never have doubted that he was gone."

"And no doubts about these?"

"Some."

"You want to sneak out after dark and dig one of them up?"

"What's the point? There'll be somebody in the grave, and no way to prove it isn't who it's supposed to be."

"They were killed by other Taken and by members of the Circle. That's a little different than getting worked on by a no-talent like you."

He meant no talent for sorcery. "I know. That's what keeps me from getting obsessed with the whole mess. Knowing that those who supposedly killed them really had the power to do them in."

One-Eye stared at the ground where once a cross stood with the forvalaka nailed upon it. After a while he shivered and came back to now. "Well, it doesn't matter now. It was long ago, if not very far away. And far away is where we'll be if we ever get out of here." He pulled his floppy black hat forward to keep the sun out of his eyes, looked up at the Tower. We were being watched.

"Why does she want to go with us? That's the one I keep coming back to. What's in this for her?"

One-Eye looked at me with the oddest expression. He pushed his hat back, put his hands on his hips, cocked his head a moment, then shook it slowly. "Croaker. Sometimes you're too much to be believed. Why are you hanging around here waiting for her instead of heading out, putting miles behind?"

It was a good question and one I shied off anytime I tried to examine it. "Well, I guess I kind of like her and think she deserves a shot at some kind of regular life. She's all right. Really."

I caught a transient smirk as he turned to the unmarked grave. "Life wouldn't be half fun without you in it, Croaker. Watching you bumble through is an education in itself. How soon can we get moving? I don't like this place."

"I don't know. A few more days. There're things she has to wrap up first."

"That's what you said—"

I am afraid I got snappish. "I'll let you know when."

When seemed never to come. Days passed. Lady remained ensnared in the web of the administrative spider.

Then the messages began pouring in from the provinces, in response to edicts from the Tower. Each one demanded immediate attention.

We had been closed up in that dread place for two weeks.

"Get us the hell out of here, Croaker," One-Eye demanded. "My nerves can't take this place anymore."

"Look, there's stuff she's got to do."

"There's stuff *we*'ve got to do, according to you. Who says what we got to do has to wait on what she's got to do?"

And Goblin jumped on me. With both feet. "We put up with your infatuation for about twenty years, Croaker," he exaggerated. "Because it was amusing. Something to ride you about when times got boring. But it ain't nothing I mean to get killed over, I absodamnlutely guarantee. Even if she makes us all field marshals."

I warded a flash of anger. It was hard, but Goblin was right. I had no business hanging around there, keeping everyone at maximum risk. The longer we waited, the more certain it was that something would go sour. We were having enough trouble getting along with the Tower Guards, who resented our being so close to their mistress after having fought against her for so many years.

"We ride out in the morning," I said. "My apologies. I was elected to lead the Company, not just Croaker. Forgive me for losing sight of that."

Crafty old Croaker. One-Eye and Goblin looked properly abashed. I grinned. "So go get packed. We're gone with the morning sun."

She wakened me in the night. For a moment I thought . . .

I saw her face. She had heard.

She begged me to stay just one more day. Or two, at the most. She did not want to be here any more than we did, surrounded and taunted by all that she had lost. She wanted to go away, to go with us, to remain with me, the only friend she'd ever had—

She broke my heart.

It sounds sappy when you write it down in words, but a man has to do what a man has to do. In a way I was proud of me. I did not give an inch.

"There is no end to it," I told her. "There'll always be just one more thing that has to be done. Khatovar gets no closer while I wait. Death does. I value you, too. I don't want to leave . . . Death lurks in every shadow in this place. It writhes in the heart of every man who resents my influence." It was that kind of empire too, and in the past few days a lot of old imperials were given cause to resent me deeply.

"You promised me dinner at the Gardens in Opal."

I promised you a lot more than that, my heart said. Aloud, I replied, "So I did. And the offer still stands. But I have to get my men out of here."

I turned reflective while she turned uncharacteristically nervous. I saw the fires of schemes flickering behind her eyes, being rejected. There were ways she could manipulate me. We both knew that. But she never used the personal to gain political ends. Not with me, anyway.

I guess each of us, at some time, finds one person with whom we are compelled toward absolute honesty, one person whose good opinion of us becomes a substitute for the broader opinion of the world. And that opinion becomes more important than all our sneaky, sleazy schemes of greed, lust, self-aggrandizement, whatever we are up to while lying the world into believing we are just plain nice folks. I was her truth object, and she was mine.

There was only one thing we hid from one another, and that was because we were afraid that if it came into the open it would reshape everything else and maybe shatter that broader honesty.

Are lovers *ever* honest?

"I figure it'll take us three weeks to reach Opal. It'll take another week to find a trustworthy shipmaster and to work One-Eye up to crossing the Sea of Torments. So twenty-five days from today I'll go to the Gardens. I'll have the Camelia Grotto reserved for the evening." I patted the lump next to my heart. That lump was a beautifully tooled leather wallet containing papers commissioning me a general in the imperial armed forces and naming me a diplomatic legate answerable only to the Lady herself.

Precious, precious. And one good reason some longtime imperials had a big hate on for me.

I am not sure just how that came about. Some banter during one of those rare hours when she was not issuing

decrees or signing proclamations. Next thing I knew I
had been brought to bay by a pack of tailors. They fitted
me out with a complete imperial wardrobe. Never will I
unravel the significance of all the piping, badges, but-
tons, medals, doodads, and gewgaws. I felt silly wearing
all that clutter.

I didn't need much time to see some possibilities,
though, in what at first I interpreted as an elaborate
practical joke.

She does have that kind of sense of humor, not always
taking this great dreadfully humorless empire of hers
seriously.

I am sure she saw the possibilities long before I did.

Anyway, we were talking the Gardens in Opal, and the
Camelia Grotto there, the acme of that city's society
see-and-be-seen. "I'll take my evening meal there," I told
her. "You're welcome to join me."

Hints of hidden things tugged at her face. She said,
"All right. If I'm in town."

It was one of those moments in which I become very
uncomfortable. One of those times when nothing you say
can be right, and almost anything you do say is wrong. I
could see no answer but the classic Croaker approach.

I began to back away.

That is how I handle my women. Duck for cover when
they get distressed.

I almost made it to the door.

She could move when she wanted. She crossed the gap
and put her arms around me, rested a cheek against my
chest.

And that is how they handle me, the sentimental fool.
The closet romantic. I mean, I don't even have to know
them. They can work that one on me. When they really
want to drill me they turn on the water.

I held her till she was ready to be let go. We did not
look at one another as I turned and went away. So. She
hadn't gone for the heavy artillery.

She played fair, mostly. Give her that. Even when she was the Lady. Slick, tricky, but more or less fair.

The job of legate comes with all sorts of rights to subinfeudation and plunder of the treasury. I had drafted that pack of tailors and turned them loose on the men. I handed out commissions. I waved my magic wand and One-Eye and Goblin became colonels. Hagop and Otto turned into captains. I even cast a glamor on Murgen, so that he looked like a lieutenant. I drew us all three months' pay in advance. It all boggled the others. I think one reason One-Eye was anxious to get moving was an eagerness to get off somewhere where he could abuse his newfound privileges. For the time being, though, he mostly bickered with Goblin about whose commission carried the greater seniority. Those two never once questioned our shift in fortunes.

The weirdest part was when she called me in to present my commissions, and insisted on a real name to enter into the record. It took me a while to remember what my name was.

We rode out as threatened. Only we did not do it as the ragged band that rode in.

I travelled in a black iron coach drawn by six raging black stallions, with Murgen driving and Otto and Hagop riding as guards. With a string of saddle horses trailing behind. One-Eye and Goblin, disdaining the coach, rode before and behind upon mounts as fey and magnificent as the beasts which pulled the coach. With twenty-six Horse Guards as escort.

The horses she gave us were of a wild and wonderful breed, hitherto given only to the greatest champions of her empire. I had ridden one once, long ago, during the Battle at Charm, when she and I had chased down Soulcatcher. They could run forever without tiring. They were magical beasts. They constituted a gift precious beyond belief.

How do these weird things happen to me?

A year earlier I was living in a hole in the ground, under that boil on the butt of the world, the Plain of Fear, with fifty other men, constantly afraid we would be discovered by the empire. I had not had new or clean clothing in a decade, and baths and shaves were as rare and dear as diamonds.

Lying opposite me in that coach was a black bow, the first gift she ever gave me, so many years ago, before the Company deserted her. It was precious in its own right.

How the wheel turns.

Chapter Six:
OPAL

Hagop stared as I finished primping. "Gods. You really *look* the part, Croaker."

Otto said, "Amazing what a bath and a shave will do. I believe the word is 'distinguished.'"

"Looks like a supernatural miracle to me, Ott."

"Be sarcastic, you guys."

"I mean it," Otto said. "You do look good. If you had a little rug to cover where your hairline is running back toward your butt . . ."

He did mean it. "Well, then," I mumbled, uncomfortable. I changed the subject. "I meant what I said. Keep those two in line." In town only four days and already I'd bailed Goblin and One-Eye out of trouble twice. There was a limit to what even a legate could cover, hush, and smooth over.

"There's only three of us, Croaker," Hagop protested. "What do you want? They don't want to be kept in line."

"I know you guys. You'll think of something. While you're at it, get this junk packed up. It has to go down to the ship."

"Yes sir, your grand legateship, sir."

I was about to deliver one of my fiery, witty, withering rejoinders when Murgen stuck his head into the room and said, "The coach is ready, Croaker."

And Hagop wondered aloud, "How do we keep them

in line when we don't even know where they are?
Nobody's seen them since lunchtime."

I went out to the coach hoping I would not get an ulcer
before I got out of the empire.

We roared through Opal's streets, my escort of Horse
Guards, my black stallions, my ringing black iron coach,
and I. Sparks flew around the horses' hooves and the
coach's steel wheels. Dramatic, but riding in that metal
monster was like being locked inside a steel box that was
being enthusiastically pounded by vandalistic giants.

We swept up to the Gardens' understated gate, scattering gawkers. I stepped down, stood more stiffly erect than
was my wont, made an effete gesture of dismissal copied
from some prince seen somewhere along life's twisted
way. I strode through the gate, thrown open in haste.

I marched back to the Camelia Grotto, hoping ancient
memory would not betray me. Gardens employees
yapped at my heels. I ignored them.

My way took me past a pond so smooth and silvery its
surface formed a mirror. I halted, mouth dropping open.

I did, indeed, cut an imposing figure, cleaned up and
dressed up. But were my eyes two eggs of fire, and my
open mouth a glowing furnace? "I'll strangle those two in
their sleep," I murmured.

Worse than the fire, I had a shadow, a barely percepti-
ble specter, behind me. It hinted that the legate was but
an illusion cast by something darker.

Damn those two and their practical jokes.

When I resumed moving I noted that the Gardens
were packed but silent. The guests all watched me.

I had heard that the Gardens were not as popular as
once they had been.

They were there to see me. Of course. The new general.
The unknown legate out of the dark tower. The wolves
wanted a look at the tiger.

I should have expected it. The escort. They had had
four days to tell tales around town.

I turned on all the outward arrogance I could muster.
And inside I echoed to the whimper of a kid with stage
fright.

I settled in in the Camelia Grotto, out of sight of the
crowd. Shadows played about me. The staff came to
enquire after my needs. They were revolting in their
obsequiousness.

A disgusting little part of me gobbled it up. A part just
big enough to show why some men lust after power. But
not for me, thank you. I am too lazy. And I am, I fear, the
unfortunate victim of a sense of responsibility. Put me in
charge and I try to accomplish the ends to which the
office was allegedly created. I guess I suffer from an
impoverishment of the sociopathic spirit necessary to go
big time.

How do you do the show, with the multiple-course
meal, when you are accustomed to patronizing places
where you take whatever is in the pot or starve? Craft.
Take advantage of the covey hovering about, fearful I
might devour *them* if not pleased. Ask this, ask that, use
a physician's habitual intuition for the hinted and im-
plied, and I had it whipped. I sent them to the kitchens
with instructions to be in no haste, for a companion
might join me later.

Not that I expected Lady. I was going through the
motions. I meant to keep my date without its other half.

Other guests kept finding excuses to pass by and look
at the new man. I began to wish I had brought my escort
along.

There was a rolling rumble like the sound of distant
thunder, then a hammerclap close at hand. A wave of
chatter ran through the Gardens, followed by grave-dead
silence. Then the silence gave way to the rhythm of
steel-tapped heels falling in unison.

I did not believe it. Even as I rose to greet her, I did not
believe it.

Tower Guards hove into view, halted, parted. Goblin
came hup-two-threeing between them, strutting like a

drum major, looking like his namesake freshly
scrounged from some especially fiery Hell. He glowed.
He trailed a fiery mist which evaporated a few yards
behind him. He stepped down into the Grotto and gave
the place the fish-eye, and me a wink. He then marched
up the far side steps and posted himself facing outward.

What the hell were they up to now? Expanding on their
already overburdened practical joke?

Then Lady appeared, as fell and as radiant as fantasy,
as beautiful as a dream. I clicked my heels and bowed.
She descended to join me. She *was* a vision. She extended a hand. My manners did not desert me, despite
all the hard years.

Wouldn't this give Opal fuel for gossip?

One-Eye followed Lady down, wreathed in dark mists
through which crawled shadows with eyes. He inspected
the Grotto, too.

As he turned to go back the way he had come, I said,
"I'm going to incinerate that hat." Tricked out like a
lord, he was, but still wearing his ragpicker's hat.

He grinned, assumed his post.

"Have you ordered?" Lady asked.

"Yes. But only for one."

A small horde of staff tumbled past One-Eye, terrified.
The master of the Gardens himself drove them. If they
had been fawning with me, they were downright disgusting with Lady. *I* have never been that impressed with
anyone in any position of power.

It was a long, slow meal, undertaken mostly in silence,
with me sending unanswered puzzled glances across the
table. A memorable dining experience for me, though
Lady hinted that she had known better.

The problem was, we were too much on stage to take
any real enjoyment from it. Not only for the crowd, but
for one another.

Along the way I admitted I had not expected her to
appear, and she said my storming out of the Tower made
her realize that if she did not just drop everything and go

she would not shake the tentacles of imperial responsibility till someone freed her by murdering her.

"So you just walked? The place will be coming apart."

"No. I left certain safeguards in place. I delegated powers to people whose judgment I trust, in such fashion that the empire will acrete to them gradually, and become theirs solidly before they realize that I've deserted."

"I hope so." I am a charter member of that philosophical school which believes that if anything can go sour, it will.

"It won't matter to us, will it? We'll be well out of range."

"Morally, it matters, if half a continent is thrown into civil war."

"I think I have made sufficient moral sacrifice." A cold wind overswept me. Why can't I keep my big damned mouth shut?

"Sorry," I said. "You're right. I didn't think."

"Apology accepted. I must confess something. I've taken a liberty with your plans."

"Eh?" One of my more intellectual moments.

"I cancelled your passage aboard that merchantman."

"What? Why?"

"It wouldn't be seemly for a legate of the empire to travel aboard a broken-down grain barge. You are too cheap, Croaker. The quinquirireme Soulcatcher built, *The Dark Wings*, is in port. I ordered her readied for the crossing to Beryl."

My gods. The very doomship that brought us north. "We aren't well loved in Beryl."

"Beryl is an imperial province these days. The frontier lies three hundred miles beyond the sea now. Have you forgotten your part in what made that possible?"

I only wanted to. "No. But my attention has been elsewhere the past few decades." If the frontier had drifted that far, then imperial boots tramped the asphalted avenues of my own home city. It never occurred to me that the southern proconsuls might expand the borders beyond the maritime city-states. Only the Jewel Cities themselves were of any strategic value.

"Now who's being bitter?"

"Who? Me? You're right. Let's enjoy the civilized moment. We'll have few enough of them." Our gazes locked. For a moment there were sparks of challenge in hers. I looked away. "How did you manage to enlist those two clowns in your charade?"

"A donative."

I laughed. Of course. Anything for money. "And how soon will *The Dark Wings* be ready to sail?"

"Two days. Three at the most. And no, I won't be handling any imperial business while I'm here."

"Uhm. Good. I'm stuffed to the gills and ripe for roasting. We ought to go walk this off, or something. Is there a reasonably safe place we could go?"

"You probably know Opal better than I do, Croaker. I've never been here before."

I suppose I looked surprised.

"I can't be everywhere. There was a time when I was preoccupied in the north and east. A time when I was preoccupied with putting my husband down. A time when I was preoccupied with catching you. There never was a time when I was free for broadening travel."

"Thank the stars."

"What?"

"Meant to be a compliment. On your youthful figure."

She gave me a calculating look. "I won't say anything to that. You'll stick it all in your Annals."

I grinned. Threads of smoke snaked between my teeth. I swore I'd get them.

Chapter Seven:
SMOKE AND THE WOMAN

Willow figured you could pick Smoke for what he was in any crowd. He was a wrinkled, skinny little geek that looked like somebody tried to do him in black walnut husk stain, only they missed some spots. There were spatters of pink on the backs of his hands, one arm, and one side of his face. Like maybe somebody threw acid at him and it killed the color where it hit him.

Smoke had not done anything to Willow. Not yet. But Willow did not like him. Blade did not care one way or another. Blade didn't care much about anybody. Cordy Mather said he was reserving judgment. Willow kept his dislike back out of sight, because Smoke was what he was and because he hung out with the Woman.

The Woman was waiting for them, too. She was browner than Smoke and most anyone else in town, as far as Willow knew. She had a mean face that made it hard to look at her. She was about average size for Taglian women, which was not very big by Swan's standards. Except for her attitude of "I am the boss" she would not have stood out much. She did not dress better than old women Willow saw in the streets. Black crows, Cordy called them. Always wrapped up in black, like old peasant women they saw when they were headed down through the territories of the Jewel Cities.

They had not been able to find out who the Woman

was, but they knew she was somebody. She had connections in the Prahbrindrah's palace, right up at the top. Smoke worked for her. Fishwives didn't have wizards on the payroll. Anyway, both of them acted like officials trying not to look official. Like they did not know how to be regular people.

The place they met was somebody's house. Somebody important, but Willow had not yet figured who. The class lines and heirarchies did not make sense in Taglios. Everything was always screwed up by religious affiliation.

He entered the room where they waited, helped himself to a chair. Had to show them he wasn't some boy to run and fetch at their beck. Cordy and Blade were more circumspect. Cordy winced as Willow said, "Blade says you guys want to kick it up 'bout Smoke's nightmares. Maybe pipe dreams?"

"You have a very good idea why you interest us, Mr. Swan. Taglios and its dependencies have been pacifistic for centuries. War is a forgotten art. It's been unnecessary. Our neighbors were equally traumatized by the passage—"

Willow asked Smoke, "She talking Taglian?"

"As you wish, Mr. Swan." Willow caught a hint of mischief in the Woman's eye. "When the Free Companies came through they kicked ass so damned bad that for three hundred years anybody who even looked at a sword got so scared he puked his guts up."

"Yeah." Swan chuckled. "That's right. We can talk. Tell us."

"We want help, Mr. Swan."

Willow mused, "Let's see, the way I hear, around seventy-five, a hundred years ago people finally started playing games. Archery shoots, whatnot. But never anything man to man. Then here come the Shadowmasters to take over Tragevec and Kiaulune and change the names to Shadowlight and Shadowcatch."

"Kiaulune means Shadow Gate," Smoke said. His

voice was like his skin, splotched with oddities. Squeaks, sort of. They made Willow bristle. "Not much change. Yes. They came. And like Kina in the legend they set free the wicked knowledge. In this case, how to make war."

"And right away they started carving them an empire and if they hadn't had that trouble at Shadowcatch and hadn't got so busy fighting each other they would've been here fifteen years ago. I know. I been asking around ever since you guys started hustling us."

"And?"

"So for fifteen years you knew they was coming someday. And for fifteen years you ain't done squat about it. Now when you all of a sudden know the day, you want to grab three guys off the street and con them into thinking they can work some kind of miracle. Sorry, sister. Willow Swan ain't buying. There's your conjure man. Get old Smoke to pull pigeons out of his hat."

"We aren't looking for miracles, Mr. Swan. The miracle has happened. Smoke dreamed it. We're looking for time for the miracle to take effect."

Willow snorted.

"We have a realistic appreciation of how desperate our situation is, Mr. Swan. We have had since the Shadowmasters appeared. We have *not* been playing ostrich. We have been doing what seems most practical, given the cultural context. We have encouraged the masses to accept the notion that it would be a great and glorious thing to repel the onslaught when it comes."

"You sold them that much," Blade said. "They ready to go die."

"And that's all they would do," Swan said. "Die."

"Why?" the Woman asked.

"No organization," said Cordy. The thoughtful one. "But organization wouldn't be possible. No one from any of the major cult families would take orders from somebody from another one."

"Exactly. Religious conflicts make it impossible to

raise an army. Three armies, maybe. But then the high priests might be tempted to use them to settle scores here at home."

Blade snorted. "They ought to burn the temples and strangle the priests."

"Sentiments my brother often expresses," the Woman said. "Smoke and I feel they might follow outsiders of proven skill who aren't beholden to any faction."

"What? You going to make me a general?"

Cordy laughed. "Willow, if the gods thought half as much of you as you think of yourself, you'd be king of the world. You figure you're the miracle Smoke saw in his dream? They're not going to make you a general. Not really. Unless maybe for show, while they stall."

"What?"

"Who's the guy keeps saying he only spent two months in the army and never even learned to keep step?"

"Oh." Willow thought for a minute. "I think I see."

"Actually, you will be generals," the Woman said. "And we'll have to rely heavily on Mr. Mather's practical experience. But Smoke will have the final say."

"We have to buy time," the wizard echoed. "A lot of time. Someday soon Moonshadow will send a combined force of five thousand to invade Taglios. We have to keep from being beaten. If there's any way possible, we have to beat the force sent against us."

"Nothing like wishing."

"Are you willing to pay the price?" Cordy asked. Like he thought it could be done.

"The price will be paid," the Woman said. "Whatever it may be."

Willow looked at her till he could no longer keep his teeth clamped on the big question. "Just who the hell are you, lady? Making your promises and plans."

"I am the Radisha Drah, Mr. Swan."

"Holy shit," Swan muttered. "The prince's big sister." The one some people said was the real boss bull in those parts. "I knew you was somebody, but . . ." He was rattled right down to his toenails. But he would not have been Willow Swan if he had not leaned back, folded his hands on his belly, put on a big grin, and asked, "What's in it for us?"

Chapter Eight:
OPAL: CROWS

Though the empire retained a surface appearance of cohesion, a failure of the old discipline snaked through the deeps beneath. When you wandered the streets of Opal you sensed the laxness. There was flip talk about the new crop of overlords. One-Eye spoke of an increase in black marketeering, a subject on which he had been expert for a century. I overheard talk of crimes committed that were not officially sanctioned.

Lady seemed unconcerned. "The empire is seeking normalcy. The wars are over. There's no need for the strictures of the past."

"You saying it's time to relax?"

"Why not? You'd be the first to scream about what a price we paid for peace."

"Yeah. But the comparative order, the enforcement of public safety laws . . . I admired that part."

"You sweetheart, Croaker. You're saying we weren't all bad."

She knew damned well I'd claimed that all along. "You know I don't believe there's any such thing as pure evil."

"Yes there is. It's festering up north in a silver spike your friends drove into the trunk of a sapling that's the son of a god."

"Even the Dominator may have had some redeeming quality sometime. Maybe he was good to his mother."

"He probably ripped her heart out and ate it. Raw."

I wanted to say something like, you married him, but did not need to give her further excuses to change her mind. She was pressed enough.

But I digress. I was remarking on the changes in the Lady's world. What brought the whole thing home was having a dozen men drop in and ask if they could sign on with the Black Company. They were all veterans. Which meant there were men of military age at loose ends these days. During the war years there had been no extra bodies anywhere. If they were not with the grey boys or that lot they were with the White Rose.

I rejected six guys right away and accepted one, a man with his front teeth done up in gold inlays. Goblin and One-Eye, self-appointed name givers, dubbed him Sparkle.

Of the other five there were three I liked and two I did not and could find no sound reasons for going either way with any of them. I lied and told them they were all in and should report aboard *The Dark Wings* in time for our departure. Then I conferred with Goblin. He said he would make sure that the two I did not like would miss our departure.

I first noticed the crows then, consciously. I attached no special significance, just wondered why everywhere we went there seemed to be crows.

One-Eye wanted a private chat. "You nosed around that place where your girlfriend is staying?"

"Not to speak of." I had given up arguing about whether or not Lady was my girlfriend.

"You ought to."

"It's a little late. I take it you have. What's your beef?"

"It isn't something you can pin down like sticking a nail through a frog, Croaker. Kind of hard to get a good look around there, anyway, what with she brought a whole damned army along. An army that I think she figures on dragging along wherever we go."

"She won't. Maybe she rules this end of the world, but she don't run the Black Company. Nobody runs with this outfit who don't answer to me and only to me."

One-Eye clapped. "That was good, Croaker. I could almost hear the Captain talking. You even got to standing the way he did, like a big old bear about to jump on something."

I was not original, but I didn't think I was that transparent a borrower, either. "So what's your point, One-Eye? Why has she got you spooked?"

"Not spooked, Croaker. Just feeling cautious. It's her baggage. She's dragging along enough stuff to fill a wagon."

"Women get that way."

"Ain't women's stuff. Not unless she wears magical lacies. You'd know that better than me."

"Magical?"

"Whatever that stuff is, it's got a charge on it. A pretty hefty one."

"What am I supposed to do about it?"

He shrugged. "I don't know. I just thought you ought to know."

"If it's magical it's your department. Keep an eye out"—I snickered—"and let me know if you find anything useful."

"Your sense of humor has gone to hell, Croaker."

"I know. Must be the company I keep. My mother warned me about guys like you. Scat. Go help Goblin give those two guys the runs, or something. And stay out of trouble. Or I'll take you across the water in a nice bouncy rowboat we'll pull along behind the ship."

It takes some doing for a black man to get green around the gills. One-Eye managed it.

The threat worked. He even kept Goblin from getting into mischief.

Though not in keeping with the time sequence, I hereby make notation of four new members of the

Company. They are: Sparkle, Big Bucket (I don't know why; he came with the name), Red Rudy, and Candles. Candles came with his name, too. There is a long story to tell how he got it. It does not make sense and is not especially interesting. Being the new guys they mostly stayed quiet, stayed out of the way, did the scut work, and worked on learning what we were all about. Lieutenant Murgen was happy to have somebody around he outranked.

Chapter Nine:
ACROSS THE SCREAMING SEA

Our black iron coaches roared through Opal's streets, flooding the dawn with fear and thunder. Goblin outdid himself. This time the black stallions breathed smoke and fire, and flames sprang up where their hooves struck, fading only after we were long gone. Citizens stayed under cover.

One-Eye lolled beside me, restrained by protective cords. Lady sat opposite us, hands folded in her lap. The lurching of the coach bothered her not at all.

Her coach and mine parted ways. Hers headed for the north gate, bound toward the Tower. All the city—we hoped—would believe her to be in that coach. It would disappear somewhere in uninhabited country. The coachmen, handsomely bribed, should head west, to make new lives in the distant cities on the ocean coast. The trail, we hoped, would be a dead one before anyone became concerned.

Lady wore clothing that made her look like a doxy, the legate's momentary fancy.

She travelled like a courtesan. The coach was jammed with her stuff and One-Eye reported that a load had been delivered to *The Dark Wings* already, with a wagon to carry it.

One-Eye was limp because he had been drugged.

Faced by a sea voyage, he became balky. He always

does. Old in knowing One-Eye's ways, Goblin had been
prepared. Knockout drops in his morning brandy did the
trick.

Through wakening streets we thundered, down to the
waterfront, amidst the confusion of arriving stevedores.
Onto the massive naval dock we rolled, to its very end,
and up a broad gangway. Hooves drummed on deck
timbers. Finally, we halted.

I stepped down from the coach. The ship's captain met
me with all the appropriate honors and dignities—and a
furious scowl on behalf of his savaged deck. I looked
around. The four new men were there. I nodded. The
captain shouted. Hands began casting off. Others began
helping my men unharness and unsaddle horses. I noticed a crow perched on the masthead.

Small tugs manned by convict oarsmen pulled *The
Dark Wings* off the pier. Her own sweeps came out.
Drums pounded the beat. She turned her bows seaward.
In an hour we were well down the channel, running with
the tide, the ship's great black sail bellied with an
offshore breeze. The device thereon was unchanged since
our northward journey, though Soulcatcher had been
destroyed by the Lady herself soon after the Battle at
Charm. The crow kept its perch.

It was the best season for crossing the Sea of Torments.
Even One-Eye admitted it was a swift and easy passage.
We raised the Beryl light on the third morning and
entered the harbor with the afternoon tide.

The advent of *The Dark Wings* had all the impact I
expected and feared.

The last time that monster put in at Beryl the city's last
free, homegrown tyrant had died. His successor, chosen
by Soulcatcher, became an imperial puppet. And *his*
successors were imperial governors.

Local imperial functionaries swarmed onto the pier as
the quinquirireme warped in. "Termites," Goblin called
them. "Tax farmers and pen-pushers. Little things that

live under rocks and shy from the light of honest employment."

Somewhere in his background was a cause for a big hatred of tax collectors. I understand in an intellectual sort of way. I mean there is no lower human life-form—with the possible exception of pimps—than that which revels in its state-derived power to humiliate, extort, and generate misery. I am left with a disgust for my species. But with Goblin it can become a flaming passion, with him trying to work everybody up to go out and treat a few tax people to grotesque excruciations and deaths.

The termites were shaken and distressed. They did not know what to make of this sudden, obviously portentous arrival. The advent of an imperial legate could mean a hundred things, but nothing good for the entrenched bureaucracy.

Elsewhere, all work came to a halt. Even cursing gang leaders paused to stare at the harbinger ship.

One-Eye eyeballed the situation. "Better get us out of town fast, Croaker. Else it will turn into the Tower all over again, this time with too many people asking too damned many questions."

The coach was ready. Lady was inside. The mounts, both great and normal, were saddled. A small, light, closed wagon was brought up and assembled by the Horse Guards and filled with Lady's plunder. We were ready to roll when the ship's captain was ready to let us.

"Mount up," I ordered. "One-Eye, when that gangway goes down you make like the horns of hell. Otto, take this coach off here like the Limper himself is after you." I turned to the commander of the Horse Guards. "You break trail. Don't give those people down there a chance to slow us down." I boarded the coach.

"Wise thinking," Lady said. "Get away fast or risk falling into the trap I barely escaped at the Tower."

"That's what I'm afraid of. I can fake this legate

business only if nobody looks at me too close." Far better to roar through town and leave them thinking me a foul-tempered, contemptuous, arrogant Taken legate southward bound on a mission that was no business of the procurators of Beryl.

The gangway slammed down. One-Eye let loose the hell-horn howl I wanted. My mob surged forward. Gawkers and the privileged alike scattered before our fire-and-darkness apparition. We thundered through Beryl as we had thundered through Opal, our passage spreading terror. Behind us, *The Dark Wings* put out with the evening tide, under orders to proceed to the Garnet Roads and begin an extended patrol against pirates and smugglers. We exited the Rubbish Gate. Though the normal animals were exhausted, we carried on till darkness lent us its mask.

Despite our haste to get away from the city, we did not camp far enough out to escape its attention entirely. When I wakened in the morning I found Murgen waiting on me with three brothers who wanted to join up. Their names were Cletus, Longinus, and Loftus. They had been kids when we were in Beryl before. How they recognized us during our wild ride I do not know. They claimed to have deserted the Urban Cohorts in order to join us. I did not feel much like dealing with an extensive interrogation, so took Murgen's word that they seemed all right. "They're fools enough to want to jump in with us without knowing what's going on, let them. Give them to Hagop."

I now had two feeble squads, Otto and the four from Opal, and Hagop and the three from Beryl. Such was the Company's history. Pick up a man here, enlist two there, keep on keeping on.

Southward and southward. Through Rebosa, where the Company had seen service briefly, and where Otto and Hagop had enlisted. They found their city changed immensely and yet not at all. They had no trouble leaving it behind. They brought in another man there, a nephew, who quickly earned the name Smiley because of his consistent sullenness and sarcastic turn of phrase.

Then Padora, and on, to that great crossroads of trade routes where I was born and where I enlisted just before the Company ended its service there. I was young and foolish when I did. Yes. But I did get to see the far reaches of the world.

I ordered a day of rest at the vast caravan camp outside the city wall, along the westward road, while I went into town and indulged myself, walking streets I had run as a kid. Like Otto said about Rebosa, the same and yet dramatically changed. The difference, of course, was inside me.

I stalked through the old neighborhood, past the old tenement. I saw no one I knew—unless a woman glimpsed briefly, who looked like my grandmother, was my sister. I did not confront her, nor ask. To those people I am dead.

A return as imperial legate would not change that.

We stood before the last imperial mile marker. Lady was trying to convince the lieutenant commanding our guards that his mission was complete, that imperial soldiers crossing the frontier might be construed as an unacceptable provocation.

Sometimes her people are too loyal.

A half-dozen border militiamen, equally divided between sides, clad identically and obviously old friends, stood around a short distance away, discussing us in murmurs of awe. The rest of us fidgeted.

It seemed ages since I had been beyond imperial frontiers. I found the prospect vaguely unsettling.

"You know what we're doing, Croaker?" Goblin asked.

"What's that?"

"We're travelling backward in time."

Backward in time. Backward into our own history. A simple enough statement, but an important thought.

"Yeah. Maybe you're right. Let me go stir the pot. Else we'll never get moving."

I joined Lady, who gave me a nasty look. I pasted on my sweetest smile and said, "Look here. I'm over on the other side of the line. You got a problem, Lieutenant?"

He bobbed his head. He was more in awe of my rank and title, unearned though they were, than he was of the woman who was supposed to be his boss. And that was because he believed he owed her certain duties even she could not overrule.

"The Company has openings for a few good men with military experience," I said. "Now that we're out of the empire and don't have to have the imperial permission, we're actively recruiting."

He caught on real fast, skipped across beside me, gave Lady a big grin.

"There is one thing," I said. "You come over here and do it, you're going to have to take the oath to the Company, same as anybody else. Meaning you can't pledge yourself to any higher loyalty."

Lady gave him a nasty-sweet smile. He stepped back across, figuring he'd better do some serious thinking before he committed himself.

I told Lady, "That goes for everybody. I would not presume before. But if you come out of the empire and continue to ride with us it will be under the same conditions accepted by everyone else."

Such a look she gave me. "But I'm just a woman. . . ."

"Not a precedent, friend. It didn't happen often. The world don't have much room for female adventurers. But women have marched with the Company." Turning to the lieutenant, I said, "And if you sign on, your oath will be taken as genuine. First time you get an order and look to her for advice on yes or no, out you go. Alone in a foreign land." It was one of my more assertive days.

Lady muttered some very unladylike sniggen snaggen riddly rodden racklesnatzes under her breath, then told the lieutenant, "Go talk it over with your men." The moment he was out of hearing she demanded, "Does this mean we stop being friends? If I take your damned oath?"

"Do you reckon I stopped being friends with the others when they elected me Captain?"

"I admit I don't hear a lot of 'yes sir,' 'no sir,' 'your worship sir.'"

"But you do see them do what they're told when they know I mean what I say."

"Most of the time."

"Goblin and One-Eye need a little extra convincing once in a while. What's it going to be? You going to be a soldier?"

"Do I have a choice, Croaker? You can be a bastard."

"Of course you have a choice. You can go back with your men and be the Lady."

The lieutenant was talking to his troops and the idea of going on south was proving less popular than he or I had thought it would. Most of the bunch started getting their horses together, facing north, before he finished talking.

He finally came over and presented us with six men who wanted to go on with us. He did not include himself with the group. Evidently his conscience had shown him a way around doing what he considered to be his duty minutes before.

I questioned the men briefly and they did seem interested in going on. So I brought them over the line and swore them all in, making a production of it for Lady's sake. I do not recall doing anything particularly formal for anyone else before.

I gave the six to Otto and Hagop for dividing between them, and kept the one for me, and later entered their names into the Annals when we learned how they wanted to be known.

Lady remained content to be called Lady. It sounded like a name when heard by speakers of any language but one, anyway.

Crows watched the whole show from a nearby tree.

Chapter Ten:
SHADOWMASTERS

Though the sun stared in through a dozen vaulted windows there was darkness in that place where Darkness met.

A pool of molten stone simmered in the center of the vast floor. It cast bloody light upon four seated figures floating a few feet in the air. They faced one another over the pool, forming an equilateral triangle with a couple at its apex. Those two were leagued more often than not. They were allied now.

There had been war among the four for a long time, with nothing gained, one in relation to another. But at the moment there was an armistice.

Shadows slithered and swirled and pranced around them. Nothing could be seen of any of them except vague shapes. All four chose to conceal themselves within robes of black, behind black masks.

The smallest, one of the couple, broke a silence that had reigned an hour. "She has begun moving south. Those who served her and still bear her indelible mark are moving also. They have crossed the sea, and they come bearing mighty talismans. And their road is strewn with those who would join their destinies to that black standard. Including some whose power we would be foolish not to beware."

One angle of the triangle made a sound of contempt.

The other asked, "And what of the one in the north?"

"The Great One remains secure. The lesser one who lay in the shade of the prisoning tree does so no longer. It has been resurrected and given new form. It comes south too, but it is so insane and vengeance-starved that it is not to be feared. A child could dispose of it."

"Have we cause to fear that our presence here is known?"

"None. Even in Trogo Taglios only a few are convinced that we exist. Beyond the First Cataract we are but a rumor, and not that above the Second. But he who has made himself master in the great swamps may have sensed us stirring. It is possible he suspects there is more afoot than he knew."

The reporter's companion added, "They come. She comes. But harnessed to the pace of man and animal. We still have a year. Or more."

The one snorted again, then spoke. "The swamps would be a very good place for them to die. Take care of it. You may impress the one who rules them with the majesty and terror of my Name." He began to drift away.

The others stared hard. The anger in the place became palpable.

The other ceased his drift. "You know what sleeps so restlessly upon my southern border. I dare not relax my vigilance."

"Unless to stab another of us in the back. I note that the threat becomes secondary whenever you care to try."

"You have my pledge. Upon my Name. The peace will not be broken by me while those who bring danger from the north survive. You may speak of me as one with you when you extend your hands beyond the shadows. I cannot, I *dare* not, give you more." He resumed his drift.

"So be it, then," said the woman. The triangle rearranged itself so as to exclude him. "He spoke one truth, certainly. The swamps would be a very good place for them to die. If Fate does not take them in hand sooner."

One of the others began to chuckle. The shadows scurried about, frantic, as growing laughter tormented them.

"A very good place for them to die."

Chapter Eleven:
A MARCH INTO YESTERYEAR

At first the names were echoes from my childhood. Kale.
Fratter. Grey. Weeks. Some the Company had served,
some had been its foes. The world changed and became
warmer and the cities became more scattered. Their
names faded to legend and memories from the Annals.
Tire. Raxle. Slight. Nab and Nod. We passed beyond any
map I had ever seen, to cities known to me only through
the Annals and visited only by One-Eye previously.
Boros. Teries. Viege. Ha-jah.

And still we headed south, still making the first long
leg of our journey. Crows followed. We gathered another
four recruits, professional caravan guards from a nomad
tribe called the roi, who deserted to join us. I started a
squad for Murgen. He was not thrilled. He was content
being standard bearer and had developed hopes of taking
over the Annalist's chores from me because I had so
much to do as Captain and medic. I dared not discourage
him. The only alternative substitute was One-Eye. He
was not reliable.

And south some more, and still we were not back to
One-Eye's origin, the jungles of D'loc-Aloc.

One-Eye swore that never in his life, outside the
Company, had he heard the name Khatovar. It had to lie
far beyond the waist of the world.

There are limits to what frail flesh can endure.

Those long leagues were not easy. The black iron coach and Lady's wagon drew the eye of bandits and princes and princes who were bandits. Most times Goblin and One-Eye bluffed us through. The rest of the time we forced them to back down with a little applied terror. There was one long stretch where the magic had gone away.

If those two had learned anything during their years with the Company, it was showmanship. When they conjured an illusion you could smell its bad breath from seventy feet away.

I wished they would refrain from wasting that flash upon one another.

I decided it was time we laid up for a few days. We needed to regain our youthful bounce.

One-Eye suggested, "There's a place down the road called the Temple of Travellers' Repose. They take in wanderers. They have for two thousand years. It would be a good place to lay up and do some research."

"Research?"

"Two thousand years of travellers' tales makes a hell of a library, Croaker. And a tale is the only donative they ever require."

He had me. He grinned cockily. The old scoundrel knew me too well. Nothing else could have stilled my determination to reach Khatovar so thoroughly.

I passed the word. And gave One-Eye the fish-eye. "That means you're going to do some honest work."

"What?"

"Who do you think is going to translate?"

He groaned and rolled his eye. "When am I going to learn to keep my big damned mouth shut?"

The Temple was a lightly fortified monastery sprawled atop a low hill. It looked golden in the light of a late afternoon sun. The forest beyond and the fields before were as intense a dark green as ever I have seen. The place *looked* restful.

As we entered, a wave of well-being cleansed us. A feeling of *I have come home* washed over us. I looked at Lady. The things I felt glowed in her face, and touched my heart.

"I could retire here," I told Lady two days into our stay. Clean for the first time in months, we stalked a garden never disturbed by conflicts more weighty than the squabbles of sparrows.

She gave me a thin smile and did me the courtesy of saying nothing about the delusive nature of dreams.

The place had everything I thought I wanted. Comfort. Quiet. Isolation from the ills of the earth. Purpose. Challenging historical studies to soothe my lust to *know* what had gone on before.

Most of all, it provided a respite from responsibility. Each man added to the Company seemed to double my burden as I worried about keeping them fed, keeping them healthy, and out of trouble.

"Crows," I muttered.

"What?"

"Everywhere we go there're crows. Maybe I only started noticing them the past couple months. But everywhere we go I see crows. And I can't shake the feeling they're watching us."

Lady gave me a puzzled look.

"Look. Right over there in that acacia tree. Two of them squatting there like black omens."

She glanced at the tree, gave me another look. "I see a couple of doves."

"But . . ." One of the crows launched itself, flapped away over the monastery wall. "That wasn't any—"

"Croaker!" One-Eye charged through the garden, scattering the birds and squirrels, ignoring all propriety. "Hey! Croaker! Guess what I found! Copies of the Annals from when we came past here headed north!"

Well. And well. This tired old mind cannot find words adequate. Excitement? Certainly. Ecstasy? You'd better believe. The moment was almost sexually intense. My mind focused the way one's does when an especially desirable woman suddenly seems attainable.

Several older volumes of the Annals had become lost or damaged during the years. There were some I'd never seen, and never had known a hope of seeing.

"Where?" I breathed.

"In the library. One of the monks thought you might be interested. When we were here heading north I don't remember leaving them, but I wasn't much interested in that kind of thing then. Me and Tom-Tom was too busy looking over our shoulders."

"I might be interested," I said. "I might." My manners deserted me. I deserted Lady without so much as an "Excuse me."

Maybe that obsession was not as powerful as I'd worked it up to be.

I felt like an ass when I realized what I had done.

Reading those copies required teamwork. They had been recorded in a language no longer used by anyone but the temple monks. None of them spoke any language I understood. So our reader translated into One-Eye's native tongue, then One-Eye translated for me.

What filtered through was damned interesting.

They had the Book of Choe, which had been destroyed fifty years before I enlisted and only poorly reconstructed. And the Book of Te-Lare, known to me only through a cryptic reference in a later volume. The Book of Skete, previously unknown. They had a half dozen more, equally precious. But no Book of the Company. No First or Second Book of Odrick. Those were the legendary first three volumes of the Annals, containing our origin myths, referenced in later works but not mentioned as having been seen after the first century of the Company's existence.

The Book of Te-Lare tells why.

There was a battle.

Always, there was a battle in any explanation.

Movement; a clash of arms; another punctuation mark in the long tale of the Black Company.

In this one the people who had hired our forebrethren had bolted at the first shock of the enemy's charge. They had broken so fast they were gone before the Company realized what was happening. The outfit beat a fighting retreat into its fortified encampment. During the ensuing siege the enemy penetrated the camp several times. During one such penetration the volumes in question vanished. Both the Annalist and his understudy were slain. The Books could not be reconstructed from memory.

Oh, well. I was ahead of the game.

Books available charted our future almost to the edge of the maps owned by the monks, and those ran all the way to Here There Be Dragons. Another century and a half of a journey into our yesterdays. By the time we retraced our route that far I hoped we would stand at the heart of a map that encompassed our destination.

As soon as it was clear that we had struck gold I obtained writing materials and a virgin volume of the Annals. I could write as fast as One-Eye and the monk could translate.

Time fled. A monk brought candles. Then a hand settled on my shoulder. Lady said, "Do you want to take a break? I could do that for a while."

For half a minute I just sat there turning red. That, after I practically ditched her outside. After I never even thought of her all day.

She told me, "I understand."

Maybe she did. She had read the various Books of Croaker—or, as posterity might recall them, the Books of the North—several times.

With Murgen and Lady spelling me the translation went quickly. The only practical limit was One-Eye's endurance.

It was not all one way. I had to trade my later Annals for their older ones. Lady sweetened the deal with a few hundred anecdotes about the dark empire of the north, but the monks never connected my Lady with the queen of darkness.

One-Eye is a tough old buzzard. He held up. Four days after he made his great discovery the job was done.

I let Murgen into the game but he did all right. And I had to beg/buy four blank journals in order to get everything transcribed.

Lady and I resumed our stroll about where we had broken it, but with me a little down.

"What's the matter?" she chided, and to my astonishment wanted to know if it was a postcoital depression. Just the faintest of digs there, I think.

"No. I've just found out a ton about the Company's history. But I didn't learn anything that's really new."

She understood but she kept quiet and let me articulate my dissatisfaction.

"It's told a hundred ways, poorly and well, according to the skill of the particular Annalist, but, except for the occasional interesting detail, it was the same old march, countermarch, fight, celebrate or run away, record the dead, and, sooner or later, get even with the sponsor for betraying us. Even at that place with the unpronounceable name, where the Company was in service for fifty-six years."

"Gea-Xle." She got her mouth around it like she had had practice.

"Yeah, there. Where the contract lasted so long the Company almost lost its identity, intermarrying with the population and all that, becoming a sort of hereditary bodyguard, with arms handed down from father to son. But as it always will, the essential moral destitution of those would-be princes made itself evident and somebody decided to cheat us. He got his throat cut and the Company moved on."

"You certainly read selectively, Croaker."

I looked at her. She was laughing at me quietly.

"Yeah, well." I'd stated it pretty baldly. A prince did try to cheat our forebrethren and did get his throat cut. But the Company installed a new, friendly, beholden dynasty and did hang around a few years before that Captain got a wild hair and decided to go treasure hunting.

"You have no reservations about commanding a band of hired killers?" she asked.

"Sometimes," I admitted, sliding past the trap nimbly. "But we never cheated a sponsor." Not exactly. "Sooner or later, every sponsor cheated us."

"Including yours truly?"

"One of your satraps beat you to it. But given time we would have become less than indispensable and you would have started looking around for a way to shaft us instead of doing the honorable thing and paying us off and simply terminating our commission."

"That's what I love about you, Croaker. Your unflagging faith in humanity."

"Absolutely. Every ounce of my cynicism is supported by historical precedent," I grumped.

"You really know how to melt a woman, you know that, Croaker?"

"Huh?" I come armed with a whole arsenal of such brilliant repartee.

"I came out here with some feebleminded notion of seducing you. For some reason I'm not in the mood to try anymore."

Well. Some of them you screw up royal.

There was an observation catwalk along some parts of the monastery wall. I went up into the northeast corner, leaned on the adobe and stared back the way we had come. Busy feeling sorry for myself. Every couple hundred years that sort of thing leads to a productive insight.

The damned crows were thicker than ever. Must have

been twenty of them now. I cursed them and, I swear, they mocked me. When I threw a loose piece of adobe they all jumped up and fled toward . . .

"Goblin!" I think he was out keeping an eye on me in case I got suicidal.

"Yeah?"

"Get One-Eye and Lady and come up here. Fast." I turned and stared up the slope at the thing that had caught my eye.

It stopped moving but was unmistakably a human figure in robes so black looking at them was like looking at a rent in the fabric of existence. It carried something under its right arm, about the size of a hatbox, held in place by the natural fall of the limb. The crows swarmed around it, twenty or thirty of them, squabbling over the right to perch upon its shoulders. It was a good quarter mile from where I stood but I felt the gaze from its hooded, unseen face beating upon me like the heat from a furnace.

The crowd turned up with Goblin and One-Eye as quarrelsome as ever. Lady asked, "What is it?"

"Take a look out there."

They looked. Goblin squeaked, "So?"

"So? What do you mean, so?"

"What's so interesting about an old tree stump and a flock of birds?"

I looked. Damn! A stump . . . But as I stared there was an instant's shimmer and I saw the black figure again. I shuddered.

"Croaker?" Lady asked. She was still mad at me but concerned even so.

"Nothing. My eyes were playing tricks on me. I thought I saw the damned thing moving. Forget it."

They took me at my word, stomped off to whatever they had been doing. I watched them go and for another moment doubted my own senses.

But then I looked again.

The crows were flying off in a crowd, except for two

headed straight toward me. And the stump was hiking off across the hillside as though intent on circling the monastery.

I mumbled a little to myself but it did not do any good.

I tried giving the Temple a few more days to work its magic but the next one hundred fifty years of our journey drummed on in my mind. There was no repose now. I was too itchy to sit. I announced my intention. And I got no kickbacks. Just acquiescent nods. Maybe even relieved nods.

What was this?

I sat up and came out of myself, where I had been spending a lot of time reexamining the familiar old furniture. I had not been paying attention to the others.

They were restless, too.

There was something in the air. Something that told us all it was time to hit the road. Even the monks seemed eager to see us move out. Curious.

Them that stays alive in the soldiering business are them that listens to such feelings even when they make no sense. You feel like you got to move, you move. You stay put and get stomped, it is too late to whine about all that work for nothing.

Chapter Twelve:
THE SHAGGY HILLS

To reach One-Eye's jungle we had to pass through several miles of woods, then climb over a range of decidedly odd hills. The hills were very round, very steep, and completely treeless, though not especially high. They were covered with a short brown grass that caught fire easily, so that many bore black scars. From a distance they looked like a herd of giant, tawny, humped beasts sleeping.

I was in a state of high nerves. That sleeping-beast image haunted me. I kept half expecting those hills to waken and shrug us off. I caught up with One-Eye. "Is there something weird about these hills that you accidentally forgot to tell me about on purpose?"

He gave me a funny look. "No. Though the ignorant believe them to be burial mounds from a time when giants walked the earth. But they aren't. They're just hills. All dirt and rock inside."

"Then why do they make me feel funny?"

He glanced back the way we had come, puzzled. "It's not the hills, Croaker. It's something back there. I feel it, too. Like we just dodged an arrow."

I did not ask him what it was. He would have told me if he had known.

As the day wore on I realized the others were as jumpy as I was.

Worrying about it did as much good as worrying ever does.

Next morning we ran into two wizened little men of One-Eye's race. They both looked a hundred years old. One of them kept hacking and coughing like he was about to croak. Goblin cackled. "Must be old Lizard Lips's illegitimate grandchildren."

There was a resemblance. I suppose that was to be expected. We were just accustomed to One-Eye being unique.

One-Eye scowled at Goblin. "Keep it up, Barf Bag. You'll be grocery shopping with the turtles."

What the hell did that mean? Some kind of obscure shop talk? But Goblin was as croggled as the rest of us.

Grinning, One-Eye resumed gabbling with his relatives.

Lady said, "I presume these are the guides the monks sent for?"

They had done us that favor on learning our intentions. We would need guides. We were near the end of any road we could call familiar. Once past One-Eye's jungle we would need somebody to translate for One-Eye, too.

Goblin let out a sudden aggrieved squawk.

"What's your problem?" I demanded.

"He's feeding them a pack of lies!"

So what was new about that? "How do you know? You don't talk that lingo."

"I don't have to. I've known him since before your dad was whelped. Look at him. He's doing his classic mighty-sorcerer-from-a-faraway-land act. In about twenty seconds he's going to . . .". A wicked grin spread his mouth around his face. He muttered something under his breath.

One-Eye raised a hand. A ball of light formed within his curled fingers.

There was a pop like that of a cork coming out of a wine bottle.

One-Eye held a hand full of swamp bottom. It oozed between his fingers and ran down his arm. He lowered his hand and stared in disbelief.

He let out a shriek and whirled.

Innocent Goblin was faking a conversation with Murgen. But Murgen was not up to the deceit. His shifty eyes gave Goblin away.

One-Eye puffed up like a toady frog, ready to explode. Then a miracle occurred. He invented self-restraint. A nasty little smile pranced across his lips and he turned back to the guides.

That was the second time in my experience that he had controlled himself when provoked. But, then, it was one of those rare times when Goblin had initiated the process of provocation. I told Otto, "This could get interesting."

Otto grunted an affirmative. He was not thrilled.

Of One-Eye, I asked, "Have you finished telling them you're the necromancer Voice of the North Wind come to ease the pain in their hearts brought on by worry about their wealth?" He'd actually tried to sell that once, to a tribe of savages coincidentally in possession of an eye-popping cache of emeralds. He found out the hard way that primitive does not mean stupid. They were fixing to burn him at the stake when Goblin decided to bail him out. Against his better judgment, he always insisted afterward.

"It ain't like that this time, Croaker. I wouldn't do it to my own people."

One-Eye does not have an ounce of shame. Nor even the sense not to lie to those who know him well. Of course he would do it to his own people. He would do it to anybody if he thought he could get away with it. And he has so little trouble conning himself on that.

"See that you don't. We're too few and too far from safety to let you indulge yourself in your usual line of shit."

I got enough menace into my voice to make him gulp.

His tone was markedly different when he resumed gobbling at our prospective guides.

Even so, I decided I would pick up a smatter of the language. Just to keep an ear on him. His often misplaced self-confidence has a way of asserting itself at the most unpropitious moments.

Straight for a time, One-Eye negotiated a deal that pleased everyone. We had ourselves guides for the passage through the jungle and intermediary interpreters for the land that lay beyond.

Relying on his usual moronic sense of humor, Goblin dubbed them Baldo and Wheezer, for reasons that were self-evident. To my embarrassment, the names stuck. Those two old boys probably deserved better. But then again . . .

We wended our way between the shaggy, hump-backed hills the rest of that day, and as darkness approached we topped the cleavage between the pair that flanked the summit of our passage. From there we could see the sunset, reflecting bloody wounds of a broad river, and the rich green of the jungle beyond. Behind us lay the tawny humps, and beyond them a hazy sprawl of indigo.

My mood was reflective, flat, almost down. It seemed we might have reached a watershed in more than a geographical sense.

Much later, unable to sleep for thoughts that questioned what I was doing here in an alien land, thoughts that replied that I had nothing else to do and nowhere else to go, I left my bedroll and the remaining warmth of our campfire. I headed for one of the flanking hills, moved by some vague notion of going up where I could get a better view of the stars.

Wheezer, who had the watch, gave me a gap-toothed leer before spitting a wad of brown juice into the coals. I heard him start wheezing before I was halfway up the hill.

A lunger I got, yet.

* * *

The moon threatened to rise soon. It would be fat and bright. I picked me a spot and stood looking at the horizon, waiting for that fat orange globe to roll over the lip of the world. The faintest of cool, moist breezes stirred my hair. It was so damned peaceful it hurt.

"You couldn't sleep, either?"

I jerked around.

She was a dark glob on the hillside just ten feet away. If I had noted her at all, it was as a rock. I stepped closer. She was seated, her arms wrapped around her knees. Her gaze was fixed on the north.

"Sit down."

I sat. "What are you looking at so hard?"

"The Reaper. The Archer. Vargo's Ship." And yesterdays, no doubt.

Those were constellations. I considered them, too. They were very low, seen from here. This time of year they would be quite high in the sky up north. What she meant began to sink in.

We had come a far piece, indeed. With many a mile to go.

She said, "It's intimidating when you think about it. It's a lot of walking."

It was.

The moon clambered over the horizon, monstrous in size and almost red. She whispered "Wow!" and slipped her hand into mine. She was shivering, so after a minute I slid over and put my arm around her. She leaned her head against my shoulder.

That old moon was working its magic. That sucker can do it to anybody.

Now I knew what made Wheezer grin.

The moment seemed right. I turned my head—and her lips were rising to meet mine. When they touched mine I forgot who and what she had been. Her arms surrounded me, pulled me down. . . .

She shivered in my grasp like a captive mouse. "What is it?" I whispered.

"Shh," she said. And that was the best thing she could have said. But she could not leave it there. She had to add, "I never . . . I never did this. . . ."

Well, shit. She sure knew how to distract a man, and put a thousand reservations into his mind.

That moon climbed the sky. We began to relax with each other. Somehow, there were fewer rags separating us.

She stiffened. The mist went out of her eyes. She lifted her head and stared past me, face slack.

If one of those clowns had sneaked up to watch I was going to break his kneecaps. I turned.

We did not have company. She was watching the flash of a distant storm. "Heat lightning," I said.

"You think so? It doesn't seem much farther off than the Temple. And we never saw a storm the whole time we were crossing that country."

Jagged lightning bolts ripped down like a fall of javelins.

That feeling I had discussed with One-Eye redoubled.

"I don't know, Croaker." She began gathering her clothing. "The pattern seems familiar."

I followed her lead, relieved. I am not sure I would have been able to finish what we started. I was distracted now.

"Another time will be better, I think," she said, still staring at that lightning. "That is too distracting."

We returned to camp to find everyone awake yet totally uninterested in the fact that we had been away together. The view was not as good from below, but flashes could be seen. They did not let up.

"There's sorcery out there, Croaker," One-Eye said.

Goblin nodded. "The heavy stuff. You can feel the screaming edges of it from here."

"How far away?" I asked.

"About two days. Close to that place we stopped."

I shivered. "Can you tell what it's about?"

Goblin said nothing. One-Eye shook his head. "All I

can tell you is I'm glad I'm here and not there."

I agreed, even in my ignorance of what was happening.

Murgen blanched. He pointed over the book he was studying, which he held out like a protective fetish. "Did you *see* that?"

I was looking at Lady and brooding about my luck. The others could sweat the little stuff, like some bloody sorcerers' duel fifty miles away. I had troubles of my own.

"What?" I grumbled, knowing he wanted a response.

"It looked like a giant bird. I mean, like one with a twenty-mile wingspan. That you could see through."

I looked up. Goblin nodded. He had seen it, too. I looked to the north. The lightning ended, but some pretty fierce fires had to be burning up there. "One-Eye. Your new buddies there got any idea what's going on?"

The little black man shook his head. He had the brim of his hat pulled forward, cutting his line of sight. That business up there—whatever it was—had him rattled. By his own admission he is the greatest wizard ever produced by his part of the world. With the possible exception of his dead brother, Tom-Tom. Whatever that was out there, it was alien. It did not belong.

"Times change," I suggested.

"Not around here, they don't. And if they did, these guys would know about it." Wheezer nodded vigorous agreement although he could not have understood a word. He hawked and spat a brown glob into the fire.

I had a feeling I was going to have as much fun with him as I did with One-Eye. "What is that crap he's all the time chewing? It's disgusting."

"Qat," One-Eye said. "A mild narcotic. Doesn't do his lungs any good, but when he's chewing it he doesn't care how much they hurt him." He said it lightly, but he meant it.

I nodded uncomfortably, looked away. "Quieting down up there."

No one had anything to say to that.

"We're all awake," I said. "So get packing. I want to move out as soon as we can see to walk."

I did not get a bit of argument. Wheezer nodded and spat. Goblin grunted and started getting his things together. The others followed his example, Murgen putting the book away with a care that I approved. The boy might make an Annalist after all. We all kept sneaking looks at the north when we thought our uneasiness would go unnoticed.

When I was not looking that way, or tormenting myself with glances at Lady, I tried to get an estimate of the reactions of the newer men. We had encountered no sorcery directly yet, but the Company has a way of stumbling into its path. They seemed no more uncomfortable than the old hands.

Glances at Lady. I wondered if what seemed inevitable on the one hand and foredoomed on the other would ever cease crackling between us. So long as it did it would distort everything else in our relationship. Hell. I liked her fine as a friend.

There is nothing so unreasonable and irrational and blind—and just plain silly-looking—as a man who works himself into an obsessive passion.

Women do not look as foolish. They are expected to be weak. But they are also expected to become savage bitches when they are frustrated.

Chapter Thirteen:
WILLOW'S LAST NIGHT LITTLE

Willow, Cordy Mather, and Blade still had their tavern. Mainly because they had the countenance of the Prah-brindrah Drah. Business wasn't good now. The priests found out they couldn't control the foreigners. So they put them off limits. A lot of Taglians did what the priests told them.

"Shows you how much sense people have," Blade said. "They had any, they would take the priests to the river and hold them under an hour to remind them they drone like termites."

Willow said, "Man, you got to be the sourest son of a bitch I ever seen. I bet if we hadn't dragged you out, those crocs would of thrown you back. Too rancid to eat."

Blade just grinned as he went through the door to the back room.

Willow asked Cordy, "You reckon it was priests that throwed him in?"

"Yeah."

"Good house tonight. For once."

"Yeah."

"Tomorrow's the day." Willow took a long drink. Cordy's brew was getting better. Then he stood up and hammered the bar with his empty mug. In Taglian he said, "We who are about to die salute you. Drink and be merry, children. For tomorrow, and so forth. On the house." He sat down.

Cordy said, "You know how to cheer a place up, don't you?"

"You figure we got anything to be cheerful about? They'll screw it up. You know they will. All those priests mucking about in it? I tell you right out, I get my chance there's a couple accidentally ain't going to come back from out there."

Cordy nodded and kept his mouth shut. Willow Swan was a lot more bark than bite.

Swan grumbled, "Up the river if this works out. I'll tell you something, Cordy. These feet get to moving that direction they're just going to keep on shuffling."

"Sure, Willow. Sure."

"You don't believe me, do you?"

"I believe everything you tell me, Willow. If I didn't, would I be here, up to my neck, wallowing in rubies and pearls and gold doubloons?"

"Man, what do you expect of someplace nobody ever heard of six thousand miles past the edge of any map anybody ever seen?"

Blade came back. "Nerves getting you guys?"

"Nerves? What nerves? They didn't put no nerves in when they made Willow Swan."

Chapter Fourteen:
THROUGH D'LOC ALOC

We moved out as soon as there was a ghost of light. It was an easy downhill trail with only a few places where we had trouble with the coach and Lady's wagon. By noon we reached the first trees. An hour later the first contingent were aboard a ferry raft. Before sundown we were inside the jungle of D'loc Aloc, where only ten thousand kinds of bugs tormented our bodies. Worse on our nerves than their buzzing, though, was One-Eye's suddenly inexhaustible store of praises and tales of his homeland.

From my first day in the Company I had been trying to get a fix on him and his country. Every lousy detail had had to be pried out. Now it was everything anyone ever wanted to know, and more. Except specifics of why he and his brother had run away from such a paradise.

From where I sat swatting myself the answer to that seemed self-evident. Only madmen and fools would subject themselves to such continuous torment.

So which was I?

For all there was a route through, we spent almost two months in that jungle. The jungle itself was the biggest problem. It was huge, and getting the coach through was, shall we say politely, a chore. But the people were a problem, too.

Not that they were unfriendly. Too much the opposite. Their ways were much easier than ours in the north.

Those sleek, delectable little brown beauties had never seen anything like Murgen and Otto and Hagop and their boys. They all wanted a taste of novelty. The guys were cooperative.

Even Goblin got lucky often enough to keep an ear-to-ear grin on his ugly clock.

Poor hapless, inhibited old Croaker planted himself firmly among the spectators and longed his heart out.

I do not have the hair it takes to pursue a little casual funtime bouncy-bouncy while a more serious proposition is watching from the wings.

My attitude caused no direct verbal comment—those guys have some tact, sometimes—but I caught enough snide sidelongs to know what they were thinking. And them thinking made me think. When I get introspective I can become broody and unfit company for man or beast. And when I know I am being watched a natural shyness or reluctance sets in and I do not do anything, no matter how auspicious the omens.

So I sat around on my hands, getting depressed because I feared something important might be slipping away and I was constitutionally incapable of doing anything about it.

Life sure was less complicated in the old days.

My temper improved after we scaled a last excessively vegetated and overly bug-infested mountain range and broke out of the jungle onto high plateau savannah.

From there one of the more interesting aspects of D'loc-Aloc seemed to be the fact that we had not attracted a single volunteer soldier. It said something about the peace the people had with their environment. And something about One-Eye and his long-gone brother.

What the hell had they *done*? I noticed he made a point of avoiding any talk about his past, his age, or his earlier identity while in the jungle with Baldo and Wheezer. Like anybody would remember something a couple of teenagers had done that long ago.

Baldo and Wheezer planted us as soon as they had us outside the country of their own people. They claimed they had reached the limit of territory they knew. [They promised to round up a couple of trustworthy natives who could take us on.] Baldo announced that he was going to turn back despite his earlier contract. [He claimed Wheezer would do us just fine as intermediary interpreter.]

Something had happened to disenchant Baldo. I did not argue with him. His mind was made up. I just did not pay him the full fee he had been promised.

I was thrilled that Wheezer was going to stay. That guy was a second-rate soul son of One-Eye, full of ridiculous mischief. Maybe there is something in the water in the jungle of D'loc-Aloc. Except that Baldo and everyone else we met was almost normal.

I guess my magnetic personality draws the One-Eye/Wheezer types.

For sure there was fun in the offing. One-Eye had been taking it from Goblin for two months with never a spark in response. When the blowup came it was sure to be a beauty.

"The whole thing is backwards," I said as Lady and I mulled things over. "One-Eye is supposed to pick at scabs while Goblin lays in the weeds waiting like a snake."

"Maybe it's because we've crossed the equator. The seasons are reversed."

I did not understand that remark until I had given it hours of thought. Then I realized that it had no meaning. It was one of her droll, deadpan jokes.

Chapter Fifteen:
THE SAVANNAH

We waited six days at the edge of the savannah. Twice bands of dark-skinned warriors came to look us over. The first time, Wheezer told us, "Don't let them lure you off the road."

He said it to One-Eye, not knowing that I had picked up enough of the chatter to follow what they said. I have a fair gift for tongues.

Most of us old hands do. We have to learn so many.

"What road?" One-Eye demanded. "That cow path?" He indicated a track that meandered into the distance.

"Whatever is between the white stones is the road. The road is holy. As long as you stay on it you'll be safe."

On first pitching camp we were warned not to leave a circle circumscribed by white stones. I guessed the significance of the lines of white stones running southward. Trade would demand sheltered routes. Though little trade seemed to be moving these days. Seldom had we encountered any sizable caravan heading north since leaving the empire. We saw no one headed south. Except perhaps a walking stump.

Wheezer continued, "Beware the plains peoples anyway. They are treacherous. They will employ every blandishment and deceit imaginable to draw you outside. Their women are especially notorious. Remember: They are always watching. To leave the road is death."

Lady was intensely interested in the discussion. She understood, too. And Goblin cracked, "You're dead, Maggot Lips."

"What?" One-Eye squeaked.

"The first set of sweet hips that shakes your way will lead you right off to the cannibals' cookpots."

"They aren't cannibals. . . ." Sudden panic tautened One-Eye's face.

It took him that long to realize that Goblin had understood him while he was talking with Wheezer. He looked at the rest of us. Some of us gave ourselves away.

He looked that much more distraught. He whispered to Wheezer with great animation.

Wheezer cackled. His laugh seemed half chicken cluck, half peacock call. It cost him a coughing fit.

It was a bad one. One-Eye beckoned me. "You're sure you can't do something for this guy, Croaker? He busts a lung and dies, we're hurting."

"Nothing. He shouldn't be traipsing around to begin with. . . ." No point singing that song. Wheezer refused to hear it. "You or Goblin ought to be able to do him more good than I can."

"You can't help a guy who won't let you."

"Ain't it the truth," I said, looking him straight in the eye. "How long before we get us some guides?"

"All I hear is 'soon' when I ask."

Soon indeed. A pair of tall black men came up the road at a steady, hardy trot. They were the sleakest, healthiest specimens I had seen in a long time. Each carried a sheaf of javelins across his back; a short-hafted, long-bladed spear in his right hand; and a shield of some white and black striped hide upon his left arm. Their limbs moved in perfect cadence, as though each man was half of some marvelous, rhythmic machine.

I glanced at Lady. No thoughts were evident on her face. "They would make grand soldiers," she said.

The two trotted straight to Wheezer, feigning a vast indifference to the rest of us. But I felt them studying us sidelong. White people had to be rare this side of the jungle. They barked at Wheezer in an arrogant tongue filled with clicks and stops.

Wheezer did some heavy kowtowing. He responded in the same language, whining like a slave addressing an ill-tempered master.

"Trouble," Lady prophesied.

"Right-o." This contempt for the outsider was not a new experience. I had to get busy and establish who said "Jump!" and who asked "How high?"

I talked to Goblin using the finger speech of the deaf. One-Eye caught it. He cackled. That stirred our new guides' indignation.

It would be touchy. They had to give me what they themselves knew was provocation. Only then would they accept being put in their place.

One-Eye was getting big ideas. I signed him to restrain himself, to prepare some impressive illusion. Aloud, I demanded, "What's all the babble? Get into the middle of that."

He started nagging Wheezer.

Wheezer carried on like a man caught between a rock and a hard place. He told One-Eye that the K'Hlata did not bargain. He said they would go through our things and pick out what they thought was worth their trouble.

"They try that and they'll get their fingers bitten off at the elbow. Tell them that. Politely."

It was too late for polite. Those guys understood the language. But One-Eye's growling threw them. They did not know what to do next.

"Croaker!" Murgen called. "Company."

Company indeed. Some of the boys who had given us the fish-eye earlier.

They were just the specific for the bruised egos of our new friends. The boys jumped up and down and howled and banged their spears against their shields. They hurled taunts. They pranced along the stone-marked boundary. One-Eye trotted after them.

The fish were not biting. But they had a little bait of their own. Something got said.

The two warriors howled and attacked. That caught everyone off guard. Three outsiders went down. The others subdued our guides quickly, though not without further mishap.

Wheezer poised on the boundary, wringing his hands and carping at One-Eye. While crows circled high above.

"Goblin!" I snapped. "One-Eye! Get with it!"

One-Eye cackled, reached up, grabbed his hair, and yanked.

He peeled himself from under that silly hat. And the fanged and fiery thing behind the peeling was ugly enough to turn a buzzard's stomach.

Which was all show, all distraction, while Goblin got on with the meat of it.

Goblin seemed to be surrounded by giant worms. It took me a moment to realize all those squirms were lengths of rope. I shrieked when I saw the state of our gear.

Goblin howled with laughter as a hundred chunks of rope went slithering through grass and air to pester, climb, bind, garrote.

Wheezer pranced around in an absolute apoplectic fit. "Stop! Stop! You're destroying the whole concord."

One-Eye ignored him. He put the mask back over the horror while punishing Goblin with ferocious looks. He resented Goblin's ingenuity.

Goblin was not finished. Having strangled everyone not already carved up or nominally friendly, he had his ropes drag the corpses across the boundary.

"No outside witnesses," One-Eye assured me, blind to those damned crows. He glared at Goblin. "What might the little toad have been up to?"

"Say what?"

"Those ropes. That was no spur-of-the-moment piece of work, Croaker. It would take months to charm that much line. I know who he had in mind, too. No bloody more nice, polite, long-suffering One-Eye. The gloves are off now. I'm going to get my revenge before that little bastard catches me with my back turned."

"Preemptive vengeance?" There was a One-Eye concept for you.

"I told you, he's up to something. I'm not going to stand around and wait. . . ."

"Ask Wheezer what to do about the bodies."

Wheezer said bury them deep and do a prime job of camouflaging.

"Trouble," Lady said. "Any way you look at it."

"The animals are rested. We'll outrun it."

"I hope so. I wish . . ." There was something in her voice that I could not decipher. I did not get it till later. Nostalgia. Homesickness. Longing for something irrevocably lost.

Goblin dubbed our new guides the Geek and the Freak. Despite my displeasure the names clung.

We crossed the savannah in fourteen days, without mishap, though Wheezer and the guides panicked each time they heard distant drums.

The message they dreaded did not come till we had left the savannah for the mountainous desert bounding it on the south. Both guides immediately begged to be allowed to stay with the Company. An extra spear is an extra spear.

One-Eye told me, "The drums said they've been declared outlaws. What they said about us you don't want to hear. You decide to go back north again you'd better think about another way to get there."

Four days later we made camp on some heights overlooking a large city and a broad river that flowed southeast. We had come to Gea-Xle, eight hundred miles below the equator. The mouth of that river, sixteen hundred miles farther south, lay at the edge of the world on the map I had made at the Temple of Travellers' Repose. The last place name marked, with great uncertainty, was Troko Tallio, a ways upriver from the coast.

Once camp was set to my satisfaction I went looking for Lady. I located her among some high rocks. But instead of studying the view she was staring into a tin teacup. For an instant the cup appeared to contain a pinprick spark. Then she sensed my approach. She looked up, smiled.

There was no spark in the cup when I looked again. Must have been my imagination.

"The Company is growing," she said. "You've accumulated twenty men since leaving the Tower."

"Uhm." I sat down, stared at the city. "Gea-Xle."

"Where the Black Company was in service. But where wasn't the Company in service?"

I chuckled. "You're right. We're wading around in our own past. We put the present dynasty in power down there. When we left it was without the usual hard feelings. What would happen if we rode in with Murgen showing our true colors?"

"There's only one way to find out. Let's try it."

Our gazes met and locked. The multiple meaning sparked between us. It had been a long time since that lost moment. We had been evading moments like this, a sort of delayed adolescent shyness and guilt.

The sun settled in a glorious conflagration, the only fire there was that evening.

I just could not get past who she used to be.

She was angry with me. But she hid it well and joined me in watching the city put on its night face. That was a cosmetic job worthy of an aging princess.

She did not need to waste energy getting mad at me. I was doing a fine job being mad at myself. "Strange stars, strange skies," I observed. "The constellations are completely out of whack now. Much more and I'll start feeling like I'm in the wrong world."

She made a snorting sound.

"More than I do already. Hell. I'd better rummage the
Annals to see what they say about Gea-Xle. I don't know
why, but the place bothers me." Which was true, though
I'd only just realized it. That was unusual. People
intimidate me, not places.

"Why don't you do that?" I could almost hear her
thinking, *Go hide in your books and your yesterdays. I'll
sit here staring today and tomorrow in the eye.*

It was one of those times when no matter what you say,
it will be the wrong thing. So I did the second worst thing
and went away without saying anything at all.

I almost tripped over Goblin going back to camp.
Though I was making a racket stumbling through the
dark, he was so intent he did not hear me.

He was peeping over a rock, eyeballing the slump of
One-Eye's back. He was so obviously up to no good I
could not resist. I bent and whispered, "Boo!"

He let out a squawk and jumped about ten feet, stood
there giving me the evil eye.

I tramped on into camp and started digging for the
book I wanted to read.

"Why don't you mind your own business, Croaker?"
One-Eye demanded.

"What?"

"Mind your own business. I was laying for the little
toad. If you hadn't stuck your nose in, I'd have had him
strung up like an antelope ready for gutting." A rope
slithered out of the darkness and curled up in his lap.

"I won't let it happen again."

The Annals did nothing to relieve my apprehension. I
got really paranoid, getting that nervous itch between the
shoulder blades. I began studying the darkness, trying to
see who was watching.

Both Goblin and One-Eye had a big sullen on. I asked,
"Can you guys come up for a little serious business?"

Well, yes, they could, but they could not admit that
their pouting was not of earthshaking significance, so

they just stared at me and waited for me to get on with it. "I've got a bad feeling. Not exactly a premonition, but the same family, and it keeps getting worse."

They stared, stone-faced, refusing comment.

But Murgen volunteered, "I know what you mean, Croaker. I've had the heebie-jeebies since we got here."

I gave the rest a scan. They stopped yakking. The Tonk games came to a halt. Otto and Hagop had small nods to admit that they felt unsettled, too. The rest were too macho to admit anything.

So. Maybe my collywobbles were not imaginary.

"I get a feeling going down there could become a watershed of Company history. Can one of you geniuses tell me why?"

Goblin and One-Eye looked at each other. Neither spoke.

"The only thing the Annals say that's weird is that Gea-Xle was one of those rare places the Company walked away from."

"What does that mean?" That Murgen was a natural shill.

"It means our forebrethren didn't have to fight their way out. They could have renewed their commission. But the Captain heard about a treasure mountain up north where the silver nuggets were supposed to weigh a pound."

There was more to the tale but they did not want to hear it. We were not really the Black Company anymore, just rootless men from nowhere headed the same direction. How much was that my fault? How much the fault of bitter circumstance?

"No comment?" They both looked thoughtful, though. "So. Murgen. Break out the real colors tomorrow. With all the honors."

That jacked up some eyebrows.

"Finish the tea, guys. And tell your bellies to get ready for some real brew. They make the genuine elixir down there."

That sparked some interest.

"You see? The Annals are good for something after all."

I set about doing some writing in the latest of my own volumes, occasionally peeking at one or another of the wizards. They had forgotten their feud, were using their heads for something more than the creation of mischief.

During one of my upward glances I caught a silvery yellow flash. It seemed to come from the rocks where I had been a while back, watching the city lights.

"Lady!"

I barked my shins a dozen times getting there, then felt like a fool when I found her seated on a rock, arms around her legs, chin on her knees, contemplating the night. The light of a newly risen moon fell upon her from behind. She was astonished by my wild stumble to the rescue.

"What happened?" I demanded.

"What?"

"I saw some weird flashes up here."

Her expression, in that light, seemed honestly baffled.

"Must have been a trick of the moonlight. Better turn in pretty soon. I want to get an early start."

"All right," she said in a small, troubled voice.

"Is something wrong?"

"No. I'm just lost."

I knew what she meant without her having to explain.

Going back I ran into Goblin and One-Eye moving up carefully. Fireflies of magic danced in their hands and dread smoldered in their eyes.

Chapter Sixteen:
WILLOW'S WAR

Willow was amazed. It actually went pretty much the way it was supposed to. The Taglians gave up their territories below the Main without a finger raised to resist. The army of the Shadowmasters came over the river and still met no resistance. It dissolved into its four elements. Still meeting no opposition, those forces broke up into companies, the better to plunder. The looting was so good all discipline collapsed.

Taglian marauders began picking off foragers and small raiding parties, suddenly, everywhere. The invaders suffered a thousand casualties before they understood. Cordy Mather engineered that phase, claiming to emulate his military idols, the Black Company. When the invaders responded with larger foraging parties he countered by leading them into traps and ambushes. At his peak he twice suckered entire companies into densely built and specially prepared towns that he burned down around them. The third time he tried that, though, the invaders did not take the bait. His overconfident Taglians got whipped. Wounded, he went back to Taglios to contemplate the fickleness of fate.

Willow, meantime, was marching around the eastern Taglian territories with Smoke and twenty-five hundred volunteers, keeping close to the enemy commander, trying to look like a menace that would become nemesis the moment the invaders made a mistake. Smoke had no intention of fighting, and was so stubborn even Willow was tempted to grumble.

Smoke claimed he was waiting for something to happen. He wouldn't say what.

Blade got stuck down south, in the territories yielded without a fight, along the Main River. He was supposed to get the locals together and keep any messengers from going back and forth. It was an easy job. There were no bridges across the river and only four places where it could be forded. The Shadowmasters must have been preoccupied. Their suspicions were not aroused. Or maybe they just assumed no news was good news.

What Smoke was waiting for happened.

Like Blade said, Taglios was hag-ridden by its priests. Three major religions existed there, not in harmony. Each had its splinters, factions, and subcults that feuded among themselves when they weren't feuding with the others. Taglian culture centered upon religious differences and the efforts of the priests to get ahead of each other. A lot of lower-class people weren't signed up with anybody. Especially out in the country. Likewise the ruling family, who did not dare get religion if they wanted to stay in charge.

Old Smoke was waiting for one of the boss priests to get the idea he could make a name for himself and his tribe by getting out and busting the heads of the invaders nobody else would fight. "Purely a cynical political maneuver," Smoke told Willow. "The Prahbrindrah's waited a long time to show someone what can happen if they don't do things his way."

He showed them.

One of the priests got the bright idea. He conned about fifteen thousand guys into thinking they could handle experienced professionals, heads up. He led the mob out to look for the invaders. They didn't have any trouble finding them. The Shadowmasters' commander thought this was what he was waiting for, too. The Shadow-masters' other conquests had all been settled by one big brawl.

Willow and Smoke and a few others stood on top of a hill where both sides could see them and spent an afternoon watching two thousand men massacre fifteen thousand. The Taglians that got away did so mostly because the invaders were too tired to chase them.

"Now we'll fight," Smoke said. So Willow moved his force up and poked till the invaders got aggravated and came after him. He ran till they stopped. Then he poked again. And ran again. And so forth. He got the notion from a poorly remembered version of a time when the Black Company ran for a thousand miles and led their enemies into a trap where they died almost to a man, thinking they had it won almost to the end.

Maybe these guys heard the same story. Anyway, they didn't want to be led. First time they balked they just camped and wouldn't move. So Willow talked it over with Smoke and Smoke rounded up some volunteers from the countryside and started building a wall around the invaders.

Next time the invaders just turned and marched off toward Taglios, which is what they should have done at the start, instead of trying to get rich. So Willow jumped on them from behind and kept making a nuisance of himself till he convinced the enemy commander that he had to be gotten rid of or there just wouldn't be any rest.

He told Smoke, "I don't know squat about strategy or tactics or anything, but I figure I only got to work on one guy, really. The head guy over there. I get him to do what I want, he brings everybody else with him. And I know how to aggravate a guy till he'll fight me."

Which is what he did.

The Shadowmaster's general finally chased him into a town that had been getting ready all along. It was a bigger version of Cordy's game. Only this time there wasn't going to be a fire. All the people had been got out and about twelve thousand volunteers put in their place. While Willow and Smoke were running the invaders around, those guys were building a wall.

Willow ran into the town and thumbed his nose. He did everything he could to get the enemy chief mad. The man did not get mad fast, though. He surrounded the town, then got every man he had in Taglian territory that could still walk. Then he attacked.

It was a nasty brawl. The invaders had it bad because in the tight streets they could not take advantage of better discipline. They always had guys shooting arrows at them off the rooftops. They always had guys with spears jumping out of doors and alleys. But they were better soldiers. They killed a lot of Taglians before they realized they were in a box, with about six times as many Taglians after them as they expected. By then it was too late for them to get out. But they took a lot of Taglians with them.

When it was over Willow went back to Taglios. Blade came home too, and they opened the tavern back up and celebrated for a couple weeks. Meantime, the Shadow-masters figured out what happened and got thoroughly pissed. They made all kinds of threats. The prince, the Prahbrindrah Drah, basically thumbed his nose and told them to put it where the sun don't shine.

Willow, Cordy, and Blade got a month off, then it was time for the next part, which was to take a long trip north with the Radisha Drah and Smoke. Willow didn't figure this part was going to be a lot of fun, but nobody could figure a better way to work it.

Chapter Seventeen:
GEA-XLE

I got them all up and decked out in their second best. Murgen had the standard out. There was a nice breeze to stretch it. Those great black horses stamped and champed, eager to get on down the road. Their passion communicated itself to their lesser cousins.

The gear was packed and loaded. There was no reason to hold movement—except that rattling conviction that the event would be something more than a ride into a city.

"You in a dramatic mood, Croaker?" Goblin asked. "Feel like showing off?"

I did and he knew it. I wanted to spit defiance in the face of my premonition. "What have you got in mind?"

Instead of answering directly, he told One-Eye, "When we get down there and come over that saddleback where they can get their first good look at us, you do a couple of thunders and a Trumpet of Doom. I'll do a Riding Through the Fire. That ought to let them know the Black Company is back in town."

I glanced at Lady. She seemed partly amused, partly patronizing.

For a moment One-Eye looked like he wanted to squabble. He swallowed it and nodded curtly. "Let's do it if we're going to do it, Croaker."

"Move out," I ordered. I did not know what they had in mind, but they could get flashy when they wanted.

They took the point together, Murgen a dozen yards behind with the standard. The rest fell into the usual file, with me and Lady side by side leading our share of pack animals. I recall eyeing the gleaming bare backs of the Geek and the Freak and reflecting that we had us some real infantry now.

The beginning of it was tight twists and turns on a steep, narrow path, but after a mile the way widened till it was almost a road. We passed several cottages evidently belonging to herdsmen, not nearly as poor and primitive as one would suspect.

Up we went into the backside of the saddle Goblin mentioned, and the show started. It was almost exactly what he prescribed.

One-Eye clapped his hands a couple of times and the results were sky-shaking crashes. Then he set them to his cheeks and let fly a trumpet call just as loud. Meantime, Goblin did something that filled the saddleback with a dense black smoke that turned into ferocious-looking but harmless flames. We rode through. I fought down a temptation to order a gallop and tell the wizards to have the horses breathe fire and kick up lightnings. I wanted a showy announcement of the Company's return, but not the appearance of a declaration of war.

"That ought to impress somebody," I said, looking back at the men riding out of the flames, the ordinary horses prancing and shying.

"If it doesn't scare hell out of them. You should be more careful how much you give away, Croaker."

"I feel daring and incautious this morning." Which was maybe the wrong thing to say after my failure of daring and lack of incaution the night before. But she let it pass.

"They're talking about us up there." She indicated the pair of stocky watchtowers flanking the road, three hundred yards ahead. There was no way to avoid riding between them, through a narrow passage filled with the shadow of death. Up top, heliographs chatted tower to tower and presumably with the city as well.

"Hope they're saying something nice, like hurray, the boys are back in town." We were close enough so I could make out the men up there. They did not look like guys getting ready for a fight. A couple sat on the merlons with their legs dangling outside. One that I took to be an officer stood in a crenel with one foot up on a merlon, leaning on his knee, watching casually.

"About the way I'd do it if I had me a really sneaky trap set," I grumped.

"Not everyone in the world has the serpentine sort of mind you do, Croaker."

"Oh yeah? I'm plain simple compared to some I could name."

She gave me one of her sharp old-time Lady-on-fire withering looks.

One-Eye was not there to say it himself, so I said it for him. "That snake's probably got more smarts than you do, Croaker. The only trouble he goes hunting is breakfast."

We were close to the one tower now, with Goblin and One-Eye and Murgen already past. I raised my hat in a friendly salute.

The officer reached down beside him, picked up something, tossed it down. It came tumbling toward me. I snatched it out of the air. "What an athlete! Maybe I'll go for two out of three."

I looked at what I caught.

It was a black stick about an inch and a quarter in diameter and fifteen inches long, carved from some heavy wood, decorated all over with ugly what-is-its. "I'll be damned."

"No doubt. What is it?"

"An officer's baton. I've never seen one before. But they're mentioned all through the Annals, up through the fall of Sham, which was some sort of mysterious lost city up on the plateau we just crossed." I lifted the baton in a second salute to the man above.

"The Company was there?"

"It's where it ended up after it left Gea-Xle. The

Captain didn't find his silver mountain. He did find Sham. The Annals are pretty confused. The people of Sham are supposed to have been a lost race of whites. It seems that about three days after the Company found Sham, so did the ancestors of the Geek and the Freak. They got themselves worked up into some kind of religious frenzy and jumped all over the city. The first horde to get there killed damned near everybody, including most of the Company officers, before the Company finished killing them. The guys who survived headed north because there was another mob closing in from the south, keeping them from heading back this way. These batons aren't mentioned after that."

To which her only response was, "They knew you were coming, Croaker."

"Yeah." It was a mystery. I do not like mysteries. But it was only one of a herd and the bellies of most of them would never come floating up where I could give them the eyeball.

There were two guys waiting down the road from the watchtowers, a third of a mile from the city wall. The surrounding countryside was pretty barren for so close to a city. I guess the ground was poor. Farther north and south there was plenty of green. One of the two guys gave Goblin an old Company standard. There was no doubt what it was, though I did not recognize any of the honors. It was damned ragged, as you would expect of something as old as it had to be.

What the hell was going on here?

One-Eye tried talking to those guys but it was like starting a conversation with a stone. They faced their mounts around and got out front. I gave One-Eye a nod when he looked back to see if we should follow.

A twelve-man honor guard presented arms as we passed through the gate. But nobody else greeted us. Silence ran with us as we moved through the streets, people stopping to stare at the pale-faced strangers. Lady got half the attention.

She deserved it. She looked damned good. Very

damned good. Black and tight both became her. She had the body to pull it off.

Our guides led us to a barracks and stable. The barracks part had been maintained but not used for a long time. It seemed we were supposed to make ourselves at home. All right.

Our guides did a fade while we were checking the place out.

"Well," Goblin said. "Bring on the dancing girls."

There were no dancing girls. There was not a lot of anything else either, unless you count apparent indifference. I had everybody stick tight the rest of the day, but nothing happened. We had been shelved and forgotten. Next morning I turned loose our two most recent recruits, along with One-Eye and Wheezer, on a mission meant to find a barge that would take us down the river.

"You just sent the fox to get a new latch for the chicken coop," Goblin protested. "You should've sent me along to keep him honest."

Otto busted out laughing.

I grinned but kept the rest inside. "You aren't brown enough to get by out there, little buddy."

"Oh, horse hockey. You bothered to look outside since we got here? There's white folks around, Fearless Leader."

Hagop said, "He's right, Croaker. Ain't a lot of them, but I seen a few."

"Where the hell did they come from?" I muttered, going to the door. Sparkle and Candles got out of my way. They were there to ambush any surprise unwanted guests. I went outside and leaned against the white-washed wall, chewed a piece of horse sorrel I plucked from the edge of the street.

Yeah. The boys were right. There were a pair of whites, an old man and a twenty-fivish woman, skulking down the way. They made a production of being indifferent to me while everyone else gawked.

"Goblin. Get your tail out here."

He stumped outside, sulky. "Yeah?"

"Take a discreet look down there. You see an old man and a younger woman?"

"White?"

"Yes."

"I see them. So what?"

"Ever seen them before?"

"At my age everybody looks like somebody I've seen before. But we've never been in this part of the world. So maybe they look like somebody we seen somewhere else. She does, anyway."

"Hunh. Other way around for me. Something about the way he moves rings alarms."

Goblin plucked his own horse sorrel. I watched. When I looked back the odd couple were gone. Headed our way were three black guys who looked like trouble on the hoof. "Gods. I didn't know they made them that big."

Goblin muttered, stared past them. He wore a puzzled frown. He cocked his head like he was having trouble hearing.

The three big guys marched up, stopped. One started talking. I did not understand a word. "No spikee, pal. Try another lingo."

He did. I did not get any of that, either. He shrugged and checked his buddies. One of them tried a clicky tongue.

"You lose again, guys."

The biggest broke into a ferocious dance of frustration. His buddies gabbled. And Goblin wandered away on me without a fare-thee-well Croaker. I caught a glimpse of his back as he scooted into a passage between buildings.

Meantime, my new friends decided I was deaf or stupid. They yelled at me, slowly. Which brought Sparkle and Candles outside, followed by the others. The three big guys cussed each other some more and decided to go away.

"What was that all about?" Hagop asked.

"You got me."

Goblin came trooping back wearing a big smug frog grin.

"I'm amazed," I said. "I figured I was going to lose a week while I hunted down the local hoosegow and sold my soul to dig you out."

He put on a show of being hurt. He squeaked, "I thought I saw your girlfriend sneaking off. I just went to check."

"Judging by your smugness, you did see her."

"Sure did. And I saw her meet up with your old man and his fluff."

"Yeah? Let's go inside and give it a think."

I checked around in there just to make sure Goblin was not seeing things. Lady was gone, sure enough.

What the hell?

One-Eye and his crew came strutting in late that afternoon. One-Eye smirked like a cat with feathers in his whiskers. Geek and Freak lugged a big closed basket between them. Wheezer hacked and chewed and smiled like there was big mischief afoot and he maybe had a big hand in it.

Goblin jumped up from a nap with a squawk of protest before One-Eye got started. "You get right on back out that door with that whatever-it-is, Buzzard Breath. Before I turn that spider's nest you call a brain into toys for tumblebugs."

One-Eye did not give him a look. "Check this out, Croaker. You ain't going to believe what I found."

The boys set the basket down and popped the lid.

"I probably won't," I agreed. I snuck up on that basket, expecting a gross of cobras, or something such. What I saw was a pint-sized ringer for Goblin. . . . Better say demitasse-sized, since Goblin is not much more than a half-pint himself. "What the hell is it? Where'd it come from?"

One-Eye stared at Goblin. "I been asking myself that for years." He had the biggest "Gottcha!" grin I ever saw.

Goblin howled like a leopardess in heat, started making mystical passes. His fingers raked furrows of fire out of the air.

Even I ignored him. "What is it?"

"It's an imp, Croaker. An honest-to-god imp. Don't you know an imp when you see one?"

"No. Where'd it come from?" I was not sure I wanted to know, knowing One-Eye.

"Heading down to the river we come on this little bunch of shops around an outdoor bazaar where they got all kinds of neat stuff for wizards, fortune-tellers, spirit talkers, Ouija workers, and such. And right there in the window of this dinky hole-in-the-wall shop, just begging for a new home, was this little guy. I couldn't resist. Say hello to the Captain, Frogface."

The imp piped, "Hello to the Captain, Frogface." It giggled just like Goblin, in a higher voice.

"Jump on out of there, bitty buddy," One-Eye said. The imp popped into the air as if shot up. One-Eye chortled. He caught it by a foot and stood there with it dangling head down like a toddler with a doll. He eyeballed Goblin, who was positively apoplectic, so fussed he could not go on with the magical funny business he had started.

One-Eye dropped the imp. It flipped and landed on its feet, sped across and stared up at Goblin like a young bastard having a sudden epiphany about the identity of its sire. It did cartwheels back to One-Eye, said, "I'm going to like it here with you guys."

I snagged One-Eye by the collar and lifted him off the floor. "What about the damned boat?" I shook him a little. "I sent you out to hire a goddamned boat, not to buy talking knick-knacks." It was one of those flashes of rage that last about three seconds, rare for me but usually strong enough to let me make an ass of myself.

My father had them a lot. When I was little I would hide under the table for the minute or so they took to pass.

I set One-Eye down. Looking amazed, he told me, "I found one, all right? Pulls out day after tomorrow, at first light. I couldn't get an exclusive charter because we couldn't afford anything big enough to haul us and the animals and coaches if that was all the barge would be carrying. I ended up making a deal."

The imp Frogface was behind Wheezer, clinging to and peeking around his leg like a frightened child— though I got the feeling it was laughing at us. "All right. I apologize for blowing up. Tell me about the deal."

"This is only good to what they call the Third Cataract, understand. That's a place eight hundred sixty miles down that a boat can't get past. There's about an eight-mile portage, then you have to hire passage again."

"To the Second Cataract, no doubt."

"Sure. Anyway, we can get the long first leg free, with food and fodder provided, if we serve as guards on this commercial barge."

"Ah. Guards. What do they need guards for? And why so many?"

"Pirates."

"I see. Meaning we'd end up fighting even if we did pay for our passage."

"Probably."

"Did you get a good look at the boat? Is it defensible?"

"Yeah. We could turn it into a floating fort in a couple days. It's the biggest damned barge I ever seen."

A tinkle of alarm began nagging in the back of my thoughts. "We'll give it another look in the morning. All of us. The deal sounds too good to be true, which probably means it is."

"I figured. That was one of the reasons I bought Frogface. I can send him sneaking around to check things out." He grinned and glanced at Goblin, who had gone into a corner to plot and pout. "Also, with Frogface along we don't have to waste no coin on guides and interpreters. He can do all that for us."

That sent my eyebrows up. "Really?"

"That's right. See? I do do something useful once in a while."

"You're threatening to. You say the imp is ready to use?"

"As ready as he can be."

"Come on outside where it's private. I got about ten jobs for it."

Chapter Eighteen:
THE BARGE

I took the outfit to the waterfront before the sun got its rump over the hills beyond the river. The city remained somnolent, except for traffic headed the way we were. The nearer the river the worse it got. And the waterfront was a frenzied hive.

There were crows.

"Looks like they've been at it all night," I said. "Which one is it, One-Eye?"

"That big one over there."

I headed the direction he pointed. The barge was a monster, all right. It was a giant wooden shoe of a thing meant mainly to drift with the current. Travel would be slow on a fat, sluggish river like this. "It looks new."

We moved in an island of silence and stares. I tried to read the faces of the laborers we passed. I saw little but a slight wariness. I noted a few armed men, as big as my visitors of yesterday, boarding some of the lesser barges. I eyed the stevedores marching aboard our craft. "Why the lumber, do you suppose?"

"My idea," One-Eye said. "It's to build mantlets. The only protection from missile fire they had was wicker screens. I'm surprised they listened and went to the bother and expense. Maybe they took me up on all my suggestions. We're set if they did."

"I'm not surprised." I was now sure that not only had

our arrival been foreseen, it had been calculated into the schemes of an entire city. That pirate infestation was more than a nuisance. These folks meant to hammer it down using a band of expendable adventurers.

I did not understand why they thought they had to run a game on us. That was our trade. And we had to go down that river anyway.

Maybe it was the way the society worked. Maybe they could not believe the truth.

With Frogface's help it took about six minutes to straighten out the bargemaster and the committee of bigwigs waiting with him. I wrangled the promise of a huge fee on top of our passage. "We go to work as soon as we see the money," I told them. Lo. It appeared almost magically.

One-Eye told me, "You could have held them up."

"They're desperate," I agreed. "Must be something they have to get through. Let's get to work."

"Don't you want to know what?"

"It doesn't matter. We're going anyway."

"Maybe. But I'll have Frogface look around."

"Whatever." I toured the main deck. Otto and Hagop tagged along. We talked upgraded defensibility. "We need a better idea of what we're up against. We want to be prepared for pirate tactics. For example, we might set up engines behind the mantlets if they attack from small boats."

I paused along the wharf side rail. It was obvious a convoy would follow our barge, which as obviously had been constructed to lead the way. Never would they get it back upriver. It had only enough oars to keep it pointed the right direction.

There were crows over the chaos. I ignored them. I had begun to suspect I was obsessed.

Then I spied an island of emptiness against a warehouse wall. People avoided it without noting what they were doing. A vague shape stood in shadow. Crows fluttered up and down.

I felt like someone was staring at me. *Was* it my imagination? No one else saw the damned crows. "Time I found out what the hell is going on. One-Eye! I need to borrow your new pet."

I told Frogface to go over and take a gander. He went. And in a minute he was back, giving me a funny look. "What was I supposed to see, Captain?"

"What did you see?"

"Nothing."

I looked over there. Nothing was what I saw now. But then I spotted the three big guys who had tried to talk to me yesterday. They had a bunch of cousins with them, getting in the way. They were watching our barge. I presumed they were interested in us still. "Got a translating job for you, runt."

The biggest guy's name was Mogaba. Him and his buddies wanted to sign on with the Company. He said there were more at home like them if I would have them. Then he claimed a right. He told me that all the big men I saw wandering around with sharp steel were descendants of the Black Company men who had served Gea-Xle in olden times. They were the Nar, the military caste of the city. I got the impression that to them I was something holy, the real Captain, a demigod.

"What do you think?" I asked One-Eye.

"We could use guys like them. Look at them. Monsters. Take all you can get if they're for real."

"Can Frogface find out?"

"You bet." He instructed the imp, sent him scooting.

"Croaker."

I jumped. I had not heard One-Eye coming. "What?"

"Those Nar are the real thing. Tell him, Frogface."

The imp piped away in that high Goblin voice.

The Nar were indeed descendants of our forebrethren. They did form a separate caste, a warrior cult built around the myths the Company left behind. They kept their own set of Annals and observed the ancient traditions better than we did. Then Frogface hit me with the kicker.

Somebody called Eldon the Seer, a famous local wizard, foretold our coming months ago, about the time we were crossing those shaggy-backed hills headed for D'loc-Aloc. The Nar (a word meaning black) had initiated a series of contests and trials to select the best man of each hundred to rejoin the father standard and make the pilgrimage to Khatovar. If we would have them.

Eldon the Seer had deciphered our mission from afar, too.

I do not like it when things are going on that I do not understand. Understand?

Mogaba was chosen commander of the delegation by virtue of being the champion of the caste.

While the Nar prepared for a holy hadj the lords and merchants of Gea-Xle began setting up to use us to break through a pirate blockade that had become impenetrable in recent years.

The great hope from the north. That was us.

"I don't know what to say," I told One-Eye.

"I'll tell you one thing, Croaker. You aren't going to be able to tell those Nar guys no."

I did not have that inclination. These pirates, about whom nobody would say much, sounded increasingly nasty. Somewhere down the line, without it having been stated explicitly, I had come on the notion that they had big magic they could call out when the going got hairy. "Why not?"

"Those guys are serious, Croaker. Religious serious. They'd do something crazy like throw themselves on their swords because the Captain found them inadequate to march with the Company."

"Come on."

"Really. I mean it. It's a religious thing with them. You're always telling about old ways. When the standard was a tutelary deity and whatnot. They've gone the other direction from what we did. The Company that went north turned into your basic gang of cutthroats. The kids they left behind turned them into gods."

"That's scary."

"Better believe."

"They're going to be disappointed in us. I'm the only one left who takes the traditions seriously."

"Horseapples, Croaker. Spit and polish and beating the drum for the olden days ain't all there is to it. I got to go find that little geek Goblin and see if he can stop pouting long enough for us to do a layout on how we work this scow if it gets hit. Hell. The pirates know everything that's going on up here. Maybe our reputation will scare them into letting us slide through."

"Think so?" It sounded like a nice idea.

"No. Frogface! Get over here. Acts like a damned kid, getting into things. Frogface, I want you to stick with Croaker. You do what he tells you just like if he was me. Got it? You don't and I'll paddle your butt."

For all its talents, the imp had the mind of a five-year-old. With an attention span to match. It told One-Eye it would behave and help me, but I did not expect that to be easy.

I went down to the wharf and accepted thirty-two recruits into our brotherhood of arms. Mogaba was so pleased I thought he might hug me.

They were a damned impressive thirty-two men, every one a monster and quick and lithe as a cat. If they were the mongrel children of the men who had served in Gea-Xle, what must those old-timers have been like?

First thing after I swore them in, Mogaba asked if it was all right if his caste brothers did guard duty aboard the other boats. So they could tell their sons that they had followed the hadj as far as the Third Cataract.

"Sure. Why not?" Mogaba and his boys had my head spinning. For the first time since I got stiffed with the job, I really *felt* like I was the Captain.

The gang dispersed to get their gear and to spread the good news.

I noted the master of the barge watching from up forward. He was wearing a big poo-eating grin.

Things were going just dandy for his crowd. They thought they had us by the short hairs and broken to the bridle.

"Hey, Croaker. Here comes your prodigal girlfriend."

"You too, Pup? I ought to toss you in the river." If I could run the imp down. He had the energy of a five-year-old, too.

I spotted her by the commotion she caused. Or the lack of it. Where she passed men paused to look and sigh and shake their heads wistfully. It did not occur to them to whistle, catcall, or make crude remarks.

I looked around and picked a victim. "Murgen!"

Murgen ambled over. "What do you need?"

"When Lady gets here show her her quarters. The attached room is for her guests."

"I thought . . ."

"Don't think. Just do."

I made myself scarce. I was not yet ready for the inevitable battle.

Chapter Nineteen:
THE RIVER

Night on the river. A moon splattering the dark mirror of water. A stillness at times almost supernatural, then the cacophony of a festival in hell: crocodiles grunting, fifty kinds of frogs singing, birds hooting and squawking, hippos snorting; the gods only knew what all.

And bugs buzzing. The bugs were almost as bad as they had been in the jungle. They would get worse once we entered the wetlands farther south. The river was said to flow imperceptibly through a swamp ten to eighty miles wide and three hundred miles long. Here the west bank was still tame. The east was three-quarters wild. The people we saw watching from boats in the mouths of sloughs and creeks were as poorly tamed as their land.

I was assured that they, living in the shadow of the city, were harmless. When they came whooping out it was to hawk crocodile hides and parrot-feather cloaks. On impulse I bought one of the cloaks, the biggest and most outrageously colorful one available. It must have weighed sixty pounds. Wearing it I became the very image of a savage chieftain.

Mogaba examined the cloak and pronounced it a wise buy. He told me it would shed darts and arrows better than armor of steel.

Some of the Nar bought croc hides to toughen their shields.

Goblin got a wild hair and bought him a couple of

preserved croc heads. One was so big it looked like it had
been lopped off a dragon. While I was seated up top
contemplating the nighttime river, wondering about
crows, he was up forward mounting his monster pur-
chase as a figurehead. I supposed he had some drama up
his sleeve.

He came to me with the smaller head. "I want to fit
you out to wear this."

"You what?"

"I want to fit you out to wear this. So when the pirates
come you can strut around up here in your feather coat
breathing fire like some mythological beast."

"That's a great gimmick. I really like it. In fact, I love
it. Why don't we see if we can't get some dope like Big
Bucket to try it."

"But—"

"You don't think *I'm* going to stand up there and let
people snipe at *me*, do you?"

"You'll have plenty of protection from me and One-
Eye."

"Yeah? Then my prayers are answered at last. For
years I've wanted nothing more than protection from
you and One-Eye. 'Preserve me, O sainted fathers of the
Company!' I've cried a thousand times. Yea, ten thousand times have I called—"

Sputtering, he cut me off and changed the subject. He
squeaked, "Those people your girlfriend brought
aboard—"

"Next fool who calls Lady my girlfriend gets to throw a
saddle on a croc and see if they can be broken. You get
my drift?"

"Yeah. You got your feelings hurt on account of reality
is catching up with you."

I kept my mouth shut, but just barely.

"Bad news, those two are, Croaker." He whispered in
the no-breath whisper we use when we are creeping past
enemy sentries. "There's big mojo brewing down in their
cabin."

He was trying to make himself useful. He had been

overshadowed since the appearance of Frogface. So I did not tell him I was on to that already and had had me a thought or two about what could be done.

A fish jumped up and skipped across the water to get away from some predator. For his effort he got his reward: some night bird snagged him on the bounce.

I grunted. Should I let Goblin know how much I knew and suspected? Or should I just go on looking dumb while setting the moment up? Building a mystique had become important now that the Company was on the grow. It should work for a while. The old hands should not suspect me of taking as cynical and pragmatic an approach to command as I planned.

I listened to Goblin's outpouring of fact, suspicion, and speculation. Little that he said was new. What *was* new only more thoroughly framed the picture I had. I told him, "I think it's time you came up with the masterpiece of your life, Goblin. Something plain, direct, and powerful, that you can cut loose in a second."

He turned on the famous Goblin grin. "I'm way ahead of you, Croaker. I've got a couple of things in the works that are going to amaze people when I use them."

"Good." I had a feeling One-Eye was in for a shock somewhere down the line.

The journey to the Third Cataract takes a minimum two weeks because the current does not exceed a slow walk. Adding pirate trouble could make the trip last forever.

By the end of our fourth day the barge was as defensible as possible. Timber shields protected the main deck. Their lower ends projected over the water to make boarding from boats difficult. None of the embrasures in that shielding were big enough for a man to weasel through. The guys had put together four ballistae for each side. Thanks to One-Eye's foresight we had the makings for firebombs by the score, and ready bombs in well-protected nests atop the deckhouse. The three brothers from Beryl built us a dolphin, which is a fish-shaped weight attached to a long chain. It is swung out on a boom and dropped through the bottoms of boats. My favorite engine, though, was thought up by Patience, a former caravan guard.

A springboard would slap the base of a cartridge filled with poisonous darts, throwing a hail of missiles. The poison needed only the tiniest cut to cause quick paralysis. The engine's one shortcoming was that it was immobile. You had to wait for your target to cross your aim.

Once construction was finished I treated everyone to a rich diet of my own pet peeves from my days as a follower instead of chieftain. Drills and exercises. And intense language study. I kept One-Eye and his pet in a sweat trying to establish at least one common tongue among the men. There was plenty of grumbling. Only the Nar were impressed favorably.

Lady did not appear. She might not have existed for all we could tell.

We entered the wetlands, mostly cypress swamp, early the sixth morning. Everyone became more alert.

There was no sign of pirates for another two days. When they did come we had plenty of warning from One-Eye and Goblin.

We were passing through a place where the cypress crowded the channel. The attackers, in twenty boats, came at us head-on, around a bend. I could bring only two ballistae to bear. Those stopped just one boat. Arrows from those of us atop the deckhouse—which ran most of the length and width of the barge—did no good. The boats had canopies of crocodile hide.

They rushed in alongside. Grapnels on chains not easily cut caught on the top of the shielding. Pirates began clambering up.

I had them where I wanted them.

The shields were perforated with small holes. Mogaba's Nar stabbed through those at legs. The few pirates reaching the top had to balance on a four-inch width of timber before leaping to the deckhouse roof.

It was a turkey shoot. None survived to make the jump.

Goblin and One-Eye did not lift a sorcerous finger. They amused themselves throwing firebombs. The pirates had not encountered those before. They fled sooner than they would have had the boys not gotten into the game.

My guess is the pirates lost fifty to sixty men. Not a small hurt, but smaller than it could have been, and the good merchants of Gea-Xle hoped we would break the pirates.

The bargemaster appeared out of nowhere, like a ghost, as the pirates hauled ass. Neither he nor his crew had been visible during the skirmish. We had been drifting free, at the whim of the river.

Frogface appeared coincidentally. I used him to give the man nine kinds of hell. My rage took the edge off the complaining he did about us letting so many pirates get away.

"You'll have to fight them again, now. Next time they'll know what to expect."

"The way I heard, the first attack is just a probe. What the hell is going on out there?" The river had begun to foam with underwater excitement. Something began thumping against the barge's hull.

"Needleteeth." The bargemaster shuddered. Even Frogface seemed unsettled. "A fish as long as your arm. Heads for blood in the water. When there's a lot they go mad and attack everything. They can devour a hippo, bones and all, in a minute."

"Is that so?"

The river grew wilder. The dead pirates, and the wounded who had not gotten aboard boats and away, vanished. Broken and burning boats and driftwood went down piscine gullets. At least the needleteeth gave it the heroic try.

Once I was convinced the crew would participate in wreaking their own salvation next time, I went and had me a powwow with my tame wizards.

The second attack came at night. This time those guys were serious.

Their earlier asskicking had them feeling no-prisoners mean.

We had plenty of warning, of course. Goblin and One-Eye were on the job.

It was in another narrow place and this time they had a boom across to catch and hold us. I screwed them up by having anchors dropped when Goblin detected the boom. We stopped two hundred yards above the heart of the trap. We waited.

"Goblin? One-Eye? You guys set?" We had our surprises.

"Ready, Mom."

"Cletus. You on the dolphin?"

"Yes sir."

We had not used that before. "Otto. I don't hear that goddamned pump. What the hell is going on back there?"

"I'm looking for the crew guys now, Croaker."

All right. They wanted to chicken out again, eh? Hoped they could buy off the pirates by not resisting? "Murgen, dig that barge boss out of his hiding hole." I knew where he was. "I want him up here. One-Eye. I need your pet."

"Soon as he gets back from scouting."

Frogface showed first. He was telling me that every adult male in the swamp was out there when Murgen brought the bargemaster to me whimpering in a hammerlock. As the first pirate arrows fell I said, "Tell him he goes over the side if his people aren't on the job in two minutes. And that I'll keep throwing guys out till I get what I want." I meant what I said.

The message got through. I heard the pumps begin squeaking and clinking when Murgen and I were getting set to see how far we could throw a man.

The arrow fall picked up. It was ill-directed and did no harm, but its only purpose was to keep our heads down.

There was a big outbreak of cussing and caterwauling yonder when Goblin tested a favorite gimmick from his White Rose days, a spell that started every insect in a small area noshing on the nearest human flesh.

The whoop and holler died quickly. Test fulfilled, question answered. They had somebody capable of undoing trivial witcheries.

One-Eye was supposed to sneak along to spot the guy responsible, if one turned up, so he and Goblin could gang up and nail his hide to the nearest cypress.

The arrow fall stopped. And speak of the devil, here came One-Eye. "Big trouble, Croaker. That guy over there is a heavyweight. I don't know what we can do about him."

"Do what you can. Blindside him. Did you notice? The arrows stopped?" There was a lot of carrying on in the swamp, to cover the sounds of oars.

"Right." One-Eye ran to his place. A point of pink light soared upward. I donned the crocodile head Goblin had fixed. It was time for the show.

Half of winning a battle is showmanship.

The pink point grew up fast and shed light on the river.

There must have been forty boats sneaking toward us. They had extended their croc-hide protection in hopes of shedding firebombs.

I was glowing and breathing fire. Bet I made a hell of a sight from over there.

The nearest boats were ten feet away. I saw the ladder boxes and grinned behind my croc teeth. I had guessed right.

I threw my hands up, then down.

A single firebomb arced out to shatter upon a boat.

"Stop pumping, you goddamned idiots!" I yelled.

The bomb was a dud.

I did my act again.

Second time had the charm. Fire splattered. In seconds the river was aflame except for a narrow strip around the barge.

The trap was almost too good. The fire sucked most of the air away and heated what was left till it was almost unbearable. But the burning did not last long, thanks to the lack of enthusiasm of the oil pumpers.

Fewer than half the attack wave succumbed, but the survivors had no stomach left for combat. Especially after the dolphin and ballistae started knocking their boats apart. They headed for cover. Slowly. Painfully. The ballistae and dart throwers left their sting.

A big, big howl went up over there. It took them a while to get the anger worked out.

A rattle, clank, and slap of oars against water announced a second wave.

I was laying for these guys, too. It was the third wave that would be the bitch, if they did not get it out of their systems right away. The third wave and that unknown quantity that One-Eye had discovered were what worried me.

The pirate boats were a hundred feet from the barge when Goblin gave me the high sign.

He had the needleteeth gathering in baffled thousands.

The lead boats got close enough. I went into my dance.

The dolphin went down, shattering a large wooden swamp boat. Every engine cut loose. Fire bombs and javelins flew.

The idea was to get some wounded pirates into the water with the needleteeth.

Some got.

The river went mad.

Half the pirate boats were hides stretched on wooden

frames. Those did not last at all. Wooden boats fared better, but only the heaviest withstood repeated strikes. And even they were at the mercy of the panic of the men aboard.

The smartest and quickest pirates charged the barge. If they could get aboard and take control . . . But that was the chance I wanted them to see.

They had come prepared with ladders that had planks fixed to their backs. Thrown up on our mantlets and nailed into place the ladder backing would protect pirate arms and legs from the stabbing Nar.

Except that I had had the Nar driving spikes and sharpened wooden slats through the cracks between the mantlet timbers. Those made it hard to put the ladders up. Cletus and his brothers smashed several boats before the pirates discovered what wonderful hand and foot holds the spikes made.

The Nar had instructions to leave them alone as long as they did nothing but hang there. Their presence would discourage sniping by their brothers and fathers and cousins.

It took a while, but silence came to the night and stillness to the river. The wreckage drifted off to pile up against the boom. My men sat down to rest. One-Eye pulled his pink lights out of the sky. He, Goblin, Frogface, my squad leaders, Mogaba, and, lo!, the barge's master, joined me for a powwow. The latter suggested we up anchor and roll.

"How long have we been here?" I asked.

"Two hours," Goblin said.

"We'll let it rest a while." The convoy was supposed to have fallen back till it was an estimated eight hours behind, the theory being that if they overtook us because we were in action, they would arrive with the pirates in a state of exhaustion and would be able to overcome them if we had been wiped out. "One-Eye. What's the situation with the sorcerer over there?"

He did not sound well when he replied, "We could be

in big trouble, Croaker. He's even more potent than we guessed at first."

"You tried getting him?"

"Twice. I don't think he even noticed."

"If he's that bad why's he laying off instead of stomping us?"

"We don't know."

"Should we take the initiative? Should we bait him and try to draw him out?"

Murgen asked, "Why don't we just break the boom and go? We got enough of them to keep the swamp in mourning for a year."

"They won't let us, that's why. They can't. One-Eye. Can you find that wizard?"

"Yeah. Why should I? I agree with the kid. Break the boom. They might surprise us."

"They'd surprise us, all right. What the hell do you think the boom is there for, dummy? Why do you think I stopped us up here? Can you put one of your little pink balls in his hair?"

"If I have to. For maybe half a minute."

"You have to. When I tell you." I had been trying to find unusual parameters to the situation and thought I had one. I was set for an interesting, if potentially fatal, experiment. "Hagop. You and Otto get all the ballistae around to the east side. Take forty percent of the tension off them so they can throw firebombs without breaking them in the trough." With Frogface's help I told Mogaba I wanted his archers on the deckhouse roof. "When One-Eye spots our target I want half high-angle, plunging fire, half flat trajectory. And I want firebombs flying like we're trying to burn the swamp down."

A pirate let out a cry of despair as he lost his grip and fell from the shielding. A riot in the water told us the needleteeth knew a good thing and had hung around.

"Let's get at it."

Goblin hung on till the others had gone. "I think I

know what you're trying to do, Croaker. I hope you don't regret it."

"You hope? I blow it and we're all dead."

I gave the command. One-Eye's rangefinder squirted across the water. The moment it blossomed everyone cut loose.

For a minute I thought we had the sucker.

Suddenly, Lady materialized on the deckhouse roof. I removed my crocodile head. "Heck of a show there, eh?" Cypress and moss *will* burn, liberally primed.

"What do you think you're doing?"

"You finally deign to report for duty, soldier?"

Her left cheek twitched. My tactic had not been deployed against the pirate sorcerer at all.

An arrow burred between us, not six inches from either of our noses. Lady jumped.

Then the pirates clinging to the shielding finally tried coming on up and over to the deckhouse roof. The half dozen not swept away by the archers just threw themselves into a hedgehog of spears set to receive them.

"I think I've fixed it so there's only one way they can take us." I gave her a moment to think. "They have a sorcerer who's a heavy hitter. So far he's laid low. I've just told him I know he's there and I'm going to get him if I can."

"You don't know what you're doing, Croaker."

"Wrong. I know exactly what I'm doing."

She spat an epithet of disbelief, stamped away.

"Frogface!" I called.

He materialized. "Better put that croc hat back on, chief. The spell won't keep the arrows off if you don't." One whimpered past as he spoke.

I grabbed the head. "You do the job on her stuff?"

"All taken care of, chief. I rolled it over into a place that isn't this place. You'll hear them howling in a minute."

The fires among the cypress winked out like snuffed candles. Several of One-Eye's pink fireflies sailed across and simply vanished. The night began to fill with an oppressive and dreadful sense of presence.

The only light left flickered around me and around the mouth of the croc head mounted on the bow.

Lady came at a run. "Croaker! What did you do?"

"I told you I knew what I was doing."

"But—"

"All gone all your little toys from the Tower? Call it intuition, love. Reaching a conclusion from inadequate and scattered information. Though I think it helped being familiar with the people I'm playing with."

The darkness grew deeper. The stars vanished. But the night had a gleam on, like a polished piece of coal. You could see glimmers though there was no light at all—not even from the figurehead.

"You're going to get us killed."

"That possibility has existed since I was elected Captain. It existed when we left the Barrowland. It existed when we walked away from the Tower. It existed when we sailed from Opal. It existed when you swore your oath to the Black Company. It became highly probable when I accepted this hasty and misrepresented commission from the merchants of Gea-Xle. Nothing new there, friend."

Something like a large, flat black stone came skipping across the water, throwing up sprays of silver. Goblin and One-Eye scuttled it.

"What do you want, Croaker?" Her voice was taut, maybe even edged with fear.

"I want to know who runs the Black Company. I want to know who makes the decisions about who travels with us and who doesn't. I want to know who gives members of the Company permission to wander off for days at a time, and who gives out the right to hide out for a week, shirking all duties. Most of all, I want to know who decides which adventures and intrigues will involve the Company."

The skipping stones kept coming, leaving their sprays and ripples of silver. Each came nearer the barge.

"Who's going to run things, Lady? You or me? Whose game are we going to play? Yours or mine? If not mine, all your treasures stay where you can't get at them. And we go to the needleteeth. Now."

"You're not bluffing, are you?"

"You don't bluff when you're sitting across the table from somebody like you. You bet everything you've got and wait to see if you're called."

She knew me. She had had her looks inside me. She knew I could do it if I had to. She said, "You've changed. Gone hard."

"To be the Captain you have to *be* the Captain, not the Annalist or the Company physician. Though the romantic is still alive back in there somewhere. You might have pulled it off if you'd gone through with it that night on that hill."

One of the skipping stones nudged the barge.

I said, "You had me going for a while."

"You idiot. That night didn't have anything to do with this. Back then I didn't think there was a chance this would work. That was a woman on that hill with a man she cared about and wanted, Croaker. And she thought that was a man who—"

The next stone *whamm*'d home. The barge shuddered. Goblin yelled, "Croaker!"

"Are we going to make a move?" I asked. "Or should I shuck down so I can try to outswim the needleteeth?"

"Damn you! You win."

"Your promise good this time? For them, too?"

"Yes, damnit."

I took a chance. "Frogface. Roll it over. Bring the stuff back."

A stone hit the barge. Timbers groaned. I staggered and Goblin yelled again.

I said, "Your stuff is back, Lady. Get Shifter and his girlfriend up here."

"You knew?"

"I told you. I figured it out. Move."

The old man called Eldron the Seer appeared, but now he wore his true guise. He was the supposedly slain Taken called Shapeshifter, half as tall as a house and half as wide, a monster of a man in scarlet. Wild, stringy hair whipped around his head. His jungle of a beard was matted and filthy. He leaned upon a glowing staff that was an elongated, improbably thin female body, perfect in its detail. It had been among Lady's things and had been the final clue that had convinced me when Frogface reported its presence. He pointed that staff across the river.

A hundred-foot splash of oily fire boiled up amidst the cypress.

The barge reeled at the kiss of another flat stone. Timbers flew. Below, the horses shrieked in panic. Some of the crew sang with them. My companions looked grim in the light of the fires.

Shapeshifter kept laying down splash after splash, till the swamp was immersed in a holocaust that beggared both of mine put together. The screams of the pirates became lost in the roar of the flames.

I won my bet.

And Shifter kept laying it down.

A great howling rose within the fire. It faded into the distance.

Goblin looked at me. I looked at him. "Two of them in ten days," I muttered. We had heard that howling last during the Battle at Charm. "And not friends anymore. Lady, what would I have found if I *had* opened those graves?"

"I don't know, Croaker. Anymore, I don't. I never expected to see the Howler again. That's for sure." She sounded like a frightened, troubled child.

I believed her.

A shadow passed the light. A night-flying crow? What next?

Shifter's companion saw it, too. Her eyes were tight and intense.

I took Lady's hand. I liked her a lot better now that she had her vulnerability back.

Chapter Twenty:
WILLOW UP THE CREEK

Willow scowled at the boat. "I'm so thrilled I could shit."

"What's wrong?" Cordy asked.

"I don't like boats."

"Why don't you walk? Me and Blade will cheer you on whenever we see you puffing along the riverbank."

"If I had your sense of humor, I'd kill myself and save the world the pain, Cordy. Hell, we got to do it, let's do it." He headed out the wharf. "You seen the Woman and her pup?"

"Smoke was around earlier. I think they're on already. Low profile. On the sneak. They don't want anybody knowing the Radisha is leaving town."

"What about us?"

Blade grinned. "Going to cry because the girls didn't come down to drag him back."

"Going to cry a lot, Blade," Cordy said. "Old Willow can't go anywhere without bitching to keep his feet moving."

The boat wasn't that bad. It was sixty feet long and comfortable for its cargo, which consisted only of the five passengers. Willow got in his gripe about that too, as soon as he discovered that the Radisha hadn't brought a platoon of servants. "I was sort of counting on having somebody take care of me."

"Getting soft, man," Blade said. "Next thing, you be wanting to hire somebody to fight in your place when you get trouble."

"Sounds good to me. We done enough of that for somebody else. Haven't we, Cordy?"

"Some."

The crew poled the boat into the current, which was almost nonexistent that far down the river. They upped a linen sail and swung the bow north. There was a good breeze. They gained on the current about as fast as a man moving at a lazy stroll. Not fast. But no one was in a big hurry.

"I don't see why we got to start now," Willow said. "We ain't going where she wants. I bet you the river's still blockaded above the Third Cataract. There won't be no way we can get past Thresh. That's far enough to suit me, anyway."

"Thought you was going to keep on hiking," Cordy said.

"He remembered they laying for him in Gea-Xle," Blade said. "Moneylenders got no sense of humor."

It took two weeks to reach Catorce, below the First Cataract. They hardly saw Smoke or the Radisha the whole time. They got damned tired of the crew, as humorless a bunch of river rats as ever lived, all of them fathers and sons and brothers and uncles of each other so nobody ever dared loosen up. The Radisha would not let them put in at night. She figured somebody would shoot his mouth off and the whole world would find out who was on the river without benefit of armed guards.

That hurt Willow's feelings from a couple different directions.

The First Cataract was an obstacle to navigation only to traffic coming up the river. The current was too swift for sail or oars and the banks too far and boggy for a towpath. The Radisha had them leave the boat at Catorce, with the crew to wait there for their return, and they made the eighteen-mile journey to Dadiz, above the cataract, on foot.

Willow looked out at river barges coming down, riding the current, and griped.

Blade and Cordy just grinned at him.

The Radisha hired another boat for the passage to the Second Cataract. She and Smoke stopped trying to stay out of sight. She figured they were too far from Taglios for anybody to recognize them. The First Cataract was four hundred eighty miles north of Taglios.

Half a day out of Dadiz Willow joined Cordy and Blade in the bows. He said, "You guys notice some little brown guys back in town? Kind of watching us?"

Cordy nodded. Blade grunted an affirmative. Willow said, "I was afraid it was my imagination. Maybe I'll wish it was. I didn't recognize the type. You guys?"

Cordy shook his head. Blade said, "No."

"You guys don't break a jaw chinning."

"How would they know to be watching us, Willow? Whoever they are? Only one who knows where we're headed is the Prahbrindrah Drah, and even he don't know why."

Willow started to say something, decided he should shut his mouth and think. After a minute, he grunted. "The Shadowmasters. They might know somehow."

"Yeah. They might."

"You think they might give us some trouble?"

"What would you do if you was them?"

"Right. I better go nag on Smoke." Smoke could be the hole card. Smoke claimed the Shadowmasters didn't know about him. Or if they did, they had no good estimate of his competence.

Smoke and the Radisha had made themselves comfortable in the shade of the sail and were watching the river go by. The river was something worth seeing, Willow would admit. Even here it was half a mile wide. "Smoke, old buddy, we maybe got us a problem."

The wizard stopped chewing on something he had had in his mouth all morning. He peered at Willow with narrowed eyes. Willow's style was getting to him.

"Back in Dadiz there was these little brown guys about so high, skinny and wrinkly, that was watching us. I asked Cordy and Blade. They seen them, too."

Smoke looked at the woman. She looked at Willow. "Not someone you made an enemy of coming south?"

Willow laughed. "Hey. I don't have no enemies. No. There's nobody like these guys anywhere between Roses and Taglios. I never saw anybody like them before. I figure that means it's not me they're interested in."

She looked at Smoke. "Did you notice anyone?"

"No. But I wasn't watching. It seemed unnecessary."

"Hey. Smoke. You always watch," Willow said. "This here's your basic unfriendly old world. You better always be on the lookout when you're travelling. There's bad guys out here. Believe it or not, not everybody's as polite as you Taglians."

Swan returned to the bow. "That dolt wizard never even noticed the brownies. The guy's got lard for brains."

Blade took out a knife and whetstone and went to work. "Better sharpen up. Edge might dull down before the old boy wakes up and sees we're under attack."

It was a three-hundred-mile passage to the Second Cataract, where the river scampered nervously between dark and brooding hills, as though too wary to stay in one place long. On the right bank the haunted ruins of Cho'n Delor stared down on the flood, reminding Willow of a heap of old skulls. No traffic had passed along the right bank since the fall of the Paingod. Even animals shunned the area.

On the hilltops beyond the left bank were the ruins of the Triplet Cities, Odd the First, Odd the Second, and Odd the Third. Stories Cordy had heard coming south said they had sacrificed themselves to bring the Paingod down.

Now people lived only along a narrow strip beside the Cataract, in a walled city one street wide and ten miles long, perpetually nervous about ghosts from the wars that were. They called their bizarre city Idon, and had the weirdest bunch of quirks anyone ever saw. Travellers stayed in Idon only as long as absolutely necessary. Likewise, many of the people of Idon themselves.

Passing through, keeping his eyes open while pretending to be gawking at the weirdos, Willow noticed little brown guys skulking everywhere. "Hey. Smoke. You eagle-eyed bastard. You see them now?"

"What?"

"He don't," Blade said. "Better sharpen me a couple more knives."

"Pay attention, old man. They're all over like roaches." Actually, Willow had seen only eight or nine. But that was plenty enough. Especially if they had the Shadowmasters behind them.

They had somebody behind them. They made that clear soon after the Radisha found a boat for the trip to Thresh and the Third Cataract.

They got around a bend in the river, where it flowed through country that looked like it was left over from the war between the Triplet Cities and Cho'n Delor, and here came two fast boats loaded down with little brown guys rowing like the winner of the race got to become immortal.

The crew the Radisha had hired took maybe twenty seconds to decide it wasn't their squabble. They dived overboard and headed for the bank.

"You see them now, Smoke?" Willow asked, starting to ready his weapons. "I hope you're half the wizard you think you are." There were at least twenty brown men in each boat.

Smoke's jaw went high speed as he chomped whatever he chewed all the time. He did nothing till the boats began creeping up to either side. Then he stuck out both hands toward one, closed his eyes and wriggled his fingers.

All the nails and pegs holding the boat together flew around like swarming swallows, pattered into the water.

Brown men hollered and gurgled. It didn't look like many of them knew how to swim.

Smoke took a moment to catch his breath, then turned on the other boat. The brown men there were turning already, heading for shore.

Smoke took that boat apart, too. Then he gave Willow one dark look and went back to his seat in the shadow of the sail. He smirked forever afterward whenever he heard Willow bitching about having to work ship.

"At least we know he's the real thing now," Willow grumbled to himself.

The situation in Thresh was exactly what Willow had predicted. The river was closed to the north. Pirates. The Radisha could find no one willing to hazard the long run north to Gea-Xle, which is where she was determined to go, to wait. Nothing she offered would get anybody to risk the journey. Not even her companions, whom she urged to steal a boat.

She was furious. You would have thought the hinges of the world would lock up if she didn't get to Gea-Xle.

She did not get.

For months they hung around Thresh, staying out of the way of little brown guys, hearing rumors that the merchants of Gea-Xle had gotten desperate enough to try doing something about the river pirates. Thresh was a snake's nest of gloom. Without trade upriver it would wither. Any hope that the northerners would break through seemed absurd. Everyone who tried died.

One morning Smoke came to breakfast looking thoughtful. "I had a dream," he announced.

"Oh, wonderful," Willow snapped. "I been sitting around here for months now just praying you'd have another one of your nightmares. What do we do this time? Storm the Shadowlands?"

Smoke ignored him. He had been doing that a lot, communicating through the Radisha. It was the only way he could deal with Swan without getting violent. He told the woman, "They've departed Gea-Xle. A whole convoy."

"Can they break through?"

Smoke shrugged. "There's a power as mighty and cruel as the Shadowmasters in the swamps. Maybe greater than the Shadowmasters. I haven't been able to find it in my dreams."

Willow muttered, "I hope the brownies aren't smoking something, too. They figure we're going to connect up they might get more ambitious."

"They don't know why we're here, Swan. I poked around. I found out that much. They just want you and me and Cordy. Would have done it to us in Taglios if they caught us there."

"Comes to the same thing. How long before that convoy gets here?"

The Radisha said, "Smoke? How long?"

The wizard responded with all the steely certitude of his breed. He shrugged.

The lead boat was spotted by somebody fishing upriver. The news reached Tresh a few hours before the barge. Willow and his group went down to the piers with half the city to wait for it. People howled and cheered until those aboard began disembarking. Then a deep, dread silence fell.

The Radisha grabbed Smoke's shoulder in a grip obviously painful. "*These* are your saviors? Old man, I'm about out of patience with you. . . ."

Chapter Twenty-one:
THRESH

We broke the boom. We headed for the trading city Thresh, which lies above the Third Cataract. It was a quiet river going down. There might have been no other human beings in the world outside of us on the barge. But the wreckage that kept pace was a screaming reminder that we were not alone, that we belonged to a bleak and bloody-minded species. I was not fit company for man or beast, as they say.

One-Eye joined me where I stood under the battered croc head Goblin had mounted in the bows. "Be there in a little bit, Croaker."

I dipped into my trick bag of repartee and countered with an unenthusiastic grunt.

"Me and the runt been trying to get a feel for the place up ahead."

I cracked him up with another grunt. That was his job.

"Don't got a good feel to it." We watched another small fishing boat hoist anchor and raise sail and skitter south with the news of our coming. "Not a real danger feel. Not an all-bad feel. Just not a right feel. Like there's something going on."

He sounded puzzled around the edges. "You figure it's something that might concern us, send your pet to find out what. That's what you bought him for. Isn't it?"

He smirked.

The current in a lazy turn of the river held us close to

the right bank. Two solemn crows watched our progress from a lone dead tree. Gnarled and ugly, the tree made me think of nooses and hanged men.

"Now why didn't I think of that, Croaker? Here I just sent him into town to check on the quiff situation."

Teach your grandmother to suck eggs, Croaker.

The imp came back with a disturbing report. There were people in Thresh waiting for us. Specifically us, the Black Company.

How the hell did everybody know we were coming?

The waterfront was mobbed when we warped in, though nobody really believed we had come from Gea-Xle. I guess they figured we spontaneously generated on the river up around the bend. I kept everyone aboard and mostly out of sight till the rest of the convoy arrived.

It came through untouched. Its guards and crews were simmering with stories of the devastation they had found in our wake. Rejoicing spread through Thresh. The blockade had been strangling the city.

I watched the good citizens from behind a mantlet. Here and there I noted hard-eyed little brown men who seemed less than enchanted with our advent.

"Those the guys you were talking about?" I asked One-Eye.

He gave them the fish-eye, then shook his head. "Ours should be over that way. There they are. Weird."

I saw what he meant. A man with long blond hair. What the hell was he doing down here? "Keep an eye on them."

I collected Mogaba and Goblin and a couple of the guys who looked like they ate babies for breakfast and went into conference with the bosses of the convoy. They surprised me. They not only did not argue about paying the balance of our fee, they tossed in a bonus on account of every barge got through. Then I got my key people together and told them, "Let's get off-loaded and hit the road. This place gives me the creeps."

Goblin and One-Eye complained. Naturally. They wanted to stay and party.

They came around when the iron coach and the great black horses and the Company standard hit the wharfside road. The joy went out of the grand celebration almost immediately. I'd figured it would.

Blank faces watched the unforgotten standard pass.

Thresh had been on the other side when the Company was in service in Goes. Our forebrethren had kicked their butts good. So good they recalled the Company this long after the fact, though Goes itself no longer existed.

We paused in an open market toward the south edge of Thresh. Mogaba had a couple of his lieutenants dicker for supplies. Goblin went stomping around in a squeaking rage because One-Eye had set Frogface to following him, aping his every word and move. The imp was trudging behind him at the moment, looking deep in thought. Otto and Hagop and Candles were trying to thrash out the details of a pool that would pay off big to the guy who guessed closest to when Goblin would come up with a definitive counterstroke. The trouble was a definition of what could be considered definitive.

One-Eye observed proceedings with a benign, smug smile, certain he had attained ascendancy at last. The Nar stood around looking grimly military and still a little baffled because the rest of us had less rigid, absolute standards. They had not been disappointed in us on the river.

One-Eye ambled over. "Them people are giving us the eye again. Got them all picked out now. Four men and a woman."

"Round them up and bring them over. We'll see what's on their minds. Where's Wheezer?"

One-Eye pointed, then did a fade. As I approached Wheezer I noted that a dozen of my men had disappeared. One-Eye wasn't going to take any chances.

I told Wheezer to tell Mogaba we weren't stocking up

for a six-month campaign. We just wanted enough stuff for a meal or two getting past the Cataract. We yakked it back and forth, Mogaba struggling with the Jewel Cities dialect he had begun to pick up already. He was a sharp, smart man. I liked him. He was flexible enough to understand that our two versions of the Company could have arisen easily over two hundred years. He worked at being nonjudgmental.

So did I.

"Hey, Croaker. Here you go." Here came One-Eye, grinning like a possum, bringing in his catch. The three younger men, two of whom were whites, seemed baffled. The woman looked angry. The old man looked like he was daydreaming.

I eyeballed the white men, again wondering how the hell they had gotten here. "They got anything to say for themselves?"

Mogaba drifted over. He looked at the black man thoughtfully.

About then the woman had plenty to say. The darker haired white man wilted slightly but the other just grinned. I said, "Let's check them on languages. Between us we've got most of them they speak up north."

Frogface popped up. "Try them out on Rosean, chief. I got a hunch." Then he rattled something at the old man. The guy jumped about a foot off the ground. Frogface chortled. The old man stared like he was seeing a ghost.

Before I could ask what verbal stunt he'd pulled, the blond man asked, "You the captain of this outfit?" He spoke Rosean. I understood him, but my Rosean was rusty. I hadn't used it in a long time.

"Yeah. You got any other languages you use?"

He had. He tried a couple. His Forsberger was not good, but my Rosean was worse. He asked, "What the hell happened to you guys?" He regretted saying it immediately.

I looked at One-Eye. He shrugged. I asked, "What do you mean?"

"Uh . . . coming down the river. You done the impossible. Ain't nobody gotten through in a couple years. Me and Cordy and Blade, we were about the last ones."

"Just lucky."

He frowned. He had heard the stories spread by the boatmen.

Mogaba said something to one of his lieutenants. They looked the black man, Blade, over good. The Geek and the Freak, who had confessed to being brothers and having the real names Claw-of-the-Lion and Heart-of-the-Lion, also moved in to look him over. He wasn't pleased. I asked Heart, "Is there something special about that guy?"

"Maybe, Captain. Maybe. Tell you later."

"Right." Back to Forsberger. "You've been watching us. We want to know why."

He had an answer all ready. "My buddies and me, we been hired to take the broad and the old boy down the river. We was kind of hoping we could hook on with you guys as far as Taglios. For the extra protection, you know what I mean?" He looked at Murgen and the standard. "I seen that somewhere before."

"Roses. Who are you?" How stupid did I look? Maybe I needed to check a mirror.

"Oh. Yeah. Sorry. I'm Swan. Willow Swan." He stuck out a hand. I didn't take it. "This here's my buddy Cordy Mather. Cordwood. Don't ask. Even he don't know why. And this's Blade. We been doing what you might call freelancing, up and down the river. Taking advantage of being exotic. You know how it is. You guys been about everywhere."

He was rattled. You couldn't have tortured it out of him, maybe, but he was scared half to death. He kept looking at the standard and the coach and the horses and the Nar and shuddering.

He was a lot of things, maybe, that he was not going to admit. A liar was the biggest. I thought it might be interesting, even entertaining, to have him and his bunch along. So I gave him what he wanted. "All right. Tag along. As long as you pull your weight and remember who's in charge."

He broke out in smiles. "Great. You got it, chief." He started chattering at his pals. The old man said something sharp that shut him up.

I asked Frogface, "He give anything away there?"

"Nah. He just said, 'I did it!,' chief. And went to bragging on his golden tongue."

"Swan. Where the hell is this Taglios? I don't have a Taglios on my maps."

"Let me see."

Half an hour later I knew his Taglios was a place my best map named Troko Tallios. "Trogo Taglios," Swan told me. "There's this monster city, Taglios, that surrounds an older one that was called Trogo. The official name is Trogo Taglios but nobody ever calls it anything but Taglios anymore. It's a nice place. You'll like it."

"I hope so."

One-Eye said, "He's going to try to sell you something, Croaker."

I grinned. "We'll have some fun with him while he tries. Watch them. Be friendly with them. Find out whatever you can. Where's Lady gotten off to now?"

I was too fussed. She wasn't far off. She was standing aside, inspecting our new acquisitions from another angle. I beckoned her. "What do you think?" I asked when she joined me. Swan's eyes popped when he got a good look at her. He was in love.

"Not much. Watch the woman. She's in charge. And she's used to getting her own way."

"Aren't you all?"

"Cynic."

"That's me. To the bone. And you're the one made me that way, love."

She gave me a funny look, forced a smile.

I wondered if we'd ever recover that moment on that hillside so many miles to the north.

We were just coming back to the river, after having walked past the Third Cataract, when Willow joined me as I walked my horse. He eyed the big black nervously and got around where I would be between it and him. He asked, "Are you guys *really* the Black Company?"

"The one and only. The evil, mean, rude, crude, nasty, and sometimes even unpleasant Black Company. You never spent any time in the military, did you?"

"As little as I could. Man, last I heard there was a thousand of you guys. What happened?"

"Times got hard up north. A year ago we were down to seven men. How long ago did you leave the empire?"

"Way back. Me and Cordy bugged out of Roses maybe a year after you guys were in there after that Rebel general, Raker. I wasn't much more than a kid. We sort of drifted from one thing to another, headed south. First thing you know, we was across the Sea of Torments. Then we got into some trouble with the imperials, so we had to get out of the empire. Then we just kept drifting, a little bit this year, a little bit that. We hooked up with Blade. Next thing you know, here we are down here. What're you guys doing here?"

"Going home." That was all I needed to tell him.

He knew plenty about us if he had come to us knowing Taglios was on our itinerary but not our final destination.

I said, "In a military outfit it's not acceptable behavior for just anybody to walk up and start shooting the shit with the commander any time they feel like it. I try to keep this outfit looking military. It intimidates the yokels."

"Yeah. Gotcha. Channels, and all that. Right." He went away.

His Taglios was a long way off. I figured we had time to sort his bunch out. So why press?

Chapter Twenty-two:
TAGLIOS

We returned to the river and sailed down to the Second Cataract. Faster traffic had carried the word that the boys were back. Idon, a bizarre strip of a town, was a ghost city. We saw not a dozen souls there. Once again we had come to a place where the Black Company was remembered. That made me uncomfortable.

What had our forebrethren done down here? The Annals went on about the Pastel Wars but did not recall the sort of excesses that would terrify the descendants of the survivors forever.

Below Idon, while we waited to find a bargemaster with guts enough to take us south, I had Murgen plant the standard. Mogaba, as serious as ever, got a ditch dug and our encampment lightly fortified. I swiped a boat and crossed the river and climbed the hills to the ruins of Cho'n Delor. I spent a day roaming that haunted memorial to a dead god, alone except for crows, always wondering about the sort of men who had gone before me.

I suspected and feared that they had been men very much like me. Men caught in the rhythm and motion and pace, unable to wriggle free.

The Annalist who recorded the epic struggle that took place while the Company was in service to the Paingod had written a lot of words, sometimes going into too great a detail about daily minutiae, but he had had very little to say about the men with whom he had served.

Most had left their mark only when he recorded their passing.

I have been accused of the same. It has been said that too often when I bother to mention someone in particular it is only as a name of the slain. And maybe there's truth in that. Or maybe that's getting it backward. There is always pain in writing about those who have perished before me. Even when I mention them only in passing. These are my brethren, my family. Now, almost, my children. These Annals are their memorial. And my catharsis. But even as a child I was a master at damping and concealing my emotions.

But I was speaking of ruins, the spoor of battle.

The Pastel Wars must have been a struggle as bitter as that we had endured in the north, confined to a smaller territory. The scars were still grim. They might take a thousand years to heal.

Twice during that outing I thought I glimpsed the mobile stump I had seen from the wall of the Temple of Travellers' Repose. I tried getting closer, for a better look, but it always disappeared on me.

It was never more than a glimpse from the corner of my eye, anyway. Maybe I was imagining it.

I did not get to explore as thoroughly as I wanted. I was tempted to hang around but the old animal down inside told me I did not want to be stranded in those ruins after dark. It told me wicked things stalked Cho'n Delor's night. I listened. I went back over the river. Mogaba met me at the shore. He wanted to know what I had found. He was as interested in the Company's past as I was.

I liked and respected the big black man more with every hour. That evening I formalized his hitherto *de facto* status as commander of the Company infantry. And I resolved to take Murgen's Annalist training more seriously.

Maybe it was just a hunch. Whatever, I decided that it was time I got the Company's internal workings whipped into order.

All these natives, lately, were afraid of us. They carried

old grudges. Maybe farther down the river there was somebody with less fear and a bigger grudge.

We were on the brink of lands where the Company's adventures were recalled in the early lost volumes of the Annals. The earliest extant picked up our tale in cities north of Trogo Taglios—cities that no longer exist. I wished there was some way I could dig details of the past out of the locals. But they were not talking to us.

While I moped around Cho'n Delor One-Eye found a southern bargemaster willing to carry us all the way to Trogo Taglios. The man's fee was exorbitant, but Willow Swan assured me I was unlikely to get a better offer. We were haunted by our historical legacy.

I got no help from Swan or his companions unearthing that.

My notion for unmasking Swan and his gang gradually made very little headway. The woman forced them to stay to themselves, which did not please Cordy Mather. He was hungry for news from the empire. I did find out that the old man was called Smoke, but never got a hint of the woman's name. Even with Frogface on the job.

They were cautious people.

Meantime, they watched us so closely I felt they were taking notes whenever I bellied up to the rail to increase the flow in the river.

Other concerns plagued me, too. Crows. Always, crows. And Lady, who hardly spoke these days. She pulled her turns at duty with the rest of the Company but stayed out of the way otherwise.

Shifter and his girlfriend were not to be seen. They had disappeared while we unloaded at Thresh—though I held the disturbing certainty that they were still around, close enough to be watching.

What with the crows and all our arrivals anticipated I had the feeling I was being watched all the time. It was not hard to get a little paranoid.

We rode the rapids of the First Cataract and swept on down the great river, into the dawn of Company history.

* * *

My maps called it Troko Tallios. Locally they called it Trogo Taglios, though those who lived there used the shorter Taglios, mostly. As Swan said, the Trogo part refers to an older city that has been enveloped by the younger, more energetic Taglios.

It was the biggest city I had ever seen, a vast sprawl without a protective wall, still growing rapidly, horizontally instead of vertically. Northern cities grow upward because no one wants to build outside the wall.

Taglios lay on the southeast bank of the great river, actually inland a little, straddling a tributary that snakes between a half-dozen low hills. We debarked in a place that was really a satellite of the greater city, a riverport town called Maheranga. Soon Maheranga would share the fate of Trogo.

Trogo retained its identity only because it was the seat of the lords of the greater principiate, its governmental and religious center.

The Taglian people seemed friendly, peaceable, and overly god-ridden, much as Swan and Mather had described in brief exchanges during our journey. But underneath that they seemed to be frightened. And Swan had told us nothing about that.

And it was not the Company that was their terror. They treated us with respect and courtesy.

Swan and party vanished as soon as we tied up. I did not have to tell One-Eye to keep an eye on them.

The maps showed the sea only forty miles from Taglios, but that was along a straight line to the nearest coast, west across the river. Down the river's meander and delta it was two hundred miles to salt water. On the map the delta looked like a many-fingered, spidery hand clawing at the belly of the sea.

It is useful to know a little about Taglios because the Company ended up spending a lot more time there than any of us planned. Maybe even more than the Taglians themselves hoped.

* * *

Once I was convinced we would be secure doing so I ordered a break at Taglios. The rest was overdue. And I needed to do some heavy research. We were near the edge of the maps in my possession.

I discovered that I had come to count on Swan and Mather to show me around. Without them I was forced to rely on One-Eye's pet devil. And that I did not like. For no reason I could finger, I did not entirely trust the imp. Maybe it was because his sense of humor so closely reflected his owner's. The only time you trusted One-Eye was when your life was at stake.

I hoped we were now far enough south that I could chart the rest of our course to Khatovar before we resumed travelling.

Lady had been the perfect soldier since the encounter on the river, though not much of a companion otherwise. She was shaken badly by the Howler's return and enmity. He had been a staunch supporter in the old days.

She was still caught in the purgatory zone between the old Lady and the new that had to be, and the heart was not bound in the same direction as the head. She could not find her way out and, much as I ached for her, I did not know how to take her hand and show her.

I figured she deserved a distraction. I had Frogface shop for a local equivalent of Opal's Gardens and he astonished me by finding one. I asked Lady if she would be interested in a real social evening out.

She was amenable, if not excited after so many months of neglect. Not thrilled. Just, "I don't have anything better to do, so why not."

She never was the social sort. And both my maneuver on the river and my evasions through attention to duty had not left her pleased with me.

We did it decked out, with drama, though without as much uproar as we had raised in Opal. I did not want the local lords taking offense. One-Eye and Goblin behaved. Frogface was the only clear evidence of sorcery. None of that nastiness we had shown in Opal. Frogface went along in his capacity as universal translator.

One-Eye decked his pet out in a costume as flamboyant as his own, one that mocked Goblin's dress subtly. It seemed to state that this was how nice Goblin could look if he would get over being a slob.

Taglios's elite went to see and be seen in an olive grove past its prime bearing years. The grove bestrode a hill near old Trogo. A hot spring fed a score of private baths. It cost a bundle to get in when you were not known, most of that in bribes. Even so, it was two days after I asked before room could be found for us.

We went in the coach with Goblin and One-Eye up top and squads of four Nar each marching before and behind. Murgen drove. He took the coach away after he delivered us. The others accompanied us into the grove. I wore my legate's costume. Lady was dressed for the kill, but in black. All the time with the black. It looked good on her, but times were I wished she would try another color.

She said, "Our presence has stirred more interest than you expected." Our advent had caused very little stir in the streets of Taglios.

She was right. Unless the grove was a major *in* place to spend an evening a lot of class folks had come out just to give us the eye. It looked like everyone who might be anyone was there. "Wonder why?"

"There's something going on here, Croaker."

I am not blind. I knew. I knew after a few minutes with Willow Swan way back upriver. But I could not find out what. Even Frogface was no help. If they did any scheming they did it when he was not around.

Except for the Nar, who had lived with ceremony in Gea-Xle, we were all uncomfortable under the pressure of so many eyes. I admitted, "This might not have been one of my brighter ideas."

"On the contrary. It confirms our suspicions that there's a greater interest in us than should be for simple travellers. They mean to use us." She was disturbed.

"Welcome to life in the Black Company, sweetheart," I said. "Now you know why I'm cynical about lords and such. Now you know one of the feelings I've been trying to get across."

"Maybe I get it. A little. I feel demeaned. Like I'm not human at all but an object that might be useful."

"Like I said, welcome to the Black Company."

That was not all her problem. I harken back to the rogue Taken Howler, the dead unexpectedly alive and inimical. No amount of tall talking would convince me his appearance on the river was chance. He had been there to do us hurt.

Moreover, there had been an odd and unusual interest in us at least since Opal. I looked for crows.

There were crows in the olive trees, quiet and still. Watching. Always watching.

Shapeshifter's presence in Gea-Xle, the dead again living, waiting for Lady. There were hidden schemes brewing. Too much had happened to let me believe otherwise.

I had not pressed her. Yet. She was being a good soldier. Maybe waiting . . .

For what?

I had learned long ago that I can find out more around her sort by watching and listening and thinking than I ever do by asking. They lie and mislead even when there is no need. More, except in her own case, I did not think she had any better idea what was stirring than I did.

The grove staff showed us to a private bower with its own hot mineral bath. The Nar spread out. Goblin and One-Eye found themselves inconspicuous posts. Frogface stayed close, to interpret.

We settled.

"How is your research coming?" Lady asked. She toyed with some plump purple grapes.

"Strangely is the only way to describe it. I think we're right up next to the place where you come to the end of the earth and fall off the edge."

"What? Oh. Your sense of humor."

. "Taglios is infested with chartmakers. They do good work. But I can't find one map that will get me where I want to go."

"Maybe you haven't been able to make them understand what you need."

"It wasn't that. They understood. That's the problem. You tell them what you need and they go deaf. New maps only run to the southern borders of Taglian territory. When you can find an old one, it fades to blank eight hundred miles southeast of the city. It's the same even with maps so good they show damned near every tree and cottage."

"They're hiding something?"

"A whole city? Don't seem likely. But it does look like there's no other explanation."

"You asked the appropriate questions?"

"With the silver-tongued cunning of a snake. When the blank space comes up translation problems develop."

"What will you do?"

Dusk had come. Lamplighters were at work. I watched a moment. "Maybe use Frogface somehow. I'm not sure. We're far enough back that the Annals are almost useless. But the indicators are that we head straight for that blank space. You have any thoughts about it?"

"Me?"

"You. Things are happening around the Company. I don't think that's because *I* strut so pretty."

"Phooey."

"I haven't pressed, Lady. For all there's reason. And I won't—unless I have to. But it *would* be nice to know why we've got one dead Taken hanging around watching us out of the bushes and another one that used to be your buddy trying to kill us back in those swamps. Might be interesting to know if he knew you were aboard that barge, or if he was working on a grudge against Shifter, or if he just wanted to keep traffic from moving down the river. Might be interesting to know if we're likely to run into him again. Or somebody else who didn't die on time."

I tried to keep my tone gentle and neutral but some of my anger got through.

The first food arrived, bits of iced melon soaked in brandy. While we nibbled, some thoughtful soul gave our guardians food as well. Less elegant fare, perhaps, but food nevertheless.

Lady sucked a melon ball and looked thoughtful. Then her whole stance changed. She shouted, "Don't eat that stuff!" She used the tongue of the Jewel Cities, which by now even the most thick-witted of the Nar understood.

Silence grabbed the grove. The Nar dropped their platters.

I rose. "What is it?"

"Someone has tampered with their food."

"Poison?"

"Drugged, I'd guess. I'd have to check more closely."

I went and got the nearest's platter. He looked grim behind his Nar mask of indifference. He wanted to hurt somebody.

He got his chance when I turned back with my plunder.

A quick shuffle of feet. A *thwack!* of wood against flesh. A cry of pain that was little more than a whimper. I turned. The Nar had his spearpoint resting on the throat of a man sprawled before him. I recognized one of the lamplighters.

A long knife lay not far from his outflung hand.

I surveyed our surroundings. Bland faces watched from every direction.

"One-Eye. Frogface. Come here." They came. "I want something low-key. Something that won't disturb anybody's dinner. But something that will have him in a mood to talk when I'm ready. Can do?"

One-Eye snickered. "I know just the thing." He rubbed his hands in wicked glee while Goblin, left out, pouted. "I know just the thing. Go enjoy your dinner and sweet nothings. Old One-Eye will take care of everything. I'll have him ready to sing like a canary."

He gestured. An invisible force snagged the lamplighter's heels. Up he went, wriggling like a fish on a line, mouth stretched to scream but nothing coming out.

I settled opposite Lady. A jerk of my head. "One-Eye's idea of low-key. Don't let the victim scream." I popped a melon ball into my mouth.

One-Eye stopped lifting the lamplighter when his nose was twenty feet off the ground.

Lady began poking through the Nar's food.

The expedient of turning my back on One-Eye did not let me attain the mood I'd had in mind when arranging the evening. And Lady remained troubled.

I glanced over my shoulder occasionally.

The captive shed bits of clothing like dead leaves peeling away. The flesh beneath, betrayed, crawled with tiny lime and lemon glowing worms. When two of different hues butted heads they sparked and the failed assassin tried to shriek. When the mood took him, One-Eye let the man fall till his nose was a foot off the ground. Frogface whispered into his ear till One-Eye hoisted him up again.

Real low-key. What the hell would he have done if I'd asked for a show?

Goblin caught my eye. I raised an eyebrow. He used deaf sign to tell me, "Company coming. Looks like big stuff."

I pretended no greater interest than my meal while watching Lady intently. She seemed possessed of no special awareness.

There were two of them, well dressed and courteous. One was a native, walnut brown but not of negroid stock. The people of Taglios were dark but not negroid. The negroid peoples we had seen there were all visitors from up the river. The other one we knew already, Willow Swan, with the hair as yellow as maize.

Swan spoke to the Nar nearest him while his companion appraised One-Eye's efforts. I nodded to Goblin, who went to see if he could get any sense from Swan.

He came back looking thoughtful. "Swan says the guy with him is the boss wog around here. His choice of words, not mine."

"I guess it was bound to come." I exchanged glances with Lady. She had on her empress's face, readable as a rock. I wanted to shake her, to hug her, to do *something* to free up the passion that had appeared so briefly before going underground. She shrugged.

I said, "Invite them to join us. And tell One-Eye to send the imp over. I want him to check on Swan's translations."

The serving staff got down on their faces as our guests approached. It was the first time I had seen that kind of behavior in Taglios. Swan's prince was the real thing.

Swan got right to it. "This here's the Prahbrindrah Drah, the head guy around here."

"And you work for him."

He smiled. "In a left-hand sort of way. Drafted. He wants to know if you're looking for a commission."

"You know we're not."

"I told him. But he wanted to check it out personal."

"We're on a quest." I thought that sounded dramatic enough.

"A mission from the gods?"

"A what?"

"These Taglians are superstitious. You ought to know that by now. That would be the way to get the quest idea across. Mission from the gods. Sure you couldn't stick around for a while? Take a break from the road. I know how rough it is, travelling and travelling. And my man needs somebody to do his dirty work. You guys got a rep for handling that stuff."

"What do you really know about us, Swan?"

He shrugged. "Stories."

"Stories. Hunh."

The Prahbrindrah Drah said something.

"He wants to know why that guy is hanging up in the air."

"Because he tried to stab me in the back. After somebody tried to poison my guards. After a while I'm going to ask him why."

Swan and the Prahbrindrah chattered. The Prahbrindrah looked irked. He glanced at One-Eye's pet, chattered some more.

"He wants to know about your quest."

"You heard it all coming down the river. You told him already."

"Man, he's trying to be polite."

I shrugged. "How come so much interest in a few people just passing through?"

Swan started looking nervous. We were starting to move in toward it. The Prahbrindrah said several sentences.

Swan said, "The Prahbrindrah says you've talked about where you've been—and he would like to hear more about your adventures because far peoples and places intrigue him—and your quest, but you haven't really said where you're going." He sounded like he was trying to translate very accurately. Frogface gave me a shallow nod.

We had told Swan's bunch little during the passage south from the Third Cataract. We had hidden from them as much as they from us. I decided to pronounce the name maybe better kept to myself. "Khatovar."

Willow did not bother translating.

The Prahbrindrah chattered.

"He says you shouldn't do that."

"Too late to stop, Swan."

"Then you got troubles you can't even imagine, Captain." Swan translated. The Prince replied. He got excited.

"Boss says it's your neck and you can shave with an axe if you want, but no sane man says that name. Death could strike you down before you finished." He shrugged and smirked as he spoke. "Though it's likely more mundane forces will slaughter you if you insist on chasing that chimera. There's bad territory between here and there." Swan looked at the Prince and rolled his eyes. "We hear tales of monsters and sorcery."

"Hey, really." I plucked a morsel from a small bird, chewed, swallowed. "Swan, I brought this outfit here all the way from the Barrowland. You remember the Barrowland. Monsters and sorcery? Seven thousand miles. I never lost a man. You remember the river? Folks who got in my way didn't live to be sorry. Listen close. I'm trying to say a couple of things here. I'm eight hundred miles from the edge of the map. I won't stop now. I can't." It was one of the longest speeches I've ever made, outside reading to the men from the Annals.

"Your problem is those eight hundred miles, Cap. The other seven thousand were a stroll in the country."

The Prahbrindrah said something short. Swan nodded but did not translate. I looked at Frogface. He told me, "Glittering stone."

"What?"

"That's what he said, chief. Glittering stone. I don't know what he meant."

"Swan?"

"It's a local expression. 'The walking dead' is the closest way to say it in Rosean. It has something to do with old times and something called the Free Companies of Khatovar, which was bad medicine back when."

I raised an eyebrow. "The Black Company is the last of the Free Companies of Khatovar, Swan."

He gave me a sharp look. Then he translated.

The Prince chattered back. He stared at One-Eye's victim as he did.

"Cap, he says he supposes anything is possible. But a returning company ain't been spotted since his granddaddy's granddaddy was a pup. He wonders, though. Says maybe you're real. Your coming was foretold." Quick glance at Frogface, with a scowl, like the imp was a traitor. "And the Shadowmasters have warned him against dealing with you. Though that would be the natural inclination, considering the devastation and despair spread by the fanatics of old."

I glanced at Frogface. He nodded. Swan was striving for exactitude.

Lady said, "He's playing games, Croaker. He wants something. Tell him to get to the point."

"That would be nice, Swan."

He continued translating, "But yesterday's terror means nothing today. You are not those fanatics. That was seen on the river. And Trogo Taglios will bow the neck to no one. If the pestilence in the south fears a band of freebooters, he is willing to forget the ancient scores and tend to those of his own time. If you too can forget."

I didn't have the foggiest what the hell he was talking about.

"Croaker!" Lady snapped, catching the scent of what was in the back of my mind almost before I did. "We don't have time for you to indulge your curiosity about the past. There's something going on here. Tend to it before we get our butts in a sling."

She was turning into one of the guys for sure.

"You getting the idea where we stand, Swan? You don't really figure we think running into you and the woman up there was by chance, do you? Talk me some plain talk."

Some not so very plain talk took a while. Darkness came and the moon rose. It climbed the sky. The operators of the grove became exasperated but were too polite to ask their ruling prince to bug off. And while we stayed, so did the scores who had come out to look at us.

"Definitely something going on," I whispered to Lady. "But how do I dig it out of him?"

The Prahbrindrah played down everything he said, but the presence of the city fathers shrieked that Taglios was approaching a perilous crossroads. An undercurrent in what I heard told me the Prince wanted to spit in the face of calamity.

Willow tried to explain. "A while back—and nobody's sure exactly when because nobody was looking for it—what you might call a darkness turned up in a place called Pityus, which is like four hundred miles southeast of Taglios. Nobody worried about it. Then it spread to Tragevec and Kiaulune, which are pretty important, and Six and Fred, and all of a sudden everybody was worried but it was too late. You had this huge chunk of country ruled by these four sorcerers that refugees called Shadowmasters. They had a thing about shadows. Changed Tragevec's name to Shadowlight and Kiaulune to Shadowcatch and nowadays most everybody calls their empire the Shadowlands."

"You're going to get around to telling me what this's got to do with us, aren't you?"

"Within a year after the Shadowmasters took over they had those cities—which hadn't practiced war since the terror of Khatovar—armed and playing imperial games. In the years since, the Shadowmasters have conquered most of the territories between Taglios's southern frontiers and the edge of the map."

"I'm starting to smell it, Croaker," Lady said. She had grown grim as she listened.

"I am, too. Go on, Swan."

"Well, before they got to us . . . Before they went to work on Taglios they had some kind of falling out down there. Started feuding. The refugees talk about the whole big show. Intrigues, betrayals, subversions, assassinations, alliances shifting all over. Whenever it looked like one of them was starting to get ahead the others would gang up. Was like that for fifteen, eighteen years. So Taglios wasn't threatened."

"But now they are?"

"Now they're all looking this way. They made a move last year but it didn't work out for them." He looked smug. "What they got here in this berg is all the guts anybody could ask—and not a bat in broad daylight's notion what the hell to do with them. Me and Cordy and Blade, we kind of got drafted last year. But I wasn't never much of a soldier and neither was they. As generals we're like tits on a boar hog."

"So this isn't about bodyguarding and dirty-tricking for your Prince at all. Is it? He wants to drag us into his fight. Did he think he could get us on the cheap or something? Didn't you make a report about our trip down here?"

"He's the kind of guy who's got to check things for himself. Maybe he figured to see if you rated yourself cheap. I told him all the stories I ever heard about you guys. He still wanted to see for himself. He's a pretty good old boy. First prince I ever seen that tries to do what a prince is supposed to do."

"Rarer than frog hair, then. I'm sure. But you said it, Swan. We're on a mission from the gods. We don't have time to mess in local disputes. Maybe when we're on our way back."

Swan laughed.

"What's so funny?"

"You really don't got no choice."

"No?" I tried to read him. I couldn't. Lady shrugged when I looked at her. "Well? Why not?"

"To get where you want to go you got to head right through the Shadowlands. Seven, eight hundred miles of them. I don't think even you guys can make it. Neither does he."

"You said they were four hundred miles away."

"Four hundred miles to Pityus, Cap. Where it started. They got everything from the border south now. Seven, eight hundred to Shadowcatch. And like I said, they started on us last year. Took everything south of the Main."

I knew the Main to be a broad river south of Taglios, a natural frontier and barrier.

Swan continued, "Their troops are only eighty miles from Taglios some places. And we know they're planning a push as soon as the rivers go down. And we don't figure they're gonna be polite. All four Shadowmasters said they would get mean if the Prahbrindrah had anything to do with you guys."

I looked at Lady. "Damned awful lot of folks know more about what I'm doing and where I'm going than I do."

She ignored me. She asked, "Why didn't he run us off, Swan? Why did he send you to meet us?"

"Oh, he never sent us. He didn't know about that part till we got back. He just figures if the Shadowmasters are scared of you guys then he ought to be friends with you."

It wasn't me who frightened them, but why give that away? Swan and his buddies and boss didn't need to know who Lady had been. "He's got guts."

"They all got guts. Out the yang-yang. Pity is, they don't know what to do with them. And I can't show them. Like he says, the Shadowmasters would come sooner or later anyway, so why appease them? Why let them pick their time?"

"What's in this for Willow Swan? You come on pretty strong for a guy just passing through."

"Cordy ain't here to hear me, so I'll tell it straight. I'm not on the run no more. I've found my place. I don't want to lose it. Good enough?"

Maybe. "I couldn't give him an answer here, now. You know that if you know anything about the Black Company at all. I don't think there's much chance. It isn't what we want to do. But I'll give the situation a fair look. Tell him I want a week and the cooperation of his people." I planned to spend another eleven days resting and refitting. I was out nothing making that promise. Nothing but some of my share of the rest.

"That's it?" Swan asked.

"What else is there? You expect me to jump in just because you're a sweet guy? Swan, I'm headed for

Khatovar. I'll do what I have to do to get there. You made your pitch. Now's the time to back off and let the customer think."

He babbled to his prince. The more the evening went on, the more I was tempted to issue a flat rejection. Croaker was getting old and cranky and not thrilled with the idea of learning yet another language.

The Prahbrindrah Drah nodded to Swan. He agreed with me. They rose. I did likewise, and gave the Prince a shallow bow. He and Swan walked away, pausing here and there to speak to other midnight diners. No telling what he said. Maybe what they wanted to hear. The faces I could see were smiling.

I got myself comfortable, leaned back to watch One-Eye at play. He had a swarm of bugs zipping around his victim's head. I asked Lady, "What do you think?"

"It's not my place to think."

"Where would you be inclined to stand?"

"I'm a soldier of the Black Company. As you're inclined to remind me."

"So was Raven. So long as it suited his convenience. Don't play games with me. Talk to me straight. Do you know these Shadowmasters? Are they Taken you sent down here to start building you a new empire?"

"No! I salvaged Shifter and sent him south, just in case, when the fury of the war and Stormbringer's enmity were enough to explain his disappearance. That's all."

"But Howler . . ."

"Had his own escape planned. Knows of my condition and nurtures ambitions of his own. Obviously. But the Shadowmasters . . . I know nothing. Nothing. You should've asked more about them."

"I will. If they're not Taken they sound close enough as makes no difference. So I want to know. Where do you stand?"

"I'm a soldier of the Black Company. They've already declared themselves my enemies."

"That's not a definitive answer."

"It's the best you're going to get."

"I figured. What about Shifter and his sidekick?" I hadn't seen them since Thresh, but had the feeling they were just around the corner. "If it's as bad as it looks we'll need all the resources we can muster."

"Shifter will do what I tell him."

Not the most reassuring answer, but I did not press. Again, it was the best I was going to get.

"Eat your dinner and stop pestering me, Croaker."

I looked down at food now so old it was no longer palatable.

Smirking, Frogface ambled off to help his master soften the will of an assassin.

One-Eye overdid it. He has that way when he has an audience. He gets too exuberant. Our prisoner expired from sheer terror. We gained nothing from him but notoriety.

As though we needed that.

Chapter Twenty-three:
WILLOW, BATS, AND THINGS

It was late. Willow yawned as he tumbled into his chair. Blade, Cordy, and the Woman looked at him expectantly. Like the Prahbrindrah couldn't talk for himself. "We talked."

"And?" the Radisha demanded.

"You maybe expected him to jump up and down and yell, 'Oh, goodie!'"

"What did he say?"

"He said he'd check it out. Which is about the best you could expect."

"I should have gone myself."

The Prahbrindrah said, "Sister, the man wouldn't have listened at all had not someone just tried to kill him."

She was astonished.

Willow said, "Those guys aren't stupid. They knew we was up to something way back when they let us hook up with them at the Third Cataract. They been watching us as close as we been watching them."

Smoke drifted in with all the racket of his namesake. It was a big room in the cellar of a friend of the Radisha, near the olive grove. It smelled moldy although it was open to the night in places. Smoke came a few steps into the light cast by three oil lamps. His face puckered into a frown. He looked around.

"What's the matter?" Cordy asked. He shivered visibly. Swan got a creepy feeling, too.

"I'm not sure. For a moment . . . like something was staring at me."

The Radisha exchanged looks with her brother, then with Willow. "Willow. Those two odd little men. One-Eye and Goblin. Fact or fraud?"

"Six of one and half a dozen of the other. Right, Blade? Cordy?"

Cordy nodded. Blade said, "The little one. Like a child. Frogface. That's dangerous."

"What is it?" the Woman asked. "The oddest child I've ever seen. There were times when it acted a hundred years old."

"Maybe ten thousand," Smoke said. "An imp. I dared not investigate lest it recognize me as more than a silly old man. I don't know its capacities. But definitely a supernatural entity of great efficacy. My question is how an adept of a capacity as limited as the One-Eye creature obtained control. I'm superior to him in talent, skill, and training, but I can neither summon nor control such a thing."

Sudden squeaks and flutters came from the darkness. Startled, everyone turned. Bats hurtled into the light, peeping, diving, dodging. A sudden larger shape flashed through, dark as a chunk of night. It ripped a bat on the fly. Another shape flung through a second later, dropping another bat. The others got away through a barred but otherwise unclosed ground-level window.

"What the hell?" Willow squawked. "What's going on?"

Blade said, "Couple of crows. Killing bats." He sounded perfectly calm. As if crows killing bats in a basement at midnight, around his head, was something that happened all the time.

The crows did not reappear.

"I don't like it, Willow," Cordy said. "Crows don't fly at night. Something's going on."

Everyone looked at everyone else and waited for somebody to say something. Nobody noticed the pan-therine shadow settle outside the window, one eye peeking inside. Nor did anybody realize that a child-sized figure lounged atop an old crate beyond the light, grinning. But Smoke began to shiver and turn in slow circles, again with that feeling of being watched.

The Prahbrindrah said, "I recall saying it wouldn't be a good idea to meet this close to the grove. I recall suggesting we get together in the palace, in a room that Smoke has sealed against prying. I don't know what just happened, but it wasn't natural and I don't want to talk here. Let's go. The delay can't hurt. Can it, Smoke?"

The old man shuddered violently, said, "It might be most wise, my Prince. Most wise. There is more here than meets the eye. . . . Henceforth we must assume we are under surveillance."

The Radisha was irked. "By who, old man?"

"I don't know. Does it matter, Radisha? There are those who are interested. The High Priests. These soldiers you wish to use. The Shadowmasters. Perhaps forces of which we are unaware."

They all looked at him. "Explain that," the Woman ordered.

"I cannot. Except to remind you that those men successfully fought their way through river pirates who have held the river closed for some time. None of them would say much about it, but a word here and a word there added together suggested that there was sorcery of the highest order involved, on both sides. And theirs was sufficient to force the blockade. But, except for the imp, there was nothing of that sort evident when we joined them. If they had it, where did it go? Could it be that well hidden? Maybe, but I doubt it. Maybe it travels with them without being with them, if you see what I mean."

"No. You're up to your old tricks. Being deliberately vague."

"I'm vague because I have no answers, Radisha. Only questions. I wonder, more and more, if the band we see isn't an illusion cast for our benefit. A handful of men, hard and tough and skilled in their murderous ways, to

be sure, but nothing that should terrify the Shadowmasters. There aren't enough of them to make a difference. So why are the Shadowmasters concerned? Either
they know more than we do or they see better than we
do. Remember the history of the Free Companies. They
weren't just bands of killers. And these men are determined to reach Khatovar. Their captain has tried everything short of violence to unearth information about the
way."

"Hey, Smoke! You said go someplace else and talk,"
Blade said. "So how about we go?"

Swan agreed. "Yeah. This dump gives me the creeps. I
don't get you guys, Radisha. You and the Prince claim
you run Taglios, but you go around hiding out in holes
like this."

"Our seats aren't secure." She started moving. "We
rule with the consent of the priests, really. And we don't
want them knowing everything we're doing."

"Every damned lord and priest who was anybody was
up in that grove tonight. They know."

"They know what we told them. Which is only part of
the truth."

Cordy eased in close to Willow. "Keep it down, man.
Can't you see what's up? They're playing for a lot more
than just turning back the Shadowmasters."

"Uhm."

Behind them, something resembling a panther padded
from one pool of darkness to another, silent as death
itself. Crows glided from one point of vantage to another. A childlike figure tagged along behind, apparently
openly but remaining unseen. But no bats darted overhead.

Willow understood, with that one admonition. The
Woman and her brother thought the struggle with the
Shadowmasters would preoccupy the priests and cults.
While they were distracted they would gather all the
reins of the state. . . .

He did not begrudge them. He had little use for priests.

He thought maybe Blade was on to something. Here, sure. They ought all to be drowned so Taglios could be put out of its misery.

Each dozen or so paces he turned, looked back. The street was always empty behind him. Yet he was sure something was watching.

"Creepy," he muttered. And wondered how he'd gotten himself into this mess.

Chapter Twenty-four:
TAGLIOS: A PRINCELY PRESSURE

That Prahbrindrah Drah might have been one of the good guys but he was as slick as any villian. Two days after our visit I couldn't go out without being hailed Guardian, Protector, and Deliverer. "What the hell is going on?" I asked One-Eye.

"Trying to lock you in." He glared at Frogface. The imp had not been much good since that night. He couldn't get near anybody—except Swan and his buddies, in a dive they owned. And they didn't talk business there. "You sure you want to go to this library?"

"I'm sure." Somehow the Taglians had gotten the idea I was a big healer as well as some kind of messianic general. "What the hell is wrong with them? I can see the Prince trying to sell them the load of sheep shit, but why are they buying it?"

"They want to."

Mothers thrust their babies at me to be touched and blessed. Young men clashed anything metal and roared songs with a martial beat. Maidens threw flowers on my path. And sometimes themselves.

"That's nice, Croaker," One-Eye said, as I disentangled myself from a daydream about sixteen years old. "You don't want her, toss her my way."

"Take it easy. Before you give in to your baser instincts think about what's going on."

He was reserved to an extreme that baffled me. I think

he saw it all as illusion. Or at least as a honeytrap. One-Eye is silly but he isn't stupid. Sometimes.

One-Eye chuckled. "Surrender to temptation. Lady can't look over your shoulder all the time."

"I might. I just might. It *is* my duty not to disappoint these people when they're trying so hard to hustle us. Isn't it?"

"There you go." But he did not sound like he believed himself. He was uncomfortable with his good fortune.

We went into the library. I found nothing. So much nothing I got even more suspicious than I was. Frogface wasn't much use, but he could eavesdrop. The conversations he reported contributed to my concern.

It was a good time for the men. Even the supreme discipline of the Nar was not proof against some temptations. Mogaba did not hold them on too tight a leash. As Goblin howled one morning, "Heaven's on fire, Croaker!"

Always there was this feeling of something happening just out of the corner of my eye.

The geopolitical situation was clear. It was just as Swan had described. Meaning that to reach Khatovar we would have to slice through seven hundred miles of country ruled by the Shadowmasters. If Shadowmasters there were.

I had some slight doubts. Everyone I talked to, through Frogface, believed they existed, but nobody provided any concrete evidence.

"Nobody has ever seen the gods, either," a priest told me. "But we all believe in them, don't we? We see their handiwork. . . ." He realized that I had scowled at his suggestion that everyone believed in gods. His eyes narrowed. He scurried away. For the first time I had found me somebody less than thrilled with my presence in Taglios. I told One-Eye it might be more profitable if we started spying on the High Priests instead of the Prince and Swan, who knew when to keep their mouths shut.

That we were being manipulated into going up against some heavyweight sorcerers did not intimidate me. Much. We had been up against the best for twenty years. What troubled me was my ignorance.

I did not know the language. I did not know the Taglian people. Their history was a mystery and Swan's bunch were no help tossing light into the shadows. And, of course, I knew nothing about the Shadowmasters or the peoples they ruled. Nothing but what I had been told, which could be worse than nothing. Worst of all, I was not acquainted with the ground where any struggle would take place. And I had too little time to learn all the answers.

Sundown of the third day. We moved to quarters farther south in the city, provided by the state. I gathered everyone but the half-dozen men on guard duty. While most of the guys ate supper—cooked and served by people provided by the Prahbrindrah—the folks at my long table got their heads together. The rest had orders to keep the Taglians hopping. I doubted they could understand us, but you don't take chances. ˙

I sat at the head of the table, Lady to my left and Mogaba to my right, he with his two leading men next to him. Goblin and One-Eye were beyond Lady on her side, tonight with Goblin in the seat nearer the head. I had to make them trade off each meal. Beyond them were Murgen and Hagop and Otto, with Murgen at the foot of the table, in his capacity as apprentice Annalist. I made like I was telling a story as we ate. The paterfamilias entertaining his children.

"I'm taking the imperial horses out tonight. Lady, Goblin, Hagop, Otto, you'll come. One of the roi. One of your lieutenants, Mogaba, and one of your men. Men who can ride."

One-Eye drew a breath to complain. So did Murgen. But Mogaba slid in ahead of both. "A sneak?"

"I want to scout to the south. These people could be selling us a pig in a poke."

I didn't think they were, but why take a man's word when you can see for yourself? Especially when he's trying to use you?

"One-Eye, you stay here because I want you working your pet. Day and night. Murgen, write down whatever he tells you. Mogaba, cover for us. If they've been telling it straight we won't be gone long."

"You told the Prahbrindrah you'd give him an answer in a week. You have four days left."

"We'll be back in time. We'll go after next watch change, after Goblin and One-Eye knock out anybody who might see us."

Mogaba nodded. I glanced at Lady. She didn't contribute much anymore. If I wanted to be the boss, I was going to be the boss and she would keep her opinion to herself.

Mogaba said, "Several of my men have approached me on a matter of some delicacy. I think we need a policy."

This was something unexpected. "A policy? About what?"

"To what extent the men can use violence to defend themselves. Several have been attacked. They want to know how much restraint they have to show, for political reasons. Or if they have permission to make examples."

"Gah! When did this start?"

"I received the first report this afternoon."

"All today, then?"

"Yes sir."

"Let's see the men involved."

He brought them to the table. They were Nar. There were five of them. It did not seem likely that such things would happen to the Nar alone. I sent Murgen around. He returned. "Three incidents. They took care of it themselves. Said they didn't figure it was something worth reporting."

Discipline. Something to be said for it.

It took half a minute to decide the attackers were not, apparently, Taglians. "Wrinkly little brown guys? We saw those on the river. I asked Swan. He said he didn't know where they came from. But they gave him the colly-wobbles. If they're not Taglians, don't take no shit. Ace them unless you can take a couple prisoners. One-Eye. If you could snag a couple and give them the works. . . ."

We did all this amidst the comings and goings of our Taglian servitors. At that point several came to collect empty plates, forestalling One-Eye from poormouthing about how he was so grossly overworked. He did not squawk fast enough when they cleared away, either.

Murgen got the first word in. "I got a problem, Croaker." Mogaba winced. Flexible man, Mogaba, but he could not get used to me letting anybody call me anything but Captain.

"What's that?"

"Bats."

Goblin snickered.

"Can it, runt. Bats? What about bats?"

"Guys keep finding dead bats around."

I noted, from the corner of my eye, that Lady had grown more attentive. "I don't follow you."

"The men have been finding dead bats every morning since we got here. Bats all torn up, not just dropped over dead. And they're only around where we are. Not all over town."

I looked at One-Eye. He looked at me. He said, "I know. I know. One more job for good old One-Eye. How's this outfit ever going to get along without me when I go?"

I don't know if the others bought it or not.

There were things One-Eye and I hadn't shared with everyone.

"Any other problems?"

Nobody had a problem, but Murgen had a question. "All right if we work on Swan a little? I checked out that place he owns. It's the kind of place some of our guys would hang out. We might find out something interesting there."

"At least you'd keep him nervous. Good idea. Have some of the Nar hang out there, too. To work on that Blade character."

"He's a spooky one," Otto said.

"The most dangerous too, I'd bet. One of those guys like Raven. Kill you without batting an eye and not even remember it five minutes later."

Mogaba said, "You must tell me more of this Raven. Each time I hear of him he sounds more intriguing."

Lady paused with fork half lifted to mouth. "It's all in the Annals, Lieutenant." The gentlest of admonitions. For all his devotion to things Company, Mogaba had yet to make a serious attempt to explore those Annals set down after the Company had departed Gea-Xle.

"Of course," he replied, voice perfectly even, but eyes hard as steel. There was a distinct coolness between them. I had sensed it before, mildly. Negative chemistry. Neither had any reason to dislike the other. Or maybe they did. I spent more time with Mogaba these days than I did with Lady.

"That's that, then," I said. "Out of here after the next watch change. Be ready."

Mostly nods as they pushed back from the table, but Goblin stayed put, scowling, for several seconds before he rose.

He suspected that he was being drafted mainly to keep him out of mischief while I was gone.

He was sixty percent right.

Chapter Twenty-five:
TAGLIOS: SCOUTING SOUTHWARD

Try sneaking someplace on a plowhorse sometime. You'll get half the idea of the trouble we had sliding out of town unnoticed on those monsters Lady had given us. We wore poor Goblin down to the nubs, covering up. By the time we cleared town I was thinking maybe we would have done as well to have taken the coach.

Getting out unnoticed was a relative notion, anyway. There were crows on watch. Seemed one of those damned birds was perched on every tree and roof we passed.

Though we hurried through it, and it could not be seen well in the dark, the countryside immediately south of Taglios seemed rich and intensively cultivated. It had to be to support an urban area so large—though there appeared to be garden areas inside the city, especially in the well-to-do neighborhoods. Surprisingly, Taglians did not eat much meat though it was food that could be walked to market.

Two of the three great religious families banned the eating of flesh.

Along with everything else, our great steeds could see in the dark. It did not bother them to canter when I could not see my hand in front of my face. Dawn caught us forty miles south of Taglios, thoroughly saddlesore.

Opened-mouth peasants watched us flash by.

Swan had told me about the Shadowmasters' invasion of the previous summer. Twice we crossed the path of that struggle, coming upon gutted villages. In each the villagers had rebuilt, but not on the same site.

We paused near the second. A hetman came to look us over while we ate. We had no words in common. When he saw he wasn't going to get anywhere he just grinned, shook my hand, and walked away.

Goblin said, "He knew who we are. And figures us the same as the people in the city."

"For dopes?"

"Nobody thinks we're stupid, Croaker," Lady said. "And maybe that's the problem. Maybe we aren't as smart as they think we are."

"Say what?" I threw a stone at a crow. I missed. She gave me a funny look.

"I think you're right when you say there's a conspiracy of silence. But maybe they aren't hiding as much as you think. Maybe they just think we know more than we know."

Sindawe, Mogaba's lieutenant and third, offered, "I feel this to be the heart of it, Captain. I have spent much time on the streets. I have seen this in the eyes of all who look upon me. They think I am much more than what I am."

"Hey. They don't just look at me. I go out they start hailing me everything but emperor. It's embarrassing."

"But they won't talk," Goblin said, starting to pack up. "They'll bow and grin and kiss your backside and give you anything but their virgin daughters, but they won't say squat if you go after a concrete answer."

"Truth is a deadly weapon," Lady said.

"Which is why priests and princes dread it," I said. "If we're more than we seem, what do they think we are?"

Lady said, "What the Company was when it came through heading north."

Sindawe agreed. "The answer would be in the missing Annals."

"Of course. And they're missing." If I had had my own along I would have paused to review what I had learned at the Temple of Traveller's Repose. Those first few books had been lost down here somewhere.

None of the names on my maps rang any bells. None of what I remembered contained any echoes. Cho'n Delor had been the end of history, so to speak. The beginning of unknown country, though there was much in the Annals from before the Pastel Wars.

Could they have changed all the names?

"Oh, my aching ass," Goblin complained as he clambered into the saddle. A sight to behold, a runt like him getting up the side of one of those horses. Every time Otto had a crack about getting him a ladder. "Croaker, I got an idea."

"That sounds dangerous."

He ignored that. "How about we retire? We're not young enough for this crap anymore."

Hagop said, "Those guys we ran into on the road down from Oar probably had the right idea. Only they were small-time. We ought to find a town and take over. Or sign on with somebody permanent like."

"That's been tried fifty times. Never lasts. Only place it worked was Gea-Xle. And there the guys got itchy feet after a while."

"Bet that wasn't the same guys who rode in."

"We're all old and tired, Hagop."

"Speak for yourself, Granddad," Lady said.

I threw a rock and mounted up. That was an invitation to banter. I did not take it up. I felt old and tired that way, too. She shrugged, mounted up herself. I rode out wondering where we were at, she and I. Probably nowhere. Maybe the spark had been neglected too long. Maybe propinquity was counterproductive.

As we moved farther south we noted a phenomenon. Post riders in numbers like we had seen nowhere else. In every village we were recognized. It was the same old salute and cheer that started in Taglios. Where they had them the young men came out with weapons.

I'm not much for morality. But I felt morally reprehensible when I saw them, as if I were somehow responsible for transmuting a pacific people into fire-eyed militarists.

Otto was of the opinion the weapons had been taken from last year's invaders. Maybe. Some. But most looked so old and rusted and brittle I would wish them only on my enemies.

The commission looked more improbable by the hour.

Nowhere did we encounter evidence that Taglians were anything but a pleasant, friendly, industrious people blessed with a land where survival was not a day-to-day struggle. But even these country folk seemed to devote most of their leisure time, whence culture springs, to their bewildering battalions of gods.

"One signal victory," I told Lady when we were about eighty miles south of the city, "and these people will be psyched up to take any hardships the Shadowmasters can dish out."

"And if we take the commission and lose the first battle it won't matter anyway. We won't be around to have to suffer the consequences."

"That's my girl. Always thinking positive."

"Are you really going to take the commission?"

"Not if I can help it. That's why we're out here. But I've got a bad feeling that what I want won't have much to do with what I'll have to do."

Goblin snorted and grumbled something about being dragged around on the claws of fate. He was right. And my only notion for breaking loose was to find a way to keep heading south, Shadowmasters be damned.

We did not press hard, and paused for lunch before our breakfasts were really settled. Our bodies were not up to the continuous abuse of a sustained ride. Getting old.

Otto and Hagop wanted to lay on a fire and fix a real meal. I told them go ahead. Sore and tired, I settled down nearby, head pillowed on a rock, and stared at clouds trudging across alien skies that by day looked no different than those whence I had come.

Things were happening too fast and too strange to wring any sense out of them. I was plagued by a dread that I was the wrong man in the wrong place and wrong time for the Company. I did not feel competent to handle the situation Taglios threatened. Could *I* presume to lead a nation to war? I did not think so. Even if every Taglian man, woman, and child proclaimed me savior.

I tried comforting myself with the thought that I was not the first Captain with doubts, and far from the first to get embroiled in a local situation armed only with a glimmer of the true problems and stakes. Maybe I was luckier than some. I had Lady, for whom the waters of intrigue were home. If I could tap her talent. I had Mogaba, who, despite those cultural and language barriers that still existed between us, had begun to look like the best pure soldier I'd ever known. I had Goblin and One-Eye and Frogface and—maybe—Shifter. And I had four hundred years of Company shenanigans in my trick bag. But none of that appeased my conscience or stilled my doubts.

What *had* we gotten into on our simple ride back into the Company's origins?

Was that half the trouble? That we were in unknown territory so far as the Annals were concerned? That I was trying to work without a historical chart?

There *were* questions about our forebrethren and this country. I'd had little opportunity to ferret out information. The hints I had gathered suggested that those old boys had not been nice fellows. I got the impression that the diaspora of the original Free Companies had been a nut religious thing. The moving doctrine, a vestige of which survived among the Nar, must have been terrible. The name of the Company still struck fear and stirred intense emotion.

The exhaustion caught up. I fell asleep, though I did not realize it till the conversation of crows awakened me.

I bounced up. The others looked at me oddly. They did not hear it. They were about finished with their meal.

Otto was keeping the pot hot for me.

I looked into a lone nearby tree and saw several crows, their ugly heads all cocked so they could look at me. They started chattering. I had a definite feeling they wanted my attention.

I ambled toward them.

Two flew when I was halfway to the tree, gaining altitude in that clumsy way crows have, gliding to the southeast toward an isolated stand of trees maybe a mile away. A good fifty crows circled above those trees.

The remaining crow left the lone tree when he was satisfied I had seen that. I turned to lunch in a thoughtful mood. Halfway through a bad stew I concluded that I had to assume I had been given a warning. The road passed within yards of those trees.

As we mounted up, I said, "People, we ride with weapons bare. Goblin. See those trees yonder? Keep an eye on them. Like your life depends on it."

"What's up, Croaker?"

"I don't know. Just a hunch. Probably wrong, but it don't cost nothing to be careful."

"If you say so." He gave me a funny look, like he was wondering about my stability.

Lady gave me an even funnier look when, as we approached the woods, Goblin squeaked, "The place is infested!"

That's all he got to say. The infestation broke cover. Those little brown guys. About a hundred of them. Real military geniuses, too. Men on foot just don't go jumping people on horseback even if they do outnumber them.

Goblin said, "Gleep!" And then he said something else. The swarm of brown men became surrounded by a fog of insects.

They should have shot us down with arrows.

Otto and Hagop chose what I considered the stupider course. They charged. Their momentum carried them through the mob. My choice seemed the wiser. The others agreed. We just turned away and trotted ahead of the brown guys, leaving them to Goblin's mercies.

My beast stumbled. Master horseman that I am, I promptly fell off. Before I could get to my feet the brown guys were all around me, trying to lay hands on. But Goblin was on the job. I don't know what he did, but it worked. After they knocked me around a little, leaving me a fine crop of bruises, they decided to keep after those who had had sense enough to stay on their horses.

Otto and Hagop thundered past, making a rear attack. I staggered to my feet, looked for my mount. He was a hundred yards away, looking at me in a bemused sort of way. I limped toward him.

Those little guys had some kind of petty magic of their own going, and no sense at all. They just kept on. They dropped like flies, but when they outnumber you a dozen to one you got to worry about more than just a favorable kill ratio.

I did not see it well, busy as I was. And when I did manage to drag my abused flesh aboard my animal's back the whole brouhaha had swept out of sight down a narrow, shallow valley.

I have no idea how, but somehow I managed to get disoriented. Or something. When I got organized and started after my bunch I could not find them. Though I never got much chance to look. Fate intervened in the form of five little brown guys on horses that would have been amusing if they hadn't been waving swords and lances and rushing at me with intent to be obnoxious.

On another day I might have stayed forty yards ahead and plinked at them with my bow. But I wasn't in the mood. I just wanted to be left alone and to get back together with the others.

I galloped off. Up and down and around a few hills and I lost them easily. But in the process I lost myself. During all the fun the sky clouded over. It started to drizzle. Just to make me that much more enchanted with my chosen way of life. I set out to find the road, hoping I would find traces of my companions there.

I topped a hill and spied that damned crow-

surrounded figure that had been haunting me since the
Temple of Travellers' Respose. It was striding along in
the distance, directly away from me. I forgot about the
others. I kicked my mount into a gallop. The figure
paused and looked back. I felt the weight of its stare but
did not slow. I would unravel this mystery now.

I charged down a shallow hill, leapt a wash in which
muddy water gurgled. The figure was out of sight for a
moment. Up the other side. When I reached the crest
there was nothing to be seen but a few random crows
circling no particular point. I used language that would
have distressed my mother immensely.

I did not slow but continued my career till I reached
the approximate point where I had seen the thing last. I
reined in, swung down, began stomping around looking
for sign. A mighty tracker, me. But, moist as the ground
was already, there had to be traces. Unless I was crazy
and seeing things.

I found traces, sure enough. And I felt the continued
pressure of that stare. But I did not see the thing I sought.
I was baffled. Even considering the probability that there
was sorcery involved, how could it have vanished so
completely? There was no cover anywhere around.

I spotted some crows starting to circle about a quarter
mile away. "All right, you son of a bitch. We'll see how
fast you can run."

There was nothing there when I got there.

The cycle repeated itself three times. I got no closer.
The last time I halted I did so atop a low crest that, from
a quarter mile, overlooked a hundred-acre wood. I
dismounted and stood beside my horse. We stared.
"You, too?" I asked. His breathing was as uneven as
mine. And those monster beasts never got winded.

That was a sight, down there. Never have I seen so
many crows except maybe on a recent battlefield.

In a lifetime of travel and study I have come upon half
a hundred tales about haunted forests. The woods are
always described as dark and dense and old or the trees

are mostly dead, skeleton hands reaching for the sky. This wood fit none of the particulars except for density. Yet it sure felt haunted.

I tossed my reins across the horse's neck, strapped on a buckler, drew my sword from its saddle scabbard, and started forward. The horse came along behind me, maybe eight feet back, head down so his nostrils were almost to the ground, like a hound on the track.

The crows were most numerous over the center of the wood. I did not trust my eyes but thought I detected some squat dark structure among the trees there. The closer I got the slower I moved, meaning maybe a part of me was still infected with common sense. The part that kept telling me that I was not cut out for this sort of thing. I wasn't some lone brawling swordsman who stalked evil into its lair.

I am a dope cursed with an unhealthy portion of curiosity. Curiosity had me by the chin whiskers and kept right on dragging me along.

There was one lone tree that approximated the stereotype, a bony old thing about half dead, as big around as me, standing like a sentinel thirty feet from the rest of the wood. Scrub and saplings clustered around its feet, rising waist high. I paused to lean against it while I talked myself into or out of something. The horse came up till his nose bumped my shoulder. I turned my head to look at him.

Snake hiss. *Thump!*

I gawked at the arrow quivering in the tree three inches from my fingers and only started to get myself down when it struck me that the shaft had not been meant to stick me in the brisket.

Head, shaft, and fletching, that bolt was as black as a priest's heart. The shaft itself had an enameled look. An inch behind the head was a wrap of white. I levered the arrow out of the tree and held the message close enough to read.

It is not yet time, Croaker.

The language and alphabet were those of the Jewel Cities.

Interesting. "Right. Not yet time." I peeled the paper off, crumpled it into a ball, tossed it at the wood. I looked for some sign of the archer. There was none. Of course.

I shoved the arrow into my quiver, swung onto my saddle, turned the horse and rode about a step. A shadow ran past, of a crow flying up to have a look at the seven little brown men waiting for me atop the hill. "You guys never give up, do you?"

I got back down, behind the horse, took out my bow, strung it, drew an arrow—the arrow just collected—and started angling across the hillside, staying behind my mount. The little brown guys turned their toy horses and moved with me.

When I had a nice range I jumped out and let fly at the nearest. He saw it coming and tried to dodge, only he did himself more harm than good. I meant to put the shaft into his pony's neck. It slammed in through his knee, getting him and the animal both. The pony threw him and took off, dragging him from a stirrup.

I mounted up fast, took off through the gap. Those little horses did not move fast enough to close it.

So we were off, them pounding after me at a pace to kill their animals in an hour, my beast barely cantering and, I think, having a good time. I can't recall any other horse I've ridden looking back to check the pursuit and adjusting its pace to remain tantalizingly close.

I had no idea who the brown guys were but there had to be a bunch of them the way they kept turning up. I considered working on this bunch, taking them out one by one, decided discretion was the better part. If need be I could bring the Company down and forage for them.

I wondered what became of Lady and Goblin and the others. I doubted they had come to any harm, what with our advantage in mounts, but . . .

We were separated and there was no point spending the remaining daylight looking for them. I would get

back to the road, turn north, find a town and someplace
dry.

The drizzle irritated me more than the fact that I was
being hunted.

But that stretch of forest bothered me more than the
rain. That was a mystery that scared the crap out of me.

The crows and walking stump were real. No doubt of
that anymore. And the stump knew me by name.

Maybe I ought to bring the Company down and go
after whatever hid there.

The road was one of those wonders that turns to mud
hip deep if somebody spits on it. There were no fences in
this part of the world, so I just rode beside it. I came to a
village almost immediately.

Call it a stroke of fate, or timing. Timing. My life runs
on weird timing. There were riders coming into town
from the north. They looked even more bedraggled than
I felt. They were not little brown men but I gave them the
suspicious eye anyway and looked for places to duck.
They were carrying more lethal hardware than I was, and
I had enough to outfit a platoon.

"Yo! Croaker!"

Hell. That was Murgen. I got a little closer and saw
that the other three were Willow Swan, Cordy Mather,
and Blade.

What the hell were they doing down here?

Chapter Twenty-six:
OVERLOOK

The one who had withdrawn everything but moral support did not give up his right to complain and criticize.

The gathering of the Shadowmasters took place in the heights of a soaring tower in that one's new capitol fortress, Overlook, which lay two miles south of Shadowcatch. It was a strange, dark fortress, more vast than some cities. It had thick walls a hundred feet high. Every vertical surface was sheathed in plates of burnished brass or iron. Ugly silver lettering in an alphabet known only to a few damascened those plates, proclaiming fearful banes.

The Shadowmasters assembled in a room not at all in keeping with their penchant for darkness. The sun burned through a skylight and through walls of crystal. The three shrank from the glare, though they were clad in their darkest apparel. Their host floated near the southern wall, seldom withdrawing his gaze from the distance. His preoccupation was obsessive.

Out there, many miles away but visible from that great height, lay a vast flat expanse. It shimmered. It was as white as the corpse of an old dead sea. The visitors thought his fear and fixation dangerously obsessive. If it was not feigned. If it was not the fulcrum of an obscure and deadly strategem. But it was impossible not to be impressed by the magnitude of the defenses he had raised.

The fortress had been seventeen years in the building and was not yet more than two-thirds completed.

The small one, the female, asked, "It's quiet out there now?" She spoke the language that was emblazoned upon the fortress walls.

"It's always quiet during the day. But come the night . . . Come the night . . ." Fear and hatred blackened the air.

He blamed *them* for his dire circumstances. *They* had mined the shadows and had awakened the terror, then they had left him to face the consequences alone.

He turned. "You have failed. You have failed and failed and failed. The Radisha went north without inconvenience. *They* sailed through the swamps like vengeance itself, so easily *she* never had to lift a finger. They go where they will and do what they will, without peril, so blithely sure they don't even notice your meddling. And now they and she are on your marches, conjuring mischief there. So you come to me."

"Who could have suspected they would have a Great One as companion? That one was supposed to have perished."

"Fool! Was he not a master of change and illusion? You should have known he was there waiting for them. How could such a one hide?"

"Did you know he was there and fail to inform us?" the female mocked.

He whirled back to the window. He did not answer. He said, "They are on your marches now. Will you deal with them this time?"

"They are but fifty mortal men."

"With her. And the Great One."

"And we are four. And we have armies. Soon the rivers will go down. Ten thousand men will cross the Main and obliterate the very Name of the Black Company."

A sound came from the one at the window, a hissing

that grew up to become cold, mocking laughter. "They will? That has been tried numberless times. Numberless. But they endure. For four hundred years they have endured. Ten thousand men? You joke. A million might not suffice. The empire in the north could not extermi- nate them."

The three exchanged glances. Here was madness. Obsession and madness. When the threat from the north was expunged perhaps this one ought to follow it.

"Come here," he said. "Look down there. Where that ghost of an old road winds through the valley up toward the brilliance." Something turned and coiled there, a blackness deeper than that of their apparel. "You see that?"

"What is it?"

"My shadow trap. They come through the gateway you breached, the great old strong ones. Not the toys you drew into your services, these. I could loose them. I might if you fail again."

The three stirred. He had to go for certain.

He laughed, reading their thoughts. "And the key to that trap is my Name, my brethren. If *I* perish the trap collapses and the gateway stands open to the world." He laughed again.

The male who spoke the least when they gathered spat angrily and made to depart. After hesitating the other two followed. There was nothing more to be said.

Mad laughter pursued them down the endless spiral of the stairs.

The woman observed, "Maybe he can't be conquered. But while he persists in facing south he offers us no peril. Let us ignore him henceforth."

"Three against two, then," her companion grumbled. The other, in the lead, grunted.

"But there is one in the swamps, whose debt of anger might be manipulated if we grow desperate. And we have gold. Always there are tools to be found in the ranks of the enemy when gold is allowed to speak. Not so?" She laughed. Her laughter was almost as crazy as that peeling out above.

Chapter Twenty-seven:
NIGHT STRIFE

I gave Murgen my dirtiest look as he rode up. He understood it. We would talk later. For the moment he said, "You told me to keep an eye on them."

Swan reached me a moment later. "Gods, you guys move fast. I'm shot." He made an obscene gesture at the sky. "We leave five minutes after you and find out you had time to take a couple of breaks and still stay ahead of us." He shook his head. "Bunch of iron men. Told you I wasn't cut out for this crap, Cordy."

"Where is everybody?" Murgen asked.

"I don't know. We got ambushed. We got separated."

Mather, Swan, and Blade exchanged glances. Swan asked, "Little brown guys? All wrinkly?"

"You know them?"

"We had a run-in with them when we were headed north. Man, I got me a brainstorm. We going to jaw, let's do it out of the rain. My lumbago is killing me."

"Lumbago?" Mather asked. "When did you come up with lumbago?"

"When I forgot my hat and it started raining on my head. Blade, you was in this place last year. They got like an inn, or something?"

Blade didn't say anything, just turned his horse and headed out. He was an odd one for sure. But Swan thought he was an all-right guy, and I liked Swan as much as I could like anybody who worked for somebody who was trying to play games with me.

I was about to follow up last, with Murgen, when Murgen said, "Hold up. Somebody's coming." He pointed.

I looked into the drizzle to the south and saw three shapes, riders coming in. Their mounts were tall enough that they could be nothing but Lady's gifts. Swan cursed the delay but we waited.

The three were Hagop, Otto, and the roi Shadid. Shadid looked ragged. And Hagop and Otto were wounded. "Damn you two. Can't you take a crap without getting hurt?" In the thirty or so years I had known them it seemed they had come up wounded about three times a year. And survived everything. I'd begun to suspect they were immortal and the blood was the price they paid.

"They piled an ambush on top of the ambush, Croaker," Hagop said. "They ran us down that valley right into another gang on horseback."

My stomach tightened. "And?"

He put on a feeble grin. "I figure they're sorry they did. We cut them up bad."

"Where are the others?"

"I don't know. We scattered. Lady said for Shadid to ride back up here with us and wait. She led them off."

"All right. Blade. Why don't you show us where to roost?"

Murgen looked at me with a question unspoken. I told him, "Yeah. We'll get them settled. Then we'll go."

The place Blade took us wasn't really an inn, just a big house where the owner made a bit taking in travellers. He was not thrilled to see us, though like everybody else in this end of the world he seemed to know who we were. The color of our coin brightened his day and livened his smile. Still, I think he let us in mainly because he thought we would get rowdy if he didn't.

I got Otto and Hagop sewed up and bandaged and

generally settled into a routine they knew all too well. Meanwhile, the householder brought food, for which Swan expressed our sincere gratitude.

Murgen said, "It's going to be getting dark, Croaker."

"I know. Swan, we're going out to find the others. Got a spare horse if you want to ride along."

"You kidding? Go out in that muck when I don't have to? Hell. All right. I guess." He started levering himself out of his chair.

"Sit down, Willow," Mather said. "I'll go. I'm in better shape than you are."

Swan said, "You talked me into it, you smooth-talking son of a bitch. I don't know how you do it, you golden-tongued bastard. You can get anything you want out of me. Be careful."

"Ready?" Mather asked me. He stifled a small smile.

"Yeah."

We went out and climbed onto the horses, who were beginning to look a little put-upon. I led out, but Shadid soon slipped past, suggesting he lead since he knew whence they had come. The day was getting on. The light was feeble. It was about as dreary as it could get. More to distract myself than because I cared, I told Murgen, "Better explain what's going on."

"Cordy can tell you better than me. I just stuck with them."

The roi was not setting a blistering pace. I fought down the growls breeding in my gut. I kept telling me she was a big girl and she'd been taking care of herself since before I was born. But the man in me kept saying that's your woman, you got to take care of her.

Sure.

"Cordy? I know you guys don't work for me and you got your own priorities, but . . ."

"Nothing to cover up, Captain. Word came that some of you guys was going to ride out. That boggled the Woman. She figured you all to make a break for the Main in a mob and learn about the Shadowmasters the hard way. Instead, you went to scout it. She didn't think you were that smart."

"We're talking about the old broad you guys brought down the river, right. The Radisha?"

"Yeah. We call her the Woman. Blade hung it on her before we knew who she was."

"And she knew we were heading out before we went. Interesting. This is a wondrous time of my life, Mr. Mather. For the last year everybody in the world has known what I was going to do before I did. It's enough to make a guy nervous."

We passed some trees. In one I spied this incredibly bedraggled crow. I laughed, and hoped aloud he was as miserable as me. The others eyed me uncertainly. I wondered if I shouldn't start cultivating a new image. Work it up slowly. All the world dreads a madman. If I played it right . . .

"Hey, Cordy, old travelling buddy. You sure you don't know anything about those little brown guys?"

"All I know is they tried to ice us when we was headed north. Nobody ever saw anybody like them before. They figure to be out of the Shadowlands."

"Why are the Shadowmasters paranoid about us?" I did not expect an answer. I did not get one. "Cordy, you guys really serious about winning it for the Prahbrindrah?"

"I am. For Taglios. I found something there I never found anywhere else. Willow too, though you could roast him and never get it out of him. I don't know about Blade. I guess he's in because we're in. He's got one and a half friends in the world and nothing else to live for. He's just going on."

"One and a half?"

"Willow he's got. I'm the half. We pulled him out when somebody threw him to the crocodiles. He stuck because he owed us a life. After what we've been through since then if you was keeping accounts you couldn't figure who owes who what anymore. I can't tell you about the real Blade. He never lets you see that."

"What are we into? Or is that something you figure you shouldn't tell me?"

"What?"

"There's more going on than your Woman and the Prahbrindrah trying to get us to keep the Shadowmasters out. Otherwise they'd make a straight deal instead of trying to con us."

We travelled a mile while he thought. He finally said, "I don't know for sure. I think they're doing the way they are because of the way the Black Company did Taglios before."

"I thought so. And we don't know what our forebrethren did. And no one will tell us. It's like one giant conspiracy where everybody in Taglios won't tell us anything. In a city that big you'd think I'd find one guy with an axe to grind."

"You'd find platoons if you looked in the right place. All them priests spend their lives looking to cut each others' throats."

He had given me something there. I wasn't sure what. "I'll keep it in mind. I don't know if I can handle priests, though."

"They're like any other guys if you get your bluff in."

The gloom closed in tighter as the day advanced. I was so soaked I no longer paid that much attention. We hit a stretch where we had to go single file. Cordy and Murgen dropped back. "I picked up a few things I'll tell you about later," Murgen said before he went.

I moved up behind the roi to ask how much farther. It was just the misery of the day, but I felt like I'd been travelling for weeks.

Something whipped across our path so suddenly that that unflappable mount of Shadid's reared and whinnied. He shouted "What the hell was that?" in his native tongue. I understood because I'd learned a few words when I was a kid.

I caught only a glimpse. It looked like a monster grey wolf with a deformed pup clinging to its back. It vanished before my eye could track it.

Do wolves do that? Carry their young on their backs?

I laughed almost hysterically. Why worry about that when I ought to be wondering if there was such a thing as a wolf the size of a pony?

Murgen and Cordy caught up and wanted to know what had happened. I said I didn't know because I was no longer sure I had seen what I had seen.

But the wonder lay back there in the shadows of my mind, ripening.

Shadid stopped two miles past the place where we'd been ambushed originally. It was getting hard to see. He peered around, trying to read landmarks. He grunted, moved out to his left, off the road. I spied signs suggesting this was the way he had come with Otto and Hagop.

After another half mile the ground dropped into a small valley where a narrow creek ran. Rocks stuck up seemingly at random. Likewise, trees grew in scatters. It was now so dark I could not see more than twenty feet.

We started finding bodies.

A lot of little brown men had died for their cause. Whatever that was.

Shadid stopped again. "We led them in from the other direction. Here's where we split. We went up that way. The others held on to give us a head start." He dismounted, began snooping around. The light was almost gone before he found the track out of the valley. It was full dark before we covered a mile.

Murgen said, "Maybe we ought to go back and wait. We can't accomplish much stumbling around in the dark."

"You go back if you want," I snapped, with a savagery that surprised me. "I'm staying till I find . . ."

I could not see him, but I suspected he was grinning through his misery. He said, "Maybe we shouldn't split up. That much more trouble getting everybody back together."

Riding through the night in unfamiliar territory is not one of the smarter things I've done. Especially with a horde out there that wanted to do me harm. But the gods take care of fools, I guess.

Our mounts stopped. Their ears pricked. After a moment mine made a sound. A moment later still that sound was repeated from our left quarter. Without being urged the animals turned that way.

We found Sindawe and the man he'd brought in a crude bough shelter, their mounts hanging around outside. Both were injured, Sindawe the worst. We talked briefly while I did some stitching and patching and bandaging. Lady had ordered them to disappear. Goblin had covered for them while the pursuit went on off to the southeast. They had planned to head north in the morning.

I told them where to meet up, then got back into my saddle.

I was dead on my butt, barely able to stay upright, but something made me go on. Something I did not want to examine too closely lest I have to mock myself for my sentiment.

I got no arguments, though I think Mather was getting a little unsure of my sanity. I heard him whispering with Murgen, and Murgen telling him to can it.

I took the lead and gave my horse his head, telling him to find Lady's mount. I'd never determined how intelligent the beasts were, but it seemed worth a try. And the animal went walking, though his pace was a little slow to suit me.

I don't know how long the ride went on. There was no way to estimate time. After a while I began drifting off and coming awake with a start, then drifting off again. Near as I could tell, the others were doing the same thing.

I could have raised hell with them and me both, but that would have been unreasonable. Reasonable men would have been in a warm room, back at that village, snoring.

I was about half awake when the crest of a hill half a mile ahead burst into flames. It was like an explosion. One moment darkness, the next several acres ablaze and men and animals scattering, burning, too. The smell of sorcery was so strong I could detect it.

"Go, horse!"

There was light enough for it to risk a trot.

A minute later I was moving over ground dotted by smoldering, twitching bodies. Little brown men. One hell of a lot of little brown men.

The flaming trees illuminated a racing silhouette, a gigantic wolf with a smaller wolf astride, clinging with paws and claws. "What the hell is that?" Mather demanded.

Murgen guessed, "That Shifter, Croaker?"

"Maybe. Probably. We know he's around somewhere. Lady!" I yelled it at the burning trees. The fire was dying in the drizzle.

A sound that might have been an answer slithered through the crackling.

"Where are you?"

"Here."

Something moved amidst an outcrop of small rocks. I jumped down. "Goblin! Where the hell are you?"

No Goblin. Just Lady. And now not enough light to see how badly she was hurt. And hurt she was, no doubt about that. A fool damned thing to do, and me a physician who ought to know better, but I sat down and pulled her into my lap and held her, rocking her like a baby.

The mind goes.

From the minute you sign on with the Company you're doing things that make no sense, drills and practices and rehearsals, so that when the crunch comes you'll do the right thing automatically, without thought. The mind goes. I was without thought of anything but loss. I did not do the right thing.

I was lucky. I had companions whose brains had not turned to mud.

They got together enough burnable wood to get a fire started, got me my gear, and with a little judicious yelling got me to stop fussing and start doing.

She wasn't as bad off as she'd seemed in the dark. A few cuts, a lot of bruises, maybe a concussion to account for her grogginess. The old battlefield reflexes took over. I became a military physician. Again.

Murgen joined me after a while. "I found her horse. No sign of Goblin, though. How is she?"

"Better than she looks. Banged around some but nothing critical. She'll hurt all over for a while."

About then her eyelids fluttered, she looked up at me, and recognized me. She threw herself at me, wrapped her arms around me, and started crying.

Shadid said something. Murgen chuckled. "Yeah. Let's see if we can find Goblin." Cordy Mather was a beat slow, but he got it and went away, too.

She settled down quickly. She was who she was, and was not in the habit of yielding to her emotions. She peeled herself off me. "Excuse me, Croaker."

"Nothing to excuse. You had a close call."

"What happened?"

"I was going to ask you."

"They had me. They had me dead, Croaker. I thought we'd given them the slip, but they knew right where we were. They split us apart and ran me up here, and there must have been a dozen of them sneaking around, jumping in on me and jumping away. They were trying to capture me, not kill me. Guess I should be glad. Otherwise, I'd be dead. But there's some time missing. I don't remember you showing up and running them off."

"I didn't. Near as I can tell, Shifter saved you." I told her about the sudden fire and the wolf."

"Maybe. I didn't know he was around."

"Where's Goblin?"

"I don't know. We split about a mile from here. He tried to baffle them with illusions. We must have killed a hundred of those men today, Croaker. I never saw anybody so inept. But they never stopped coming. When we tried to outrun them there were always more in ambush no matter which way we went. If we tried to fight they always outnumbered us and two more turned up for every one we killed. It was a nightmare. They always knew where we were." She snuggled in close again. "There had to be some kind of sorcery involved. I was never so scared."

"It's all right now. It's over." It was the best I could think to say. Now that my nerves were settled I was intensely aware of her as a woman.

What appeared to be lightning flashed to the east, several miles away. But there had been no lightning running with this petty drizzle. I heard Shadid and Murgen and Mather yelling at each other, then the sounds of their mounts moving away. "That's got to be Goblin," I said, and started to get up.

She tightened her grip, held me down. "They can handle it, Croaker."

I looked down. It did not take much light to show me what was in her face. "Yeah. I guess they can." After a moment's hesitation, I did what she wanted.

As the breathing got heavier I broke away and said, "You're not in any shape for—"

"Shut up, Croaker."

I shut up, and paid attention to business.

Chapter Twenty-eight:
BACK TO SCOUTING

The pinhead gods had other ideas.

I am not a swift worker, and Lady had her natural reluctances—and all of a sudden the sky opened up like somebody chopped open the bellies of the clouds. The downpour was heavy and cold and came with just a breath or two of chill wind for warning. I'd have thought I was already wet enough not to mind more, but . . .

We'd hardly stopped scrambling around trying to find some shelter when Murgen and the others came out of the night. Murgen said, "It was Goblin, all right, but he was gone when we got there." He assumed I knew what he was talking about. "Croaker, I know us Black Company types is tough he-men and neither rain nor snow nor little brown geeks is supposed to stop us from doing any damned thing we want, but I'm burned out on this rain. I guess I got what you call conditioned at the Barrowland. I can't handle too much of it. I get the collywobbles."

I was burned out on it, too. Especially now it was coming down serious. But . . ."What about Goblin?"

"What about him? I'll make you a bet, Croaker. That little dork is all right. Goddamned well better off than we are. Eh?"

This is where command really gets you. When you make a choice that feels like you're taking the easy way out. When you think you are taking convenience over

194

obligation. "Right, then. Let's see if we can't find our way back to town." I let go Lady's hand. We got ourselves in better array. Those guys pretended not to notice. I supposed the troops back in Taglios would know before sunrise, somehow. Rumor works that way.

Damn, I wished I was guilty as suspected.

We reached the village as the world began to turn grey. Even those fabulous mounts of ours were worn out. We boothorned them into a stable meant for half a dozen normal animals and went clumping inside. I was sure the owner would be thrilled to death to see his clientele expanded again and looking like they'd just spent the night rolling around in the mud.

The old boy wasn't around. Instead, a pudgy little woman appeared from the kitchen, looked at us like she thought the barbarians had invaded, then saw Lady.

Lady looked just as rough as the rest of us. Just as mean. But there was no mistaking her for a guy. The old gal rushed her and babbled in Taglian and reached up to pat her back and I didn't need Cordy to tell me she was doing an "Oh, you poor dear" routine. We followed them back into the kitchen.

And there was friend Goblin, leaning back with his feet up on a log in front of a fire, sipping something from a huge mug.

"Get the little bastard!" Murgen said, and started after him.

Goblin bounced up and squeaked, "Croaker!"

"Where you been, runt? Sitting here drinking toddies while we're out stomping in the mud trying to save your butt from the baddies, eh?"

Murgen got him cornered. "Hey! No! I just got here myself."

"Where's your horse? The stable was one short when we put ours in."

"It's pretty miserable out there. I left it out back and came straight inside."

"It's not miserable for a horse? Murgen, throw him out

and don't let him back inside till he takes care of his horse."

Not that we had done all that decent a job ourselves. But we'd at least gotten them in out of the wet.

"Cordy, when the old gal finishes fussing over Lady ask her how far it is to the Main."

"The Main? You're not still—"

"I'm still. As soon as I get some chow inside me and a couple hours of sleep. It's what I came down for and it's what I'm going to do. Your pals have been running a game on us, whatever their reasons, and I don't like it. If I can take the Company on without getting drafted into somebody's fight, I'm going to do it."

He sort of smiled. "All right. If you have to see for yourself, see for yourself. But be careful."

Goblin came in looking sheepish and conciliatory and wet. "Where are you going now, Croaker?"

"Where we were going in the first place. The river."

"Maybe I can save you the trouble."

"I doubt it. But let's hear it. You find out something while you were adventuring on your own?"

His eyes narrowed.

"Sorry. It wasn't one of my all-time best nights."

"You're having a lot of not-so-good times in recent years, Croaker. Being Captain gives you a sour stomach."

"Yeah."

We exchanged stares. I won the lookdown. He said, "After Lady and I split up I only got about half a mile before I realized them brown guys weren't being fooled. I knew I did a good job with the illusion. If they didn't all come after me, then they had some mojo of their own somewhere. I already suspected they did on account of how they stuck all the time even when we outran them. So I figured if I couldn't get back to Lady I'd do the next best thing and go after whoever was controlling and guiding them. When I started sniffing around for it it was damned easy to find. And they gave me no trouble. I guess they figured if I would go away from Lady they'd leave me alone. Only a few stuck with me. I turned on them and uncorked a few specials I was saving for the next time One-Eye got out of line, and after they all stopped kicking I buzzed over there and sneaked up and there was this hilltop that had been sort of hollowed out, like a bowl, and down in the bowl there was these six guys all facing a little fire. Only there was something weird. You couldn't see them right. It was like you was looking at them through a fog. Only the fog was black. Sort of. Lots of little shadows, I'd guess you'd call them. Some of them no bigger than a mouse's shadow. All buzzing around like bees."

He was talking as fast as his mouth would go, yet I knew he was having trouble telling what he had seen. That words for what he wanted to convey did not exist, at least in any languages us mundanes would understand.

"I *think* they were seeing what we were doing in the flames, then sending those shadows out to tell their boys what to do to us and how to get into our way."

"Hunh?"

"Maybe you were lucky, not dealing with them so much in the daytime."

"Right." I figured I'd had troubles enough chasing a walking treestump around the countryside. "See any crows while you were at it?"

He looked at me funny. "Yeah. As a matter of fact. See, I was laying there in the mud looking at these guys, trying to figure what I had in the trick bag that I could smack them with, and all of a sudden there's about twenty crows swooping around. The whole thing blew up like it was raining naptha instead of water. Cooked those brown guys good. Only those crows maybe weren't crows. You know what I mean?"

"Not till you tell me."

"I only saw them for a second, but it seemed like I could see right through them."

"You always do," I muttered, and he looked at me

weird again. "So you figure any of the brown guys who're still out there are wandering around lost now? Like puppies without their masters?"

"I wouldn't say that. I figure they're as smart as you or me. Well, as smart as you, anyway. They just don't have their advantage anymore."

The old woman was still fussing over Lady. She had taken her somewhere to get bathed and patched up. As if she needed patching.

"How does this save me a trip to the Main?"

"I'm not finished yet, Your Grand Impatience. Right after the blowup here came one of the guys I thought I'd finished, tracking me down, all on his lonesome, and he's stumbling around holding his head like something got ripped out. I grabbed him. And I grabbed a couple loose shadows that were hanging around and I slapped one of them around a little and sent it off to tell One-Eye I needed to borrow his little beast. I taught another shadow how to make a guy talk and when the little monster showed up we asked the brown guy a few hundred questions."

"Frogface is here?"

"He went back. Mogaba's got them working their butts off up there."

"Good for him. You asked questions. You got answers?"

"Not that made much sense. These little brown guys come from a berg called Shadowcatch. Specifically, out of some kind of superfortress called Overlook. Their boss is one of the Shadowmasters. Longshadow, they call him. He gave the shadows to the six guys that was in the bowl place. These were just wimpy little shadows not good for much but carrying messages. They supposedly got bad ones they can turn loose, too."

"We're having some fun now, aren't we? You find out what's going on?"

"This Longshadow is up to something. He's in with the whole bunch trying to keep the Company away—the brown guys didn't know why they're worried—but he's

running a game on his own, too. The impression I got
was he wanted them to capture you and Lady and have
you dragged down to his castle, where he was going to
make some kind of deal, maybe. And that's about it."

I had five hundred questions and I started asking
them, but Goblin didn't have the answers. The man he
had interrogated hadn't had them. Most of the questions
had occurred to him.

He asked, "So, are you going down to the Main?"

"You haven't changed my mind. Neither have those
brown runts. If they don't have their mojo men anymore,
they won't give me much trouble. Will they?"

Goblin groaned. "Probably not."

"So what's the matter?"

"You think I'm going to let you ride out there without
some kind of cover? I'm groaning about the state of my
butt." He grinned his big frog grin. I grinned back.

According to our hosts it was a four-hour ride to the
Ghoja ford, the nearest and best crossing over the Main.
Swan said there were four along an eighty-mile stretch of
the Main: Theri, Numa, Ghoja, and Vehdna-Bota. Theri
being the farthest upriver. Above Theri the Main
coursed through rugged canyons too steep and bleak for
military operations—though Goblin said our little
brown friends had come that way, to evade the attention
of the other Shadowmasters. They had lost a third of
their number making the journey.

Vehdna-Bota lay nearest the sea and was useful only
during the driest months of the year. The eighty miles of
river between Vehdna-Bota and the sea were always
impassable. Both Vehdna-Bota and Theri fords took
their names from Taglian villages that had been abandoned when the Shadowmasters had invaded last year.
They remained empty.

Numa and Ghoja were villages below the Main, formerly Taglian, now occupied. Ghoja appeared to be the
critical crossing, and Swan, Mather, and Blade had all
seen it. They told me what they could. I asked about the

other fords and made an amusing discovery. Each was unfamiliar with at least one. Ha!

"Me and Goblin will scout the Ghoja crossing. Murgen, you and Cordy check out Vehdna-Bota. Shadid, you and Swan go to Numa. Sindawe, you and Blade check out Theri." I was sending each of the three into strange country.

Cordy laughed. Swan scowled. And Blade . . . Well, I wonder if you could get a reaction out of Blade by sticking his feet in a fire.

We split up. Lady, Otto, Hagop, and Sindawe's man all stayed behind to recuperate. Goblin rode beside me but did not say much after he hoped the weather would not go sour again. He did not sound like he expected the drizzle to hold off.

Swan said he had heard the Shadowmasters were fortifying the south bank of the Ghoja ford. Another indication the enemy would put his main force over there. I hoped it would come out that way. On the maps the terrain looked very favorable.

Two hours after we split the drizzle resumed. Perfect weather for the dreary thoughts tramping my brain.

Despite my adventure yesterday it seemed forever since I had been alone long enough to think a thought through. So with Goblin still as the grave I expected to do some serious brooding about where Lady and I were going. But she hardly crossed my mind. Instead, I mulled over what I'd gotten me and the Company into.

I was in charge but not in control. As far back as that monastery things had been happening that I could not control and could not unravel into sense. Gea-Xle and the river worsened matters. Now I felt like driftwood tumbling through a rapid. I had only the slightest idea who was doing what to whom, and why, but I was locked into the middle of it. Unless this last frantic gesture showed me an out.

For all I knew if I let the Prahbrindrah suck me in I would be enlisting on the "wrong" side. Now I knew how the Captain felt when Soulcatcher dragged us into the Lady's service. We were fighting in the Forsberg campaigns before the rest of us began to suspect we'd made a mistake.

It is not necessary for mercenary soldiers to know what is going on. It is sufficient for them to do the job for which they have taken the gold. That had been drummed into me from the moment I enlisted. There is neither right nor wrong, neither good nor evil, only our side and theirs. The honor of the Company lies within, directed one brother toward another. Without, honor lies only in keeping faith with the sponsor.

Nothing I knew of the Company's experiences resembled our present circumstance. For the first time— mainly by my doing—we were fighting for ourselves first. Our contract, if we accepted it, would be coincidental to our own desires. A tool. If I kept my head and perspective as I should, Taglios and all Taglians would become instruments of our desires.

Yet I doubted. I liked what I had seen of the Taglian people and especially liked their spirit. After the wounds they had taken keeping their independence they were still fired up for the Shadowmasters. And I had a good notion I wouldn't like those folks if I got to know them. So before it was fairly begun I'd broken the prime rule and become emotionally involved. Fool that I am.

That damned rain had a personal grudge. It got no heavier but it never let up. Yet to east and west I saw light that indicated clear skies in those directions. The gods, if such existed, were laying on the misery especially for me.

The last tenanted place we passed lay six miles from the Ghoja ford. Beyond, the countryside had been abandoned. It had been empty for months. It was not bad land, either. The locals must have had a big fear on to uproot and flee. A change of overlords usually isn't that traumatic for peasants. The five thousand who had come north and not returned must have had a real way about them.

The country was not rugged. It was mostly cleared land that rolled gently, and the road was not awful, considering, though it had not been built to carry military traffic. Nowhere did I see any fortifications, manmade or natural. I'd seen none of the former anywhere in Taglian territory. There would be no place to run and few places to hide in the event of disaster. I became a bit more respectful of Swan and his buddies, daring what they had.

The ground, when soaked, became a clayey, clinging mud that exercised the strength and patience even of my tireless steed. Note to the chief of staff. Plan our battles for clear, dry days.

Right. And while we're at it, let's order up only blind enemies.

You have to take what is handed you in this trade.

"You're damned broody today, Croaker," Goblin said, after a long while.

"Me? You been chattering like a stone yourself."

"I'm troubled about all this."

He was troubled. That was a very un-Goblin-like remark. It meant he was worried right down to his toenails. "You don't think we can handle it if we have to take the commission?"

He shook his head. "I don't know. Maybe. You always grab something out of the trick bag. But we're getting worn out, Croaker. There's no zest in it anymore. What if we did pull it off, and broke through, and got to Khatovar, and ended up with a big nothing?"

"That's been the risk since we started. I never claimed anything for this trip. It's just something I thought had to be done because I pledged to do it. And when I turn the Annals over to Murgen I'll extract the same oath from him."

"I guess we don't have anything better to do."

"To the end of the world and back again. It's an accomplishment of sorts."

"I wonder about the first purpose."

"So do I, old friend. It got lost somewhere between here and Gea-Xle. And I think these Taglians know something about it. But they're not talking. Going to have to try some old-fashioned Company double shuffle on them sometime."

The drizzle had its good side, I suppose. It lessened visibility. We were over the last crest and headed down toward the Main and Ghoja ford before I realized we had come that far. Sentries on the south bank would have spotted us immediately in better weather.

Goblin sensed it first. "We're there, Croaker. The river's right down there."

We reined in. I asked, "You feel anything on the other side?"

"People. Not alert. But there's a couple poor fools on sentry duty."

"What kind of outfit does it feel like?"

"Sloppy. Third rate. I could get a better look if I had a little time."

"Take some time. I'm going to roam around and look it over."

The site was what I had been told it would be. The road wandered down a long, bare slope to the ford, which lay just above an elbow in the river. Below the elbow a creek ran into the river from my side, though I had to go make sure because it lay behind higher ground. The creek had a beard of the usual growth along both banks. There was also a slight rise in the other direction, so that the road to the ford ran down the center of a slight concavity. Above the ford the river arched southward in a slow, lazy curve. On my side its bank was anywhere from two to eight feet high and overgrown with trees and brush everywhere but at the crossing itself.

I examined all that very carefully, on foot, while my mount waited with Goblin beyond the ridge. I sneaked down to the edge of the ford itself and spent a half hour sitting in the wet bushes staring at the fortifications on the other side.

We were not going to get across here. Not easily.

Were they worried about us coming to them? Why?

I used the old triangulation trick to figure out that the watchtower of the fortress stood about seventy feet high, then withdrew and tried to calculate what could be seen from its parapet. Most of the light was gone when I finished.

"Find out what you need to know?" Goblin asked when I rejoined him.

"I think so. Not what I wanted, either. Unless you can cheer me up. Could we force a crossing?"

"Against what's in there now? Probably. With the water down. If we tried in the dead of the night and caught them napping."

"And when the water does go down they'll have ten thousand men hanging around over there."

"Don't look good, does it?"

"No. Let's find a place to get out of the rain."

"I can stand to ride back if you can."

"Let's try. We'll sleep dry if we make it. What do you think of the men over there? Professionals?"

"My guess is they're just a little better than men disguised as soldiers."

"They looked pretty sloppy to me, too. But maybe they don't have to be any better in these parts."

I had seen and watched four men while I was crouching near the ford. They had not impressed me. Neither had the design or construction of the fortifications. Clearly, these Shadowmasters had brought in no professionals to train their forces and they had not developed a good edge on what they did have.

"'Course, maybe we saw what we were supposed to see."

"There's always that." An interesting thought, maybe worth some consideration, because at that moment I noticed a couple of bedraggled crows watching us from a dead branch on an elm tree. I started to look around for

the stump, thought the hell with it. I would handle that
when the time came.

"You remember Shifter's woman, Goblin?"

"Yeah. So?"

"You said you thought she seemed familiar back in
Gea-Xle. Now it's all of a sudden coming on me that
maybe you were right. I'm sure we ran into her somewhere before. But I can't for the life of me think where or
when."

"Does it matter?"

"Probably not. Just one of those things that nag at you.
Let's cut off to the left here."

"What the hell for?"

"There's a town on the map, called Vejagedhya, that I
want to look at."

"I thought we were going back—"

"It'll only take a few minutes extra."

"Right." Grumble, grumble, ragglesnatz.

"Looks like we might have to fight. I need to know the
country."

Fraggin snigglebark.

We ate cold food as we rode. It is not often that I do so,
but at such moments I sometimes envy the man with a
cottage and wife.

Everything costs something. It was ghost country we
rode, spooky country. The hand of man was evident
everywhere, even in darkness. Some of the homes we
inspected looked like they had been closed up only
yesterday. But not once did we encounter another human being. "I'm surprised thieves haven't been working
all this."

"Don't tell One-Eye."

I forced a chuckle. "I guess they were smart enough to
take their valuables with them."

"These people do seem determined to pay whatever
price they have to, don't they?" He sounded impressed.

Grudgingly, I was developing a case of respect. "And it

looks like the Company is going to be their one toss of the bones with fate."

"If you let them."

There was the town, Vejagedhya. It might once have been home to as many as a thousand people. Now it was even more spooky than the abandoned farms. Out there, at least, we had encountered wildlife. In the town I saw nothing but a few crows fluttering from roof to roof.

The townsfolk had not locked their doors. We checked maybe two dozen buildings. "It would do for a head-quarters," I told Goblin.

He grunted. After a while, he asked, "You making up your mind?"

"Beginning to look made up for me. Right? But we'll see what the others have to say."

We headed north. Goblin did not have much to say after that. That gave me time to dwell on and invent deeper meanings to my roles as Captain and potential warlord.

If there was no choice but to fight, and to lead a nation, I was going to make demands. I was not going to let the Taglians put me in a position where they could second-guess and override my every decision. I had watched my predecessors get half crazy dealing with that. If the Taglians hooked me, I was going to hook them right back.

We might call it something prettier, but by damn I was going to be a military dictator.

Me. Croaker. The itinerant military physician and amateur historian. Able to indulge in all the abuses I'd damned in princes for so long. It was a sobering notion.

If we bought it, and took the commission, and I got what I would demand, I might have Wheezer follow me around and remind me that I'm mortal. He wasn't good for much else.

The rain let up as we were riding into town.

Now I knew the gods loved me.

Chapter Twenty-nine:
SMOKE'S HIDEOUT

Smoke was perched on a tall stool, bent over a huge old book. The room was filled with books. It looked like a wave of books had swept in and left tidal pools behind. Not only were there shelves dripping books, there were books stacked hip-high on the floor, books on tables and chairs, even books piled on the sill of the room's one small, high window. Smoke read by the light of a single candle. The room was sealed so tight the smoke had begun to irritate his nose and eyes.

From time to time he grunted, made a note on a piece of paper to his left. He was left-handed.

In all the Palace that room was the best protected from spying eyes. Smoke had woven webs and walls of spells to secure it. No one was supposed to know about it. It did not show on any plan of the Palace.

Smoke felt something touch the outermost of the protective spells, something as light as a mosquito's weight as it lands. Before he could swing his attention to it it was gone and he was not sure he had not imagined it. Since the incident of the crows and bats he had been almost paranoid.

Intuition told him he had reason. There were forces at work that were way beyond him. His best weapon was the fact that no one knew he existed.

He hoped.

He was a very frightened man these days. Terror lurked in every shadow.

He jumped and squeaked when the door opened.

"Smoke?"

"You startled me, Radisha."

"Where are they, Smoke? There's been no word from Swan. Have they gotten away?"

"Leaving most of their people behind? Radisha, be patient."

"I have no patience left. Even my brother is becoming unsettled. We have only weeks left before the rivers fall."

"I'm aware of that, madam. Concentrate on what you *can* do, not what you wish you could do. Every force possible is being bent upon them. But we cannot compel them to help."

The Radisha kicked over a pile of books. "I've never felt so powerless. I don't like the feeling."

Smoke shrugged. "Welcome to the world where the rest of us live."

In a high corner of the room a point no bigger than a pinprick oozed something like a black smoke. The smoke slowly filled out the shape of a small crow. "What are the rest of them doing?"

"Making preparations for war. In case."

"I wonder. That black officer. Mogaba. Could he be the real captain?"

"No. Why?"

"He's doing the things I want them to do. He's acting like they're going to serve us."

"It makes sense, Radisha. If their captain comes back convinced they can't sneak away, they'll be that much farther ahead."

"Has he made preparations to run back north?"

"Of course."

The Radisha looked vexed.

Smoke smiled. "Have you considered being forthright with them?"

She gave him a look to chill the bones.

"I thought not. Not the way of princes. Too simple. Too direct. Too logical. Too honest."

"You grow too daring, Smoke."

"Perhaps I do. Though as I recall my mandate from your brother is to remind you occasionally—"

"Enough."

"They are what they pretend to be, you know. Wholly ignorant of their past."

"I'm aware of that. It makes no difference. They could become what they were if we let them. Sooner bend the knee to the Shadowmasters than endure that again."

Smoke shrugged. "As you will. Maybe." He smiled slyly. "And as the Shadowmasters will, perhaps."

"You know something?"

"I am constrained by my need to remain unnoticed. But I've been able to catch glimpses of our northern friends. They have fallen afoul of more of our little friends from the river. Ferocious things are happening down near the Main."

"Sorcery?"

"High magnitude. Recalling that which manifested during their passage through the pirate swamps. I no longer dare intrude."

"Damn! Damn-damn-damn! Are they all right? Have we lost them?"

"I no longer dare intrude. Time will tell."

The Radisha kicked another pile of books. Smoke's bland expression cracked, became one of intense irritation. She apologized. "It's frustration."

"We're all frustrated. Perhaps *you* would be less so if you adjusted your ambitions."

"What do you mean?"

"Perhaps if you followed the course your brother has charted and aimed to climb but one mountain at a time—"

"Bah! Am I, a woman, the only rooster around here?"

"You, a woman, will not be required to pay the price of failure. That will come out of your brother's purse."

"Damn you, Smoke! Why are you always right?"

"That is my commission. Go to your brother. Talk. Recalculate. Concentrate on the enemy of the moment. The Shadowmasters must be turned now. The priests will be here forever. Unless you want shut of them badly enough to let the Shadowmasters win, of course."

"If I could frame just one High Priest for treason . . . All right. I know. The Shadowmasters have shown they know what to do with clerics. Nobody would believe it. I'm going. If you dare, find out what's happening down there. If we've lost them we'll have to move quickly. That damned Swan had to go after them, didn't he?"

"You sent him."

"Why does everybody do what I tell them? Some of the things I say are stupid. . . . Get that grin off your face."

Smoke failed. "Kick over another stack of books."

The Radisha huffed out of the room.

Smoke sighed. Then he returned to his reading. The book's author lingered lovingly over impalements and flayings and tortures visited on a generation unlucky enough to have lived when the Free Companies of Khatovar marched out of that strange corner of the world that spawned them.

The books in that room had been confiscated so they would not fall into the hands of the Black Company. Smoke did not believe their being there would keep secrets forever. But maybe long enough for him to find a way to prevent the sort of bloodshed that had occurred in olden times. Maybe.

The best hope, though, lay in the probability that the Company had mutated with time. That it was not wearing a mask. That it had indeed forgotten its grim origins and its search for its past was more a reflex than the determined return that other Companies, come back earlier, had made.

In the back of Smoke's mind, always, was the temptation to take his own advice, to bring the Company's captain in and turn him loose on the books, if only to see how he responded to the truth.

Chapter Thirty:
TAGLIOS AROUSED

We approached Taglios with the dawn, days late, all of us at the brink of collapse, Swan and his buddies maybe worse off than the rest. Their mundane mounts were wiped out. I asked Swan, "You figure the Prahbrindrah will be overly pissed because I didn't keep my appointment?"

Swan still had a little pepper left. "What the hell can he do? Put a bug down your shirt? He'll swallow it and smile. You worry about the Woman. She's the one who'll give you trouble. If anybody does. She don't always think right."

"Priests," Blade said.

"Yeah. Watch out for the priests. They sprung this whole thing on them the day you guys landed. They couldn't do anything but go along. But they been thinking about it, you can bet your butt, and when they find them an angle they're going to start messing."

"What's Blade's thing with priests?"

"I don't know. I don't want to know. But I been down here long enough to start thinking he's maybe right. The world might be better off if we drowned some of them."

One thing that made the military situation wonderfully impossible was the absence of fortifications. Taglios itself sprawled everywhere, without a thought to defense.

A people with centuries of pacifism behind them. An

enemy with experienced armies and high-power sorcerers to support them. And me with maybe a month to figure out how to help the former whip the latter.

Impossible. When those rivers went down so troops could cross the massacre would be on.

Swan asked, "You make up your mind what you're going to do?"

"Yeah. The Prahbrindrah isn't going to like it, either."

That surprised him. I did not explain. Let them worry. I took my bunch in to the barracks and sent Swan off to announce our return. As we dismounted, with half the Company hanging around waiting to hear something, Murgen said, "I guess Goblin's made up his mind."

Something had been preying on the little wizard. He had been broody and curt all the way home. Now he was grinning. He gave special attention to his saddlebags.

Mogaba joined me. "We've made major progress while you were gone, Captain. I'll report when you feel up to it." His question remained unspoken.

I saw no need to leave it hanging. "We can't sneak through. They've got us. It's fight or turn back."

"Then there is no option, is there?"

"I guess there never was. But I had to see for myself." He nodded his understanding.

Before business I tended wounds. Lady was coming back fast. Her bruises, though, did nothing to make her more attractive. I felt odd examining her. She had had little to say since our night in the rain. She was doing a lot of thinking again.

Mogaba had a lot to tell me about discussions with Taglios's religious leaders and his ideas for putting together the pretense of an army. I could find nothing in his suggestions I disapproved. He said, "There's one other thing. A priest named Jahamaraj Jah, number two man in the Shadar cult. He has a daughter he thinks is dying. It looks like a chance to make a friend."

"Or get somebody thoroughly pissed." Never underestimate the power of human ingratitude.

"One-Eye saw her."

I looked at the little witch doctor. He said, "Looked like her appendix to me, Croaker. Not that far gone yet, either. But these clowns around here don't have the foggiest. They're trying to exorcise demons."

"I haven't opened anybody up in years. How long before it bursts?"

"Another day at least, unless she's unlucky. I did what I could for the pain."

"I'll check it on the way back from the Palace. Make me a map. . . . No. You'd better tag along. You might be useful." Mogaba and I were getting dressed for a court appearance now. Lady was supposed to be doing the same.

Swan, not at all improved in appearance, showed up to take us to the Prince. I did not feel like doing anything but take a nap. I sure did not feel up to the games of politicians. But I went.

The people of Trogo Taglios had heard that the moment of decision had come. They were in the streets to watch us. They remained eerily silent.

I saw dread in all those watching eyes, but hope, too. They were aware of the risks, and maybe even of the odds against them. A pity they did not realize that a battlefield is not a wrestling ring.

Once a child cried. I shivered, hoping it was not an omen. As we neared the Trogo an old man stepped out of the crowd and pressed something into my hand. He bowed himself away.

It was a Company badge from olden times. An officer's badge, perhaps booty from some forgotten battle. I fixed it near the badge I wore already, the fire-breathing death's-head of Soulcatcher, which we had retained though we no longer served the Taken or the empire.

Lady and I had outfitted ourselves in our finest, meaning I wore my legate's duds and she her imperial rig. We impressed the mob. Beside us Mogaba looked drab. One-Eye looked like a derelict scraped off the bottom of the worst dive in the worst slum. That damned hat. He was as happy as a snail.

"Showmanship," Lady had told me. An old maxim of my own, albeit directed somewhat differently. "In politics and battle our big weapon will have to be showmanship."

She was coming to life. I think those brown guys pissed her off.

She was right. Showmanship and craft, even more than traditionally, would have to be our tools. If we were to meet and beat the veteran armies commanded by the Shadowmasters we would have to gain our triumphs inside the imaginations of enemy soldiers. It takes ages to create a force with the self-confidence to go slug it out despite the odds.

Despite our being late the Prahbrindrah Drah was a gracious host. He treated us to a dinner the likes of which I have no hope of seeing again. Afterward, he laid on the entertainment. Dancing girls, sword swallowers, illusionists, musicians whose work my ear found too alien to appreciate. He was in no hurry to get to an answer of which he was confident. During the afternoon Swan introduced me to several score of Taglios's leading men, including Jahamaraj Jah. I told Jah I would look at his daughter as soon as I could. The gratitude in the man's face was embarrassing.

Otherwise, I paid no attention to those men. I had no intention of dealing with or through them.

The time came. We were invited out of the crowd into a private chamber. Because I had brought two of my lieutenants the Prahbrindrah did the same. One was that codger Smoke, whom the Prince introduced by title. That translated out as Lord of the Guardians of Public Safety. And that turned out to mean he was boss of the city fire brigade.

Only One-Eye failed to keep a straight face.

The Prahbrindrah's other lieutenant was his enigmatic

sister. Put them together and it was obvious she was
older and probably tougher than he. Even dressed up she
looked like she had been ridden hard and put away wet.

When the Prahbrindrah asked about my companions I
introduced Mogaba as my commander of infantry and
Lady as my chief of staff. The idea of a woman soldier
amazed him. I wondered how much more amazed he
would be if he knew her history.

She concealed surprise at the designation. As much for
her benefit as the Prahbrindrah's, I said, "There's nobody in the Company more qualified. With the possible
exception of the Captain, each post is filled on merit."

Swan was doing the translating. He skirted the edge of
the Prahbrindrah's reply, which, I think, actually suggested limited agreement. His sister seemed to be his
brain trust.

"To the point," I told Swan. "Time is too tight if we're
going to stop an invasion."

Swan smiled. "Then you're going to accept the commission?"

You never doubted it for a second, you jackal. "Don't
get your hopes too high, man. I'm going to make a
counteroffer. Its terms won't be negotiable."

Swan's smile vanished. "I don't understand."

"I've looked at the land. I've talked with my people.
Despite the lay, most of them want to go on. We know
what we have to do to get to Khatovar. Meaning we'll
consider doing the job your prince wants done. But we
won't try it except on our terms. Tell him that, then I'll
give him the sad news."

Swan translated. The Prahbrindrah did not look happy. His sister looked like she wanted a fight. Swan faced
me. "Let's have it."

"If I'm supposed to run an army that I'll have to build
from scratch, I want to have the power to do it. I want to
be the boss. No interference from anybody. No political
crap. No cult feuding. Even the will of the Prince will
have to yield for the duration. I don't know if there's a

Taglian word for what I want. I can't think of a Rosean word, either. In the Jewel Cities the man in the job I want is called 'dictator.' They elect him for a year at a time. Tell him that."

Was the Prahbrindrah happy? Sure he was. About as happy as any prince in that fix. He started lawyering, trying to bury me in ifs, ands, and buts. I smiled a lot.

"I said I wouldn't negotiate, Swan. I meant it. The only chance I see is for us to do what needs doing when it's got to be done, not six weeks later, after the ruffled feathers have been smoothed, the special interests have had their say, and the graft has been got out."

Mogaba had on the biggest smile I'd ever seen from him. He was having fun listening. Maybe he'd always wanted to talk that way to his bosses in Gea-Xle.

I said, "The way I hear it, in about five weeks the rivers will be down enough that the Shadowmasters can put their troops across the Main. They won't have internal problems slowing them down. They'll have every advantage but the Black Company on their side. So if the Prahbrindrah wants even a prayer of winning, he has to give me the tools I need. If he doesn't, I walk. I find some other way. I won't commit suicide."

Swan translated. We sat around looking tough and professional and stubborn. Lady and Mogaba did fine. I thought I might blow it by being nervous, but I did not. The Prahbrindrah never tried to call my bluff. He argued, but never so hard I might lose my temper and stomp out. I never gave an inch. I honestly believed that the only chance, and that a ghost of a hope, lay in an absolute military dictatorship. And I had a little inside word, thanks to Frogface.

"Hey, Swan. Are these people in even bigger trouble than they've admitted?"

"What?" He cast a nervous glance at the imp.

"Your boss isn't trying to talk me out of anything. He's lawyering. Politicking. Wasting time. I get the feeling that down deep he's scared to death. He agrees with me.

Only he don't want to *have* to make the choice between evils. Because then he has to live with his choice."

"Yeah. Maybe. The Shadowmasters are going to be coming mean after what we did last summer. Going to make an example of us, maybe."

"I'll want the veterans of that business. We'll turn them into squad leaders. Assuming I get to be boss soldier around here."

"There is an archaic Taglian word meaning warlord. You'll get your way. It's been argued out in council. The High Priests don't like it, but they don't have any choice. Priests were the first people the Shadowmasters rubbed out wherever they took over. He can make any deal he has to. They're scared, man. After you win is when you got to start worrying."

All I had to do was go on sitting tight. But I had come into the meeting with that assurance from Frogface.

The damned imp grinned and winked at me.

The day rolled on into night and we had to have another meal, but we sealed our pact.

For the first time since Juniper the Company had a real commission.

Or vice versa.

The Prahbrindrah wanted to know my plans. He was not dumb. He knew Mogaba had been putting in twenty-hour days.

"Put together a big flashy show for the gang that comes across the Main, mostly. But we'll recruit and train for harder times down the line too, assuming we handle that first bunch. While we're at it, we'll get an idea of what resources are available and how best to employ them. We'll root out enemy agents here and try to establish our own over there. We'll learn the terrain where the fighting may take place. Swan. I keep hearing about how little time we have till the rivers go down. How long will they stay down? How long till the next grace period?"

He translated, then said, "There'll be six to seven

months when there won't be enough rain to close the fords. Even after the rainy season starts there'll be two or three months when they're passable part of the time."

"Wonderful. We got here in the middle of the safe season."

"Just about. We could get more than five weeks. That's a worst estimate."

"We can count on it, then. Tell him we'll need a lot of help from the state. We have to have weapons, armor, mounts, rations, drays, drayage, equipment. We need a census of all males between sixteen and forty-five, with their skills and occupations. I want to know who to conscript if I don't get volunteers. A census of animals would be helpful. Likewise, a census of weapons and equipment available. And a census of fortifications and places that could be used as fortresses. You should know a lot of this from last summer. Do you write the lingo here, Swan?"

He translated, then said, "No. I can't figure out the alphabet. 'Course, I never learned to read or write Rosean, neither." He grinned. "Not Cordy, neither."

"Blade?"

"You kidding?"

"Wonderful. Find me somebody who can. It's all right if he's one of the Radisha's spies. Two birds with one stone. I'll want you and him both attached to me at the hip till I learn the language. All right. What I need right now is for him to get out the word that volunteers should assemble in the Chandri Square an hour after dawn tomorrow." The Chandri Square was near our barracks and one of the biggest in Taglios. "They should bring any weapons or equipment they have. We'll pick twenty-five hundred to start training immediately and enroll the rest for later."

"You may be too optimistic."

"I thought these people were eager to get into it."

"They are. But tomorrow is a holy day for the Gunni

cults. That takes in four-tenths of the lower classes. When they sit down nobody else can do anything, either."

"There aren't any holidays in a war. They better get used to that right now. They don't show up, that's tough. They get left behind. Tell the Prince to spread the word that the guys who volunteer earliest are the guys who're going to get the best deal. But everybody starts at the bottom. Even him, if he enlists. I don't know the class structures here and I don't care. I'll make a prince carry a spear and have a farm boy command a legion if that's what the man can do best."

"That attitude's going to cause problems, Cap. And even if they elect you god you're going to have to walk careful around the priests."

"I'll deal with them when I have to. The politics I can probably handle. I can twist arms and smooth fur if I have to, though mainly I just won't put up with it. Tell the Prince he should hang around my headquarters some. Things will go smoother if people think he's part of what's happening."

Swan and the Prince chattered. The Radisha gave me a searching look, then a smile that said she knew what I was up to. The devil in me made me wink.

Her smile broadened.

I decided I should know more about her. Not because I was attracted to her but because I suspected I would like the way she thought. I like a person with a sound cynical attitude.

Old Smoke, the so-called fire chief, did nothing all evening but nod off and start awake. Being a cynic, I approved of him as a public official. The best kind are those who stay the hell out of the way and don't mess with things. Except for me, of course.

"One thing left for tonight," I told Swan. "Financing. The Black Company don't come cheap. Neither does creating, arming, training, and maintaining an army."

Swan grinned. "They got you covered, Cap. Back

when they first heard the prophecies of your coming they started raising money. It won't be a problem."

"It's always a problem."

He smiled. "You won't be able to spend like there ain't no bottom to the bucket. The Woman hangs on to the purse strings around here. And she's famous for being tight."

"Good enough. Ask the Prince if there's anything else he needs now. I've got a ton of stuff to do."

There was another hour of talk, none of it important, all of it the Prahbrindrah and Radisha trying to get an idea what I was planning, trying to get a clearer picture of my character and competence. Giving a stranger life-and-death power over their state was one long bet for them. I figured I'd do a little something to help their underground scheme.

I became impatience itself, but was proud of me. I controlled it.

Walking home after dark, without crowds, I asked Lady, "Can we count on Shifter's help?"

"He'll do what I tell him."

"You're sure?"

"Not absolutely. It looks that way, though."

"Could he do some scouting over Shadowmaster country? Shifting into something that flies?"

"Maybe." She smiled. "But he wouldn't have strength enough to carry you. And I know you. You wouldn't trust a report from anybody but you."

"Well . . ."

"You'll have to take your chances. Trust him as much as you dare. He'll serve me if I command him. But he isn't my slave. He has his own goals now. They may not be your goals."

I thought it might be a good time to sneak up on something I'd been sliding around since I'd caught her playing with fire in a cup overlooking Gea-Xle. "And your own restored talent?"

She was not fazed. "You're kidding. I might bother Goblin if I sneaked up on him and hit him with a hammer. Otherwise, I'm useless. Even small talents have to be exercised to be any good. There's no time for exercise."

"I guess we'll all just do what we can."

Mogaba said, "I have several ideas for disarming problems arising from religious friction. At least temporarily."

"Speaking of which. I need to carve on that priest's kid. One-Eye, I'll need you to back me up. Go ahead, Mogaba."

His notion was straightforward. We would raise our own army without regard to religion and use it to meet the Shadowmasters' main thrust. We would encourage the cults to raise their own forces and use them to meet threats that appeared at the secondary fords. But we would not surrender our claim to supreme command.

I laughed. "I have a feeling you're looking for a repeat of the debacle of last summer when—"

"Nothing should disarm them more thoroughly than failures and displays of incompetence. I thought we ought to give them their chances."

"Sounds good to me. Work up a couple of questions for recruits so we can get the drift of their religious commitment and tolerance when we sign them up. You want to tell me how to find this guy Jahamaraj Jah?"

Chapter Thirty-one:
TAGLIOS; A BOOT-CAMP CITY

It had been years since I hazarded internal surgery. Before I started I was shaky and filled with doubts, but habit took hold in the crunch. My hand was steady. One-Eye restrained his natural exuberance and used his talents judiciously to control bleeding and deaden pain.

As I washed my hands I said, "I can't believe it went that well. I haven't done one of those since I was a kid, practically."

"She going to pull through?" One-Eye asked.

"Should. Unless there're complications. I want you to check back every day to make sure she's doing all right."

"Hey, Croaker. I got me an idea. Why don't you buy me a broom?"

"What?"

"When I wasn't busy doing anything else I could be sweeping up."

"I'll get myself one, too." I spoke to the child's parents briefly, through Frogface, clueing them in on what had to be done. Their gratitude was stifling. I doubted it would last. People are that way. But as we were about to leave I told the father, "I'll collect on this."

"Anything."

"It won't be trivial. When the time comes."

He understood. He looked grim as he nodded.

We were about to step into the street when One-Eye said, "Hold up." He pointed.

I looked down at three dead bats arranged in a neat equilateral triangle. "Maybe the boys aren't imagining things. The bat cadavers were not neat.

A crow cawed somewhere nearby.

I muttered, "I'll take my help where I can get it." Louder, "Could you make a bat spy on people?"

One-Eye thought about it. "I couldn't. But it might be possible. Though they aren't long on brains."

"That's all I needed to know." Except for who was running the bats. The Shadowmasters, I presumed.

The twenty-hour days started. When I was not preoccupied with anything else I tried to learn the language. After you have learned enough they come easy. Or easier, anyway.

We went at it trying to keep things simple. All the evidence indicated that the Shadowmasters would use the Ghoja ford for their main crossing. I abdicated the defense of the others to the cult leaders and concentrated on what I thought I'd need to stop that main force in its tracks. If it got across the river and started rolling north, I feared we would have a repeat of Swan's campaign. Any victory at all would be at a price too dear.

I started by forming the cadres of two legions based on the model used by the Jewel Cities in early times, when their armies were citizens with little field experience. The command structure was the simplest possible. The organization was pure infantry. Mogaba was overall commander of the foot and boss of the first legion. His lieutenant Ochiba got the second legion. Each got to keep ten Nar for NCOs and each of those ten picked a hundred candidates from among the Taglian volunteers. That gave each legion a thousand-man base which would be expanded about as fast as the Nar could teach them to march in a straight line. Mogaba got Wheezer, Lion, and Heart for staff work. I did not know what else to do with those three. They were willing but had little practical value.

Sindawe and the remaining Nar were to form a third, training and reserve legion that I expected to employ only in desperation.

Otto, Hagop, the Guards, and the roi I charged with putting together a cavalry force.

Sparkle, Candles, Cletus, and the rest from Opal and Beryl got stuck with the fun stuff, quartermastering and engineering. Hagop's nephew ended up with him. He was another one who was useless.

The ideas were mostly Mogaba's recommendations, which he had worked out while I was scouting southward. I did not agree with all of them, but it seemed a sin to waste the work he had done. And we had to move in some direction. Now.

He had it all figured. Sindawe's legion would both produce new people for the leading two units and would develop as a force itself more slowly. He did not believe we could manage a force larger than three legions till we developed a lot of local talent.

Lady, Goblin, One-Eye, and I were left to handle everything else. The important, exciting stuff, like dealing with the Prahbrindrah and his sister. Like setting up an intelligence operation, finding out if there were any local wizards we could use. Charting strategy. Coming up with gimmicks. Good old Mogaba was willing to leave me the staff work and strategy.

Actually, about the way it should be. The man embarrassed me with his competence.

"Goblin, I guess you should take counterintelligence," I said.

"Har!" One-Eye said. "That fits him perfectly."

"Borrow Frogface whenever you need him." The imp moaned. He got no pleasure out of having to work.

Goblin put on a smug look. "I don't need that thing, Croaker."

I did not like that. The runt was up to something. Ever since we came back from the country he had had that smugness about him. It meant trouble. He and One-Eye could get so involved in their feud they forgot the rest of the world.

Time would tell what was up.

"Whatever you say," I told Goblin. "As long as you get the job done. Dangerous agents of the Shadowmasters I want you to take out. Small-timers set up so we can feed them false information. We've also got to keep one eye on the big priests. They're bound to give us grief as soon as they figure out how. Human nature."

Lady I put in charge of showmanship and planning. I had decided where I wanted to meet the enemy already, before I had anything to meet him with. I told her to work out the details. She was a better tactician than I. She had managed the armies of an empire with astonishing success.

I was learning that part of a captain's job is to delegate. Maybe genius lies in choosing the right person for the right task.

We had maybe five weeks. And the time was counting down. And down. And down.

I did not think we had a prayer.

Nobody got much sleep. Everybody got testy. But that is the way it is in our business. You learn to adjust to it, to understand. Mogaba kept telling me it was going great on his end, but I never got time to review his outfits. Hagop and Otto were less pleased with their progress. Their recruits were of classes that saw discipline as something imposed only upon their inferiors. Otto and Hagop had to resort to asskicking to get their people in line. They came up with a couple of interesting ideas, like adding elephants to the cavalry. The Prahbrindrah's census of animals had turned up a few hundred work elephants.

I spent my time rushing around in confusion, more often a politician than a commander. I avoided recourse to dictate when I could, preferring persuasion, but two of the High Priests gave me no choice most of the time. If I said black they said white just to let me know they considered themselves Taglios's real bosses.

If I'd had time I'd have gotten vexed with them. I didn't, so I didn't play their games. I got them and their chief boys together, with the Prahbrindrah and his sister chaperoning, and told them I didn't care for their attitude, that I would not tolerate it, and the schedule from here on in was do it Croaker's way or die. If they didn't like that, they were welcome to take their best crack at me. Then I would roast them over a slow fire in one of the public squares.

I did not make myself popular.

I was bluffing, sort of. I would do what had to be done, but did not expect to have to do it. My apparently violent nature should cow them while I got on with the job. I would worry about them after I'd turned the Shadow-masters.

Thinking positive all the time. That's me.

I'd have starved if I'd gotten a pound of bread for every minute I really believed we had a chance.

Several people made sure news of the face-off got out. I heard rumors that some temples closed their doors for lack of business. Others had to turn away angry crowds.

Great.

But how long would it last? These peoples' passion for supernatural nonsense was far older and more ingrained than their passion for militarism.

"What the hell happened?" I asked Swan, first chance I got. I was getting the language, but not fast enough to grasp religious subtleties.

"I think Blade happened." He seemed bemused.

"Say what?"

"Ever since we've been here Blade's been spreading seditious nonsense about priests should stick to taking care of souls and karma and keep their noses out of politics. Been selling that down to our place. And when he heard about your confab with the High Priests he got himself out in the streets to spread what he called 'the true story.' These people are all for their gods, you better remember that, but they ain't so hot on some of their priests. Especially the kind that grab them by the purse and squeeze."

I laughed. Then I said, "You tell him to back off. I've got troubles enough without a religious revolution."

"Right. I don't think you got to worry about that."

I had to worry about everything. Taglian society was under extreme stress, though it took an outsider to see it. Too many changes too fast in a traditionalist, restrictive society. No way for conventional mechanisms to adjust. Saving Taglios would be like riding the whirlwind. I would have to stay light on my feet to keep the frustration and fear directed against the Shadowmasters.

One-Eye wakened me in the middle of one of my four-hour snoozes. "Jahamaraj Jah is here. Says he's got to see you right now."

"His kid take a turn for the worse?"

"She's fine. He thinks he's going to pay you off."

"Bring him in."

The priest slipped in looking furtive. He bowed and scraped like a street dweller. He plied me with every title the Taglian people had been able to imagine, including Healer. Appendectomy was a piece of surgery unknown in those parts. He looked around as though expecting ears growing out of the walls. Maybe that was an occupational hazard. He did not like the sight of Frogface at all.

That suggested some people knew what the imp was. I should keep that in mind.

"Is it safe to talk?" he asked. I followed that without translation.

"Yes."

"I must not stay long. They will be watching me, knowing I owe you a great debt, Healer."

Then get on with it, I thought. "Yes?"

"The High Priest of the Shadar, my superior, Ghojarindi Ghoj, whose patron is Hada, one of whose avatars is Death. You distressed him the other night. He has told the Children of Hada that Hada thirsts for your ka."

Frogface translated, and added commentary. "Hada is the Shadar goddess of Death, Destruction, and Corruption, Cap. The Children of Hada are a subcult who dedicate themselves by way of murder and torture. Doctrine says that should be random and senseless. The way it works out, though, is that those who die have got onto the boss priest's shitlist."

"I see." I smiled slightly. "And who is your patron, Jahamaraj Jah?"

He smiled back. "Khadi."

"All Sweetness and Light, I take it."

"Hell no, chief. She's Hada's twin sister. Just as damned nasty. Got her fingers into plague, famine, disease, fun stuff like that. One of the big things the Shadar and Gunni cults squabble about is whether Hada and Khadi are separate deities or just one with two faces."

"I love it. I bet people get killed over it. And priests look at me weird when I say I can't take them seriously. One-Eye. You figure I'm guessing right when I think our buddy here is helping himself by trying to weasel out of a debt?"

One-Eye chuckled. "I figure he plans to be the next Shadar boss."

I had Frogface go straight at him. He did not blush. He admitted he was the most likely successor to Ghojarindi Ghoj.

"In that case I don't figure he's done anything but make the vig. Tell him thanks but I figure he still owes me. Tell him that if he all of a sudden finds himself boss priest of the Shadar I'd be real proud if he'd make his people mind and not get too ambitious himself for a year or two."

Frogface told him. His grin went away. His lips tightened into a wrinkly little nut. But he bobbed his head.

"Get him on the road, One-Eye. Wouldn't want him getting in trouble with his boss."

I went and wakened Goblin. "We got priest problems. Character named Ghojarindi Ghoj is siccing assassins on me. Take Murgen, go over to Swan's dive, dig out his resident priest hater, have him finger the guy. He needs promoting to a higher plane. It don't have to be spectacular, just unpleasant. Like having him shit himself to death."

Grumbling, Goblin went to find Murgen.

One-Eye and Frogface got to watch for would-be assassins.

They were professionals but they were not up to getting past Frogface. There were six of them. I had some of the Nar, who favored that sort of thing, take them to a public square and impale them.

Ghojarindi Ghoj went west a day later. He perished of a sudden, dramatic surfeit of boils. The lesson was not lost on anyone.

The lesson was, of course, don't get caught.

Nobody seemed upset or displeased. The attitude was, Ghoj had placed his bets and taken his chances. But the Radisha did give me some thoughtful looks while we fussed over whether I needed another thousand swords and especially if I needed the hundred tons of charcoal I had requisitioned.

Actually, we were to the games-playing stage already. I asked for a hundred tons knowing I wanted ten, figuring to groan and gripe and give in and get more of the arms.

The recruits were providing their own kit. The arms I most wanted financed by the state were pieces that could not be well explained to a civilian. I was having trouble enough convincing Mogaba that wheeled light artillery might be of value.

I was not sure it would myself. That depended on what the enemy did. If they behaved as they had before, artillery would be wasted. But the model was the Jewel

Cities legion. Those guys dragged light engines along to knock holes in enemy formations.

Oh, fuss. Some things you just settle by saying I'm the boss and you'll do it my way.

Mogaba did not mind.

Seventeen days to go, estimated. Lady visited me. I asked her, "Will you be ready?"

"I'm almost ready now."

"One positive report amongst the hundreds. You brighten my life."

She gave me a funny look. "I've seen Shifter. He's been across the river." One-Eye and Goblin, in their capacities as spymasters, had had little luck, mostly because the Main was just plain uncrossable. They had no lack of volunteers.

As for cleaning up the Shadowmasters' agents in Taglios, that had not taken them ten days. A bunch of little brown guys had bitten the dust. A few native Taglians remained. We were feeding them plenty of truth, and just enough bull to tempt their masters into making their major crossing effort where I wanted it.

"Ah. And did he learn anything we want to hear?"

She grinned. "He did. You get your wish. They'll bring their main force over at the Ghoja ford. And they won't be with their armies. They don't trust each other enough to leave home base unguarded."

"Beautiful. Suddenly, I feel like we've got a chance. Maybe only one in ten, but a chance."

"And now for the bad news."

"I guess it had to be. What is it?"

"They're sending an extra five thousand men. Ten thousand in the Ghoja force. A thousand each at Theri and Vehdna-Bota. The rest come across at Numa. They tell me Numa is crossable two days earlier than the Ghoja ford is."

"That's bad. They could have three thousand guys behind us when it hits."

"They will unless they're morons."

I closed my eyes and looked at the map. Numa was where I had told Jahamaraj Jah his Shadar people could make their mark. He had raised twenty-five hundred cultists only by straining. Most Shadars wanted to wait and get into our ecumenical force. Three thousand veterans would roll right over him.

"Cavalry?" I asked. "Have Jah meet them at the water's edge and do what he can, and fall back, and have our cavalry hit them from the flank as they're about to break out?"

"I was considering sneaking Mogaba's legion down, smash them, then rout march to Ghoja. But you're right. Cavalry would be more efficient. Do you trust Otto and Hagop to handle it?"

I did not. They were having their problems taking charge. Without the bloodyminded roi to kick ass where that was needed, their force would have been a travelling circus. "You want it? You done a field command?"

She looked at me hard. "Where have you been?"

Right. I'd been there often enough.

"You want it?"

"If you want me to take it."

"Singe me to a crisp in the fire of your enthusiasm. All right. But we won't tell anybody till it's time. And Jahamaraj Jah not at all. He'll try harder if he don't know help is coming."

"All right."

"Any other news from our seldom-seen friend?"

"No."

"Who is that woman he's dragging around?"

She hesitated a moment too long. "I don't know."

"Odd. Seems like I've seen her somewhere before. But I can't place her."

She shrugged. "After a while everybody gets to look like somebody you've seen before."

"Who do I look like?"

She didn't miss a beat. "Gastrar Telsar of Novok Debraken. The voice is different, but the heart could be the same. He moralized and debated with himself, too."

How could I argue? I'd never heard of the guy.

"He moralized once too often. My husband had him flayed."

"You think I moralized about Ghoj?"

"Yes. I think you put yourself through hell after the fact. A net gain. You've gotten smart enough to get them first and cry later."

"I don't think I want to play this game."

"No. You wouldn't. I need some of your time for tailors to take your measurements."

"Say what? I got me a flashy uniform already."

"Not like this one. This one is for boggling the minions of the Shadowmasters. Part of the showmanship."

"Right. Whenever. I can work while I'm being measured. Is Shifter going to be there for the show at Ghoja?"

"We'll find out the hard way. He didn't say. I told you, he has his own agenda."

"Wouldn't mind having a peek at that. He give you one?"

"No. Mogaba is staging a mock battle between legions today. You going?"

"No. I'm going to be sucking up to the Radisha for more transport. I got the charcoal. Now I got to get it down there."

She snorted. "Things were different in my time."

"You had more power."

"That's true. I'll send the tailors and fitters."

I wondered what she had in mind. . . . What? Did I see that? What was that? Did she shake her tail as she was going out? Damn me. My eyes must be starting to go.

Weekly assessment session. I asked Murgen, "How's the bat situation?"

"What?" I had caught him from the blind side.

"You brought the bat problem up. I thought you were keeping track."

"I haven't seen any for a while."

"Good. That means Goblin and One-Eye got the right people out of the way. From where I sit everything looks like it's going smooth. Probably faster than we had reason to expect." I'd had no individual complaints for a while. Lady had found time to help Otto and Hagop put the fear into their snooty horsemen. "Mogaba?"

"Twelve days left on the worst-case estimate. It's time to put teams out to watch the river stages. Worst case might not be absolutely worst."

"The Radisha is ahead of you. I talked to her yesterday. She'd just grabbed off half the post riders for that. Right now the river is running higher than expected. That may not mean anything. We'll have plenty of weather yet."

"Every day we get is another hundred men I can take into each legion."

"Where are you at now?"

"Thirty-three hundred each. I'll stop at four thousand. Be time to move out then, anyway."

"Think five days is enough to get down there? That's twenty miles a day for guys who aren't used to it."

"They'll be used to it. They do ten a day with field pack now."

"I'll get out to look them over this week. Promise. I've got the political end pretty well whipped. Hagop. You guys going to be ready?"

"It's coming together, Croaker. They've started to realize we mean it when we say we're trying to show them how to stay alive."

"It's getting close enough that they have to think about it as more than a game. Big Bucket. How about you guys?"

"Get us fifty more wagons and we can roll tomorrow, Captain."

"You look at the sketches of that town?"

"Yes sir."

"How long to set it up?"

"Depends on materials. For the palisade. And manpower. Lot of trenching. The rest, no problem."

"You'll have the manpower. Sindawe's bunch. They'll go down with you and move on later, as our reserve. I'll tell you, though, the resource situation is bleak. You'll end up depending on the trench more than the palisade. Cletus. What about artillery?"

Cletus and his brothers grinned. They looked proud of themselves. "We got it. Six mobile engines for each legion, already built. We're working the crews on them now."

"Great. I want you to go down with the quartermasters and engineers and get a look at that town. Put some of the engines in there. Big Bucket, you guys better head out as soon as you can. The roads are going to be miserable. If you really need more wagons mooch them from the citizens. Be quicker than me trying to gouge them out of the Radisha. So. Can't anybody come up with anything I can fuss myself about? You know I'm not happy unless I'm worrying."

They looked at me blankly. Finally, Murgen blurted out, "We're going to meet their ten thousand with our eight? Isn't that worry enough? Sir?"

"Ten thousand?"

"That's the rumor. That the Shadowmasters increased the invasion force."

I glanced at Lady. She shrugged. I said, "We have unreliable intelligence to that effect. But we'll be more than eight thousand with the cavalry. With Sindawe we'll actually outnumber them. We'll have the field position. And I have a trick or two up my sleeve."

"That charcoal?" Mogaba asked.

"Among other things."

"You won't tell us?"

"Nope. Word has a way of getting around. If nobody

but me knows I can't blame anybody but me if the other side finds out."

Mogaba smiled. He understood me too well. I just wanted to keep it for myself.

We commanders are that way, sometimes.

My predecessors never told anybody anything till it was time to jump.

Afterward, I asked Lady, "What do you think?"

"I think they're going to know they were in a fight. I still have grave doubts about winning, but maybe you're a better captain than you want to admit. You put every man where he can do the most good."

"Or least harm." Wheezer and Hagop's nephew still had not shown me they were good for anything.

Seven days till deadline. The quartermasters and engineers and Sindawe's reserve legion were two days gone. Incoming post riders reported their progress as disappointing. The roads were hopeless. But they were getting help from people along the way. In places the troops and locals backpacked the freight while the teams dragged the empty wagons through the mud.

We were going to get some grace. We were still getting drizzle when that should have ended a week ago. Reports had the fords way too high to cross. The watchers guessed we had at least five extra days.

I told Mogaba, who needed time more than anyone else. He grumbled that his main accomplishment to date was that he had taught his troops to march in straight lines.

I thought that was the critical lesson. If they could maintain order on the battlefield . . .

I was not comfortable with the gift of time. As each day perished in turn, and I had more reports of the trouble the advance party was having, I grew ever more antsy.

Two days before our originally planned departure I

summoned Mogaba. "Have you relaxed any because of
the extra time?"

"No."

"Not easing up at all?"

"No. If we leave five days later, they'll be five days
more prepared."

"Good." I leaned back in my chair.

"You're troubled."

"That mud. I had Frogface go scout. Sindawe is still
twenty miles from Vejagedhya. What'll it be like for the
mob we'll take down?"

He nodded. "You're thinking of leaving early?"

"I'm seriously considering leaving when we originally
planned. Just to make sure. If we're there early we can get
rested and maybe a little more trained under field
conditions."

He nodded again. Then took me by surprise. "You
play hunches sometimes, don't you?"

I lifted an eyebrow.

"I've watched you since Gea-Xle. I'm beginning to
understand how your mind works, I think. And sometimes I think you don't understand yourself well enough.
You've been troubled all week. That is a sign you have a
hunch trying to come through." He left his chair. "I'll
proceed on the assumption that you'll leave early."

He left. I thought about him knowing how my mind
works. Should I feel flattered or threatened?

I went to a window, opened it, looked at the night sky.
I saw stars between racing clouds. Maybe the cycle of
daily drizzle was over. Or maybe it was just another
pause.

I went back to work. My current project, taken catch-
as-catch-can, was one I was working on with Frogface.
We were trying to figure out what had become of the
books missing from all the libraries around town. I had
an idea that a certain anonymous official had them
squirreled away in the Prahbrindrah's palace. The ques-

tion was, how to get to them? Invoke my powers as dictator?

"Ignore the river."

"Say what?" I looked around. "What the hell?"

"Ignore the river."

A crow stood on the windowsill. Another settled beside it. It delivered the same message.

Crows are smart. But only for bird brains. I asked what they were talking about. They told me to ignore the river. I could put them on the rack and they would not tell me more. "All right. I got it. Ignore the river. Shoo."

Crows. All the time with the damned crows. They were trying to tell me something, sure. What? They had warned me before. Were they saying I should pay no attention to the river stages?

That was my inclination anyway, because of the mud.

I went to the door and yelled, "One-Eye! Goblin! I need you."

They mustered in looking surly, standing well away from one another. Not a good sign. They were feuding again. Or working up to it. It had been so long since they had eased the pressure that it might be a major blowup.

"Tonight's the night, guys. Take out the rest of the Shadowmasters' agents."

"I thought we had some extra time," One-Eye carped.

"We might have. And we might not. I want it done now. Take care of it."

Under his breath Goblin muttered, "Yessir your dictatorship, sir." I gave him a dirty look. He moved out. I went to the window and stared out at that clearing sky.

"I had a feeling things were going too good."

Chapter Thirty-two:
SHADOWLIGHT

The Shadowmasters met in a haste that left them exhausted. The meet had been set days earlier but as they travelled a cry had gone out saying it was too late for lazy, comfortable movements.

They were in the place of the pool and uncertain dimensions and shadows. The woman bobbed restlessly. Her companion was agitated. The one who spoke seldom spoke first. "What is the panic?"

"Our resources in Taglios have been exterminated. All but the newest. As suddenly as that." She snapped her fingers.

Her companion said, "They are about to march."

The woman: "They knew who our resources were. Which means everything we learned through them is suspect."

Her companion: "We have to move sooner than we planned. We cannot give them a minute more than we must."

The quiet one asked, "Have we been found out?"

The woman: "No. We have the one resource close to the heart, still undetected if mostly ineffective. It hasn't reported a hint of a suspicion."

"We should join the troops. We should leave nothing to the hazard of battle."

"We've argued this out already. No. We will not risk

ourselves. There is no cause to think they will have any
chance against our veterans. I have added five thousand
men to the invasion force. That is enough."

"There was another thing. The thing you called us here
to present."

"Yes. Our comrade of Shadowcatch and Overlook is
not as southward obsessed as he would have us think. He
infiltrated some of his people into Taglian territory the
past year. They attacked the leaders of the Black Company. And failed abysmally. Their efforts served only one
purpose—beyond betraying his thinking. They gave me
a chance to insinuate our one surviving resource into the
enemy fold."

"Then when next we meet him we can mock him in
turn."

"Perhaps. If it seems appropriate. One piece of news
comes out of his effort. Dorotea Senjak is with them."

A long stillness followed. Finally, the one who spoke
so seldom observed, "That alone explains why our friend
would send men north secretly. How dearly he would
love to own her."

The female replied, "For more reasons than the obvious. There appears to be a relationship with the
Company's Captain. She would be a valuable resource if
that relationship is strong enough to be manipulated."

"She must be killed as soon as possible."

"No! We must capture her. If he can use her, so can we.
Think what she knows. What she was. She might hold
the key to ridding the world of him and of closing the
gateway. She may be powerless but she has not lost her
memory."

The one who spoke seldom began to laugh. His laughter was as insane as that heard in Overlook. He was
thinking anyone could use the memories of Dorotea
Senjak. Anyone!

The female recognized that laugh, understood what
was happening in his mind, knew she and her companion would have to proceed very carefully. But she

pretended not to see. She asked her companion, "Have you contacted the one in the swamps?"

"He wants nothing to do with us or our troubles. He is content with his fetid, humid little empire. But he will come around."

"Good. We're agreed? We advance the schedule?"

Heads nodded.

"I will send the orders immediately."

Chapter Thirty-three:
TAGLIOS: DRUNKEN WIZARDS

It had not been a good day. It got no better because the sun went down. The high had been Frogface reporting Sindawe reaching Vejagedhya. The low followed immediately. There was no material to fortify the town. A ditch would be it.

But the ground was so sodden the walls of a ditch would keep collapsing.

Oh, well. If the gods were out to get us they were out to get us. All our wriggling on the hook wouldn't change a thing.

I was ready to collapse into bed when Murgen burst in. I was so tired I was seeing double. Two of him did not improve the state of the universe. "What now?" I snapped.

"Maybe big trouble. Goblin and One-Eye are down at Swan's place, drunk on their asses, and they've started in. I don't like the smell of it."

I got up, resigned to another sleepless night. It had been a long time brewing. It might get out of hand. "What are they doing?"

"Just the usual, so far. But there's no fun in it this time. There's an undercurrent of viciousness. Anyway, it stinks like somebody could get hurt."

"Horses ready?"

"I sent word."

I grabbed up the officer's baton some Nar had tossed me as we had approached Gea-Xle. No special reason other than that it was the nearest thing handy for thumping heads.

The barracks was quiet as we passed through. The men sensed something afoot. By the time I reached the stables Mogaba and Lady had joined the parade. Murgen explained while they cursed our Taglian stablehands into readying two more horses.

That the feud had gotten out of hand was obvious from blocks away. Fires illuminated the night. Taglians were coming out to see what was happening.

The wizards had squared off in the street outside Swan's place. That had been gutted. Fires flickered up and down the street, none major, just patches gnawing the faces of buildings, evidence of the errant aim of a couple of drunken sorcerers.

Those troublesome little shits were having difficulty standing, let alone shooting straight. So maybe the gods do watch out for fools and drunks. Had they been sober they would have murdered each other.

Unconscious bodies lay scattered around. Swan and Mather and Blade and several guys from the Company were among them. They had tried to break it up and gotten creamed for their trouble.

One-Eye and Goblin were escalating. One-Eye had a pained-looking Frogface sicced on Goblin. Goblin had something that looked like a black snake of smoke growing out of his belt pouch. It was trying to get past Frogface. When the things grappled a shower of light washed the street, revealing Taglians crouched, watching from relative safety.

I halted before they noticed me. "Lady. What's that thing Goblin's got?"

"Can't tell from here. Something he shouldn't. A match for Frogface, which I would have thought was out of One-Eye's class." She sounded vaguely troubled.

There were times I'd had that notion myself. It did not

seem reasonable that you could walk into a shop and buy a Frogface off the shelf. But it hadn't bothered One-Eye, and he was the expert.

Frogface and the snake came to grips midway between their masters. They started grunting and straining and screaming and thumping around. I wondered aloud, "Is that what Goblin brought back from the country?"

"What?"

"From the first time I saw him after his set-to with the brown guys directing the shadows he had this smugness about him. Like he finally had him some way to whip the world."

Lady thought. "If he picked it up from the Shadowmasters' men it could be a plant. Shifter could tell us for sure."

"He ain't here. Let's make the assumption."

The last fire burned itself out. Goblin and One-Eye were totally preoccupied. One-Eye stumbled over his own bootlace. For a moment it looked like Goblin would get the upper hand. Frogface barely turned the snake's strike.

"Enough. We can't do without them, much as I'd like to bury them both and have done with their crap." I spurred my horse. Goblin was nearest me. He barely started to turn. I leaned down and thumped his head. I did not see the result. I was on One-Eye already. I whacked him up side the head, too.

I turned for a second charge but Lady, Mogaba, and Murgen had them wrapped up. The battle between Frogface and the snake died out. But they did not. They eyed one another across ten feet of pavement.

I swung down. "Frogface. Can you talk? Or are you as crazy as your boss?"

"He's crazy, Cap, not me. But I got an indenture. I got to do what he says."

"Yeah? Tell me this. What's that thing growing out of Goblin's pouch?"

"A kind of imp. In another form. Where'd he come up with it, Cap?"

"I wonder myself. Murgen, check these other guys out. See if we've got any real casualties. Mogaba, drag that little shit over here. I'm going to knock some heads together."

We plunked them down side by side with Lady and Mogaba holding them sitting from behind. They began to come around. Murgen came to tell me none of the unconscious men were injured.

That was something.

One-Eye and Goblin looked up at me. I paced back and forth, smacking the baton into my hand. My dictator's stalk. I whirled on them. "Next time this happens I'm going to tie you two into a sack, face-to-face, and drop you in the river. I don't have the patience for it. Tomorrow, while your hangovers are still killing you, you're going to get up and come down here and make good the damage. The expense will come out of your pockets. Do you understand?"

Goblin looked a little sheepish. He managed a feeble nod. One-Eye did not respond.

"One-Eye? You want another whack up side the head?"

He nodded. Sullenly.

"Good. Now. Goblin. That thing you brought back from the country. Chances are it belongs to the Shadowmasters. A plant. Before you go to bed I want it stuffed in a bottle or something and buried. Deep."

His eyes bugged. "Croaker . . ."

"You heard me."

An angry, almost roaring hiss filled the street. The snake thing came up off the paving and struck at me.

Frogface flung in from the side, deflecting it.

In a sudden, drunken, bug-eyed panic Goblin and One-Eye both tried to get it under control. I backed off. It was a wild three minutes before Goblin got it squished into his pouch. He stumbled into Swan's place. A minute later he came out carrying a closed wine jar. He looked at me funny. "I'll bury it, Croaker." He sounded embarrassed.

One-Eye was getting himself together, too. He took a deep breath. "I'll give him a hand."

"Right. Try not to talk too much. Don't get started again."

He had the grace to look embarrassed, too. He gave Frogface a thoughtful look. I noted that he did not take the imp along to do the heavy work.

"What now?" Mogaba asked.

"Pains me all to hell, but now we count on their consciences to keep them in line. For a while. If I didn't need them so much I'd make it a night they'd remember the rest of their lives. I don't need this shit. What're you grinning about?"

Lady did not stop. "It's smaller scale, but this is what it was like trying to keep a rein on the Ten Who Were Taken."

"Yeah? Maybe so. Murgen, you were out here boozing anyway, you finish picking up the pieces. I'm going to get some sleep."

Chapter Thirty-four:
TO GHOJA

It was worse than I thought it would be. The mud seemed bottomless. The first day out of Taglios, after a cheering parade, we made twelve miles. I did not feel desperate. But the road was better nearer the city. After that it got worse. Eleven miles the next day, nine each of the three days following. We made that good a time only because we had the elephants along.

The day I wanted to reach the Ghoja ford I was still thirty miles away.

Then Shifter came, wearing his wolf shape, prancing in out of the wilds.

The rains had ended but the sky remained overcast, so the ground did not dry. The sun was no ally.

Shifter came with a smaller companion. It looked as though his understudy had caught on to shifting.

He spent an hour with Lady before we moved out. Then he galloped away again.

Lady did not look cheerful.

"Bad news?"

"The worst. They've put one over on us, maybe."

I did not betray the sudden tightness in my innards. "What?"

"Recall the map of the Main. Between Numa and Ghoja there's that low area that floods."

I pictured it. For twelve miles the river ran through an

area flanked by plains that flooded whenever the river rose more than a few feet. At its highest stage it could be fourteen miles wide there, with most of the flooding on the southern side. That plain became a huge reservoir, and was the reason the Numa ford became crossable before the Ghoja. But the last I'd heard it was mostly drained.

"I know it. What about it?"

"Ever since they took the south bank the Shadow-masters have been building a levee, from the downriver end, right along the normal bank. It's something that's been talked about for ages. The Prahbrindrah wanted to do it, to claim the plain for farming. But he couldn't afford the labor. The Shadowmasters don't have that problem. They have fifty thousand prisoners on it, Taglians who didn't get across the river last year and enemies from their old territories. No one's paid any attention because the project is one of those things that anyone who could would do."

"But?"

"But. They've gotten the levee run out eight miles to the east. That's not as huge a deal as it sounds because it only needs to be about ten feet tall. Every half mile they put in a larger filled area, maybe a hundred fifty yards to a side, like towers along a wall. They keep the prisoners camped there and use the platforms for materials dumps."

"I don't see where you're going."

"Shifter noticed that they'd stopped extending the levee but they were still stockpiling materials. Then he figured it out. They're going to dam the river, partially. Just enough to divert water into the flood plain so they can drop the level at the Ghoja ford sooner than we expect."

I thought about it. It was a cunning bit of business, and entirely practical. The Company had done a trick or two with rivers in its time. All it had to do was give them a day. If they got across unchallenged we were sunk. "The sneaky bastards. Can we get there in time?"

"Maybe. Even probably, considering you didn't wait to leave Taglios. But at the rate we're going it'll be just barely in time and we'll be worn out from fighting the mud."

"Have they started damming yet?"

"They start that this morning, Shifter says. It should take them two days to get the fill in and one more to divert enough water."

"Will it affect Numa?"

"Not for a week. The water will keep dropping there for now. Shifter's guess is they'll cross at Numa the day before they do at Ghoja."

We looked at each other. She saw what I saw. The Shadowmasters had robbed us of what we had in mind for the night before Ghoja. "Damn them!"

"I know. This mud being what it is, I'll have to leave today to get there in time. I probably won't get back to Ghoja. Use Sindawe in our place. That town is a waste, anyway."

"I'll have to move faster, somehow."

"Abandon the wagons."

"But . . ."

"Leave the engineers and quartermasters behind. Let them make the best time they can. I'll leave them the elephants. They're no good to me anyway. Have each man carry a little extra. Whatever is most practical. Even the wagons might get there in time if they skip stopping at Vejagehdya."

"You're right. Let's get at it." I gathered my people and explained what we were going to do. An hour later I watched Lady and the cavalry file away to the southeast. Mogaba's grumbling infantrymen, each carrying an extra fifteen pounds, started slogging toward Ghoja.

Even the old warlord carried a load.

I was glad I had had the luck or foresight to send out the bulk of the stuff several days early.

I walked with the rest of them. My horse was carrying two hundred pounds of junk and looking humiliated by the experience. One-Eye grumbled along beside me. He had Frogface out scouting for lines of advance where the earth would least resist our passage.

I kept one eye on Lady. I felt hollow, empty. We'd both come to think of the night before the Ghoja battle as *the* night. And now that would not be.

I suspected it would never be. There would always be something to stand in the way. Maybe there were gods who frowned on our admitting and consummating what we felt inside.

A pox on them and all their illegitimate children.

Someday, damnit. Someday.

But what then? Then we would have to give up a lot of pretense. Then we'd have to face some things, decide some things, examine the possibilities and implications of some commitments.

I did not spend a lot of time thinking about saving Taglios that day.

Chapter Thirty-five:
BEFORE GHOJA

Take some ground and sog it real good, all the way down to the earth's core. Bake it under a warm sun a few days. What do you get?

Bugs.

They rose in clouds as I slithered to the crest overlooking the Ghoja ford. The mosquitoes wanted to feed. The smaller guys just wanted to pitch camp in my nose.

The grass had grown since last time. It was two feet tall now. I slid my sword forward and parted it. Mogaba, Sindawe, Ochiba, Goblin, and One-Eye did the same. "*Big* mob over there," One-Eye said.

We had known that beforehand. We could smell their campfires. My own troops were eating cold. If those guys over there didn't know we were here yet, I wasn't going to yell and let them in on it.

Mob was an operative word. That bunch was undisciplined and disorderly, camped in a sprawl that began at the fortress gate and stretched back south along the road.

"What you think, Mogaba?"

"Unless that's show to fool us we have a chance. If we keep them that side of the crest." He inched forward, looked at the ground. "You're sure you want me on the left?"

"I'm assuming your legion is more ready. Put Ochiba's on the right up the steeper ground. The natural tendency

251

of an attack would be to push the direction that looks easiest."

Mogaba grunted.

"If they push either one of you much without pushing the other, they open themselves up to heavier enfilading and quartering fire. If the artillery gets here, I'm going to plant some here and the rest down on that little hump there. Have them going both ways. Long as the hinge holds." The join between legions would be at the road that split the field. "Should be good hunting for archers and javelins, too."

Mogaba grumbled, "Plans are mayflies when the steel begins to sing."

I rolled onto my side, looked at him directly. "Will the Nar stand fast?"

His cheek twitched. He knew what I meant.

Except for the thing on the river, which was a whole different show, Mogaba's men had seen no real combat. I hadn't found out till recently. Their ancestors had gotten Gea-Xle and its neighbors so tamed they just had to make noises to keep things in line. These Nar still believed they were the best that ever was, but that had not been proven on a field of blood.

"They will stand," Mogaba said. "Can they do anything else? If terror turns their spines to water? They have made their brags."

"Right." Men will do damnfool things just because they said they would.

What about the rest of my mob? Most were veterans though few had been into this kind of thing. They had handled themselves on the river. But you can't be sure what a man will do till he does it. I was not sure of myself. I have been in and out of battles all my life, but I have seen old veterans crack.

And I'd never been a general. Never had to make decisions sure to cost lives. Did I have the inner toughness it takes to send men to sure death to achieve greater goals?

I was as new to my role as the greenest Taglian soldier.

Ochiba grunted. I parted the grass.

A dozen men approached the ford on the south side. Well-dressed men. The enemy captains? "One-Eye. Time for Frogface to do a little eavesdropping."

"Check." He slithered away.

Goblin gave me a bland look that concealed intense irritation. One-Eye got to keep his toy and he didn't. I was playing favorites. Children. What difference that that snake had damned near killed me?

Frogface came back.

They were coming in the morning. Early. They expected no resistance. They were gloating about what they were going to do to Taglios.

I had the word spread.

Wasn't nobody going to get much sleep tonight.

Was my little army overprepared? I saw plenty of the anxiety that comes before the hour of blood, but also an eagerness unusual in virgins. Those Taglians knew the odds were long. So how come they were confident in the face of probable disaster?

I realized I did not understand their culture well enough.

Dip into the old trick bag, Croaker. Play the captain game. I went walking through the camp, attended by crows as always, speaking to a man here, a man there, listening to an anecdote about a favorite wife or toddler. It was the first time many had seen me up close.

I tried not to think about Lady. So naturally she would not get out of my mind.

They were coming tomorrow at Ghoja. That meant they had crossed at Numa today. She might be fighting right now. Or it might be over. She might be dead. Three thousand enemy soldiers might be racing to get behind me.

Late that afternoon the wagons began arriving. Sindawe came in from Vejagedhya. My spirits rose. I would get to try my little trick after all.

Stragglers kept coming in all night.

If we lost the fight the train was gone. There would be no getting it out in all that mud.

One-Eye kept Frogface flitting across the river. To little purpose. The enemy strategy was: cross that river. Nothing beyond it. Don't worry about the mules, just load that wagon.

After nightfall I went up and sat in the damp grass and watched the fires burn on the other side. Maybe I dozed some, off and on. Whenever I glanced up I noticed that the stars had wheeled along. . . .

I wakened to a presence. A coldness. A dread. I heard nothing, saw nothing, smelled nothing. But I knew it was there. I whispered, "Shifter?"

A great bulk settled beside me. I amazed myself. I was not afraid. This was one of the two greatest surviving sorcerers in the world, one of the Ten Who Were Taken who had made the Lady's empire all but invincible, a monster terrible and mad. But I was not afraid.

I even noticed that he did not smell as bad as he used to. Must be in love.

He said, "They come with the light."

"I know."

"They have no sorcery at all. Only the strength of arms. You might conquer."

"I was sort of hoping I would. You going to chip in?"

Silence for some time. Then, "I will contribute only in small ways. I do not wish to be noticed by the Shadowmasters. Yet."

I thought about what little things he could do that might mean a lot.

We had started to get some traffic nearby, Taglians lugging fifty-pound sacks of charcoal to the foreslope.

Of course. "How are you with fog? Can you conjure me up a little?"

"Weather is not my strength. Maybe a small patch if there's reason. Explain."

"Be real handy to have a chunk that would lie along

the river and reach maybe two hundred feet up this slope. Bottled this side of the creek over there. Just so those guys would have to come through it." I told him about my trick.

He liked it. He chuckled, a small sound that wanted to roar like a volcano. "Man, you were always sneaky, cold-blooded, cruel bastards, smarter than you looked. I like it. I'll try. It should draw no attention and the results may be amusing."

"Thank you."

I was speaking to the air. Or maybe a nearby crow. Shifter had gone without a sound.

I sat there and tormented myself, trying to think of something more I might have done, trying not to think of Lady, trying to excuse myself the dying. The soldiers crossing the ridge made very little noise.

Later, I became aware of a few tendrils of mist forming. Good.

There was a bit of rose in the east. Stars were dying. Behind me, Mogaba and the Nar were wakening the men. Across the river, enemy sergeants did the same. A little more light and I could see the artillery batteries ready to be wheeled into position. They had arrived, but so far only one wagon loaded with missiles.

Shifter had managed a mist, though not all I wanted. Fifteen feet deep at the ford, two hundred fifty yards toward me, not quite reaching the band of charcoal, ten feet wide, that the men had laid out in the night, on an arc from the riverbank in the east around to the bank of the creek.

Time to go give the final pep talk. I slithered off the crest, turned. . . . And there was Lady.

She looked like hell but she was grinning.

"You made it."

"Just got here." She grabbed my hand in hers.

"You won."

"Barely." She sat down and told me. "The Shadar did good. Pushed them back across twice. But not the third try. It broke up into a brawl and chase before we could get into it. When we did, the Shadowmasters' men formed up and held out almost all day."

"Any survivors?"

"A few. But they didn't get back across. I put some men over right away, caught them off guard, and took their fortress. Afterward I sent Jah on across." She smiled. "I gave him a hundred men to scout and told him your orders were to circle around behind them here. He could be in position this afternoon if he pushes."

"He take heavy losses?"

"Eight hundred to a thousand."

"He's dead if we blow it here."

She smiled. "That would be terrible, wouldn't it? Politically speaking."

I lifted an eyebrow. I still had trouble thinking that way.

She said, "I sent a messenger to Theri telling the Gunni to seize the crossing. Another is headed for Vehdna-Bota."

"You have the mercy of a spider."

"Yes. It's almost time. You'd better get dressed."

"Dressed?"

"Showmanship. Remember?"

We headed for camp. I asked, "You bring any of your men with you?"

"Some. More will straggle in."

"Good. I won't have to use Sindawe."

Chapter Thirty-six:
GHOJA

I felt like a fool in the getup Lady put on me. A real Ten Who Were Taken costume, baroque black armor with little threads of bloody light slithering over it. Made me look about nine feet tall when I was up on one of those black stallions. The helmet was the worst. It had big black wings on the side, a tall gismo with fluffy black feathers on the crown, and what looked like fire burning behind the visor.

One-Eye thought it would look intimidating as hell from a distance. Goblin figured my enemies would laugh themselves to death.

Lady got into an outfit just as outrageous, black, grotesque helmet, fires.

I sat there on my horse feeling weird. My people were ready. One-Eye sent Frogface to watch the enemy. Lady's helpers brought shields and lances and swords. The shields had grim symbols on them, the lances matching pennons. She said, "I've created two nasties. With luck we can turn them into something with an image like the Taken. Their names are Widowmaker and Lifetaker. Which one do you want to be?"

I closed my visor. "Widowmaker."

She fish-eyed me a good ten seconds before she told somebody to hand me my stuff. I took all my old familiar hardware along, too.

Frogface popped up. "Get ready, chief. They're about to hit the water."

"Right. Spread the word."

I glanced right. I glanced left. Everyone and everything was ready. I had done all I could. It was in the hands of the gods or the jaws of fate.

Frogface was down in the mist when the enemy hit the water. He popped back. I gave a signal. A hundred drums started pounding. Lady and I crossed the ridgeline. I guess we made a good show. Over in the fortress people scurried around and pointed.

I drew the sword Lady had given me, gestured for them to turn back. They did not. I would not have in their place. But I'll bet they were damned uneasy. I advanced down the hill and touched that burning blade to the charcoal strip.

Flame ripped across the slope. It burned out in twenty seconds but left the charcoal glowing. I got back quickly. The fumes were powerful.

Frogface popped up. "They're pouring across now, chief."

I could not yet see them through the mists. "Tell them to stop the drums."

Instant silence. Then the clangor of troops in the mist. And their cursing and coughing in the sulphur-laden air. Frogface returned. I told him, "Tell Mogaba to bring them over."

The drums started talking again. "March them in a straight line," I muttered. "That's all I ask, Mogaba. March them in a straight line."

They came. I dared not look to see how they were doing. But they passed me soon enough. And they were holding formation.

They assumed positions across the slope from the creek, then down to the river on the left, with the hinge between legions at the road. Perfection.

The enemy began coming out of the mist, swirling it, staggering, disordered, coughing furiously, cursing. They encountered the barrier of charcoal and did not know what to do.

I gestured with my sword.

Missiles flew.

It looked like pure unreasoning panic had seized the fortress. The enemy captains saw they had walked into it and did not know how to respond. They chased their tails and fussed and did not do anything.

Their soldiers just kept coming, not knowing what they were walking into until they came out of the mist and found themselves stopped by the charcoal.

The mist began to drift off downriver. Shifter could not hold it any longer. But a little had been enough.

They had some competent sergeants on the other side. They began bringing up water and cutting paths through the coals with trenching tools. They began getting their men into ragged formations, behind their shields, safer from arrows and javelins. I signalled again. The wheeled ballistae opened up.

Daring the enemy's worst, Mogaba and Ochiba rode back and forth in front of their men, exhorting them to stand fast, to maintain the integrity of their line.

My role was cruel, now. I could do nothing but sit there with the breeze playing around me, being symbolic.

They got aisles cleared through the charcoal and rushed through. A lot got dead for their trouble. The ballistae ran out of missiles and withdrew, but arrows and javelins continued to rain on those coming up from the ford, taking a terrible toll.

More and more pressure all along the line. But the legions did not bend, and gave as good as they got. Their lungs were not burned raw by sulphur gasses.

Over half the enemy had crossed the river. A third of those had fallen. The captains in the fortress remained indecisive.

The Shadowmasters' troops kept coming across. A furious desperation began to animate them. Eighty percent over. Ninety percent. The Taglians began to give a

step here and there. I remained frozen, an iron symbol.
"Frogface," I muttered into my helmet, "I need you
now."

The imp materialized, perched on my mount's neck.
"What you need, chief?" I filled him up with orders I
wanted relayed to Murgen, to Otto and Hagop, to
Sindawe, to damned near everybody I could think of.
Some ordered next steps of the plan, some involved
innovations.

The morning had been remarkably crow-free. Now
that changed. Two monsters, damned near as big as
chickens, settled on my shoulders. They were nobody's
imagination. I felt their weight. Others saw them. Lady
turned to look at them.

A flock passed over the battlefield, circled the fortress,
settled into the trees along the riverbank.

The enemy infantry was across. Their train was getting
organized to follow.

Thousands of the Shadowmasters' men were down. I
doubted they had the advantage of numbers anymore.
But experience had begun to tell. My Taglians were
giving ground. I felt the first flutters of panic nipping at
their formations.

Frogface materialized. "Couple wagons with ballista
shafts came in, chief."

"Get them up to the engines. Then tell Otto and
Hagop it's time."

Maybe seven hundred horsemen had straggled in from
Numa by then. They were dead tired. But they were in
place and ready.

They did what they were supposed to do. They stumbled up out of the cover of the creek. They sliced through
the chaos behind the enemy line like the fabled hot knife
through butter. Soft butter. Then they came back across
the hillside, cutting at the back of the enemy line. Like
scythes felling wheat.

Murgen came over the hill behind me, displaying the
Black Company standard boldly. Sindawe's bunch were

behind him. Murgen halted between Lady and me, a few
steps back.

The artillery began feeling for the range to the fortress.

Goblin and One-Eye and maybe even Shifter had been
at work, using little charms to decompose the mortar
between stones.

"It's going to work," I muttered. "I think we're going
to do it."

The cavalry sortie did it. They did not get sorted out
for another charge before men began running for the
ford. The second charge bogged down in the sheer mass
of fleeing men.

Mogaba, I love you.

The men he had trained did not break formation and
charge. He and Ochiba hustled up and down their lines,
getting the ranks dressed and the injured out of the way.

Ballista shafts were knocking stones out of the fortress
wall. The captains up top gawked. A few of feeble
courage abandoned the battlements.

I raised my sword and pointed. The drums started. I
began walking my mount forward. Lady kept pace, as
did Murgen and the standard. One-Eye and Goblin
worked up a more terrible glamor around us. My two
crows shrieked. They could be heard above the tumult.

The enemy train was all crowded up the other side of
the ford. Now the teamsters fled, leaving them blocking
the retreat of their comrades.

We had them in a bottle, the cork was in, and most of
them had their backs to us.

The grim work began.

I continued my slow advance. People stayed away
from me and Lady and the standard. Archers on the
battlements tried dropping me, but somebody had put
some pretty good spells on my armor. Nothing got
through, though for a while it was like being in a barrel
somebody was whacking with a hammer.

Enemy soldiers began jumping in the river and swim-
ming for it.

The ballistae had a good range, all their shafts striking in a small area. The watchtower creaked and grumbled. Then rumbled. A big chunk fell out, and soon the whole tower collapsed, taking parts of the fortress wall with it.

I pushed into the river, across the ford, and on up between wagons. The standard and Sindawe's men followed. The only enemies I saw were heeling and toeing it south.

Amazing. I never struck a blow myself.

It was almost workaday stuff for Sindawe's bunch to begin clearing the wagons, for some to worm through behind Murgen and cover him while he planted the standard on the fortress wall.

Fighting continued on the north bank but the thing had been decided. It was over and won and I did not believe it. It had been close to being too easy. I had not used all the arrows in my quiver.

Though chaos continued around me I took out my map case to check out what lay to the south.

Chapter Thirty-seven:
SHADOWLIGHT: COAL-DARK TEARS

Rage and panic contended in the fountained hall at Shadowlight. Moonshadow mewled dire prophecies. Stormshadow raged. One maintained a silence as deep as that within a buried coffin. And one was not there at all, though a Voice spoke for him, dark and mocking.

"I said a million men might not be enough."

"Silence, worm!" Stormshadow snarled.

"They have obliterated your invincible armies, children. They have forced bridgeheads everywhere. What will you do now, whimpering dogs? Your provinces are a prostrate and naked woman. A two-hundred-mile jaunt behind the Lance of Passion and they will be hammering at the gates of Stormgard. What will you do, what will you do, what will you do? Oh, woe, what hast befallen thee?" Insane laughter rolled out of that black absence in the air.

Stormshadow snarled, "You haven't been a whole hell of a lot of help, have you? You and your games. Trying to catch Dorotea Senjak? How well did you do? Eh? What would you have done with their Captain? Did you have a bargain in mind? Some deal to trade us for the power they bring? Did you think you could use them to close the Gate? If you did you're the greatest fool of all."

"Whine, children. Moan and wail. They are upon you. Maybe if you beg I'll save you yet again."

Moonshadow snapped, "Bold chatter from one without the ability to save himself. Yes. In the traditions of their Company they caught us off balance. They did what is for them old routine: the impossible. But the fighting along the Main was just one move in the game. Only a pawn has vanished from the board. If they come south, every step will carry them a step nearer their dooms."

Laughter.

The silent one broke his fast of words. "There are three of us, in the fullness of our power. But two great ones dog the path of the Black Company. And they have little interest in furthering its goals. And *she* is a cripple, feeble as a mouse."

More laughter. "Once upon a time someone named the true name of Dorotea Senjak. So now she is the Lady no more. She has no more powers than a talented child. But do you believe she lost her memory when she lost those powers? You do not. Or you would not accuse me as you have. Perhaps she will grow frightened enough or desperate enough to confide in the great one who changes."

No retort. That was the dread that haunted them all.

Moonshadow said, "The reports are confused. Still, a great disaster has befallen our army. But we are dealing with the Black Company. The chance has always existed. We have prepared for it. We will regain our composure. We will deal with them. But there is a mystery from the fighting at Ghoja. Two dire figures were seen there, great dark beings on giant steeds that breathed fire. Beings immune to the bite of darts. The names Widowmaker and Lifetaker have been breathed by those who stood with the Black Company."

This was news to the others. Stormshadow said, "We must learn more about this. It may explain their luck."

The hole in the air: "You must act if you do not want to be devoured. I suggest you put aside terror, eschew squabbling, and cease the dispensation of accusation. I suggest you think of a way to go for the jugular."

No one replied.

"Perhaps I will contribute myself when next fate tries to take its cut."

"Well," Stormshadow mused. "The fear has at last penetrated as far as Overlook."

The bickering resumed, but without heart. Four minds rotated toward thwarting that doom from the north.

Chapter Thirty-eight:
INVADERS OF THE
SHADOWLANDS

Tired is not quite so important when you have just beaten the odds. You've got energy to celebrate.

I did not want a celebration. Enemy soldiers were still trying to get away. I wanted my men to get on with what we had to do while they still thought they were supermen. I had my staff together before the chaos started sorting itself out.

"Otto. Hagop. Come morning you head east along the river and break up the force guarding the prisoners building this levee system. Big Bucket, Candles, you guys get this side of the ford cleaned up. Look through these wagons and see what we've got. Mogaba, get the battlefield cleaned up. Collect weapons. One-Eye, get our casualties moved back to Vejagedhya. I'll help when I get time. Don't let those Taglian butchers do anything stupid." We had a dozen volunteer physicians along. Their ideas of medicine were pretty primitive.

"Lady. What do we know about this Dejagore?" Dejagore was the nearest big city south of the Main, two hundred miles down the road. "Besides the fact that it's a walled city?"

"A Shadowmaster makes his headquarters there."

"Which one?"

"Moonshadow, I think. No. Stormshadow."

"That's it?"

"If you'd take prisoners you might find out something from them."

I raised an eyebrow. She prodding me about excesses? "Keep that in mind, Otto. Bring those prisoners when you catch up."

"All fifty thousand?"

"As many as don't run away. I'm hoping some will be mad enough to help us out. The rest we can use for labor."

Mogaba asked, "You're going to invade the Shadowlands?"

He knew I was. He wanted a formal declaration. "Yes. They supposedly only have fifty thousand men under arms. We just creamed a third. I don't think they can get another mob as big together in time if we go at them as hard as we can, as fast as we can."

"Audacity," he said.

"Yeah. Keep hitting them and don't give them a chance to get their feet under them again."

Lady chided, "They're sorcerers, Croaker. What happens when they come out themselves?"

"Then Shifter will have to kick in. Don't worry about the mules, just load the wagons. We've worked on sorcerers before."

Nobody argued. Maybe they should have. But we all felt that fate had handed us an opportunity and we would be idiots to waste it. I figured too that since we had not expected to survive the first contest, we were out nothing by pressing onward.

"I wonder how beloved these Shadowmasters are to their subjects. Can we expect local support?"

No comment. We would find out the hard way.

Talk went on and on. Eventually I left it to help with the medical work, patching and sewing while issuing orders through a procession of messengers. I got me two hours sleep that night.

The cavalry was heading out east and Mogaba's legion had begun its southward advance when Lady joined me. "Shifter has been scouting. He says you can detect an almost visible change as news of the battle spreads. The mass of people are excited. Those who collaborate with the Shadowmasters are confused and frightened. They'll probably panic and run when they hear we're coming."

"Good. Even great." In ten days we would find out for sure how much impact Ghoja had had. I meant to advance on Dejagore at twenty miles a day. The roads south of the Main were dry. How lovely that must have been for them.

Jahamaraj Jah had gotten his survivors into position in time and set a series of clever ambushes. His mob scrubbed two thousand fugitives from Ghoja.

He was not pleased with my invasion plans. He was even less pleased when I drafted his followers and distributed them as replacements for men we had lost. But he did not argue much.

We encountered no resistance. In territories formerly belonging to Taglios we received warm welcomes in villages still occupied by their original inhabitants. The natives were cooler farther south but not inimical. They thought we were too good to be true.

We encountered our first enemy patrols six days south of Ghoja. They avoided contact. I told everybody to look professional and mean.

Otto and Hagop caught up, dragging along thirty thousand people from the levee project. I looked them over. They had not been treated well. There were some very angry, bitter men among them. Hagop said they were all willing to help defeat the Shadowmasters.

"Damn me," I said. "A year and a half ago there were seven of us. Now we're a horde. Pick out the ones in the best shape. Arm them with captured weapons. Add them to the legions so every fourth man in Mogaba's and Ochiba's is a new one. That would mean trained men left over, so move them over to Sindawe. Give him one in four, too. Should bring him up to strength. Anybody else we arm we can use as auxiliaries, and garrisons for some of these smaller cities."

The countryside was not heavily populated between the river and here, but nearer Dejagore that would change. "The rest can tag along. We'll use them somehow."

But how would I feed them? We'd used up our own supplies and had started on those captured at Ghoja.

Dejagore looked less promising now. Some of the rescued prisoners hailed from that city. They said the walls were forty feet high. The resident Shadowmaster was a demon for keeping them up.

"What will be will be," I thought.

The bloom was off the rose. We'd all had time to think. Still, morale was better than it had been moving toward Ghoja.

There were skirmishes the next few days but nothing serious. Mostly Otto and Hagop's boys overhauling enemy troops not hurrying fast enough to get away. The cavalry had begun to behave professionally at last.

I allowed foraging under strict rules, looting only where people had fled. It worked, mostly. Trouble came only where I expected it, from One-Eye, whose motto is that anything not nailed down is his and anything he can pry loose isn't nailed down.

We knocked over some towns and small cities with no trouble. The last few I left to the freed prisoners, cynically letting them vent their wrath while saving my better troops.

The nearer Dejagore we got—official name Stormgard, according to the Shadowmasters—the more tamed the country became. We made the last day's march through rolling hills that had been terraced and strewn with irrigation canals. So it was startling to come out of the hills and see the city itself.

Stormgard was surrounded by a plain as flat as a tabletop extending a mile in all directions, with the

exception of several small mounds maybe ten feet tall.
The plain looked like a manicured lawn. "I don't like the
looks of that," I told Mogaba. "Too contrived. Lady.
Remind you of anything?"

She gave me a blank look.

"The approach to the Tower."

"I see that. But here there's room for maneuver."

"We got some daylight left. Let's get down there and
get set up."

Mogaba asked, "How will you fortify the camp?" We
had seen little timber lately.

"Turn the wagons on their sides."

Nothing moved on the plain. Only haze over the city
indicated life there. "I want a closer look at that. Lady,
when we get down there dig out the costumes."

My horde flooded onto the plain. Still no sign anyone
in Stormgard was interested. I sent for Murgen and the
standard. The way people thought about the Company
here in the south, maybe Stormgard would surrender
without a fight.

Lady looked terrible in her Lifetaker rig. I supposed I
looked as grim. They were effective outfits. They would
have scared me had I seen them coming at me.

Mogaba, Ochiba, and Sindawe invited themselves
along. They had dolled up in stuff they'd worn in
Gea-Xle. They looked pretty fierce themselves. Mogaba
told me, "I want to see those walls, too."

"Sure."

Then here came Goblin and One-Eye. In an instant I
saw that Goblin had had the idea and One-Eye had
decided to go lest Goblin somehow get ahead on points.
"No clowning, you guys. Understand?"

Goblin grinned his big frog grin. "Sure, Croaker. Sure.
You know me."

"That's the trouble. I know you both."

Goblin faked bruised feelings.

"You guys make these costumes look good. Hear?"

"You'll strike terror to the roots of their souls,"

One-Eye promised. "They'll flee from the walls screaming."

"Sure they will. Everybody ready?"

They were. "Around it from the right," I told Murgen. "At the canter. As close as you dare."

He rode out. Lady and I followed twenty yards behind. As I got started two monster crows plopped down on my shoulders. A flock came out of the hills and raced ahead, circling the city.

We got close enough to see the scramble on the walls. And impressive walls they were, at least forty feet high. What nobody had bothered to mention was that the city was built upon a mound that raised it another forty feet above the plain.

This was going to be a bitch.

A few arrows wobbled out and fell short.

Finesse. Cunning. Trickery. Only a dip would go up against those walls, Croaker.

I had had liberated prisoners work up maps. I had a good idea of the city's layout.

Four gates. Four paved roads approached from the points of the compass rose, like spokes of a wheel. Nasty barbicans and towers protected the gates. More towers along the wall for laying enfilading fire along its face. Not pleasant.

It was very quiet up on those walls. They had one eye on us and one on the horde still pouring out of the hills, wondering where the hell we all came from.

We got us a little surprise south of Stormgard.

There was a military camp there. A big one set maybe four hundred yards from the city wall. "Oh, shit," I said, and yelled at Murgen.

He misunderstood. On purpose, probably, though I'll never prove it. He kicked his mount into a gallop and headed for the gap between.

Arrows rose from the wall and camp. Miraculously, they fell without doing any harm. I glanced back as we entered the throat of the gap.

That little shit Goblin wa. standing on his saddle. He was bent over with his pants down, telling the world what he thought of the Shadowmasters and their boys.

Naturally, those folks took exception. As they say in the *chansons*, the sky darkened with arrows.

I was certain fate would take its cut now. But we had moved far and fast enough. The arrowstorm fell behind us. Goblin howled mockingly.

That irritated somebody bigger.

A bolt of lightning from nowhere struck ahead, ripping a steaming hole in the turf. Murgen leapt it. So did I, with my stomach creeping toward my throat. I was sure the next shot would fry somebody in his boots.

Goblin went right on mooning Stormgard. Horsemen began pouring out of the camp. They were no problem. We could outrun them. I tried to concentrate on the wall. Just in case I got out of this alive.

A second bolt seared the backs of my eyeballs. But it too went astray—though I think it shifted course just before it hit.

When my sight cleared I spied a giant wolf racing in from our right, covering ground in strides that beggared those of our black stallions. My old pal Shifter. Right on time.

Another two bolts missed. The gardner was going to be pissed about all the divots knocked out of his lawn. We completed our circuit and headed for camp. Our pursuers gave up.

As we dismounted Mogaba said, "We've drawn fire. Now we know what we're up against."

"One of the Shadowmasters is in there."

"There may be another in that camp," Lady said. "I felt something. . . ."

"Where'd Shifter get to?" He had disappeared again. Everybody shrugged. "I hoped he'd sit in on a brainstorming session. Goblin, that was a dumb stunt."

"It sure was. Made me feel forty years younger."

"Wish I'd thought of it," One-Eye grumbled.

"Well, they know we're here and they know we're bad, but I don't see them making a run for it. Guess we'll have to figure out how to kick their butts."

Mogaba said, "Evidently they mean to fight outside the walls. Otherwise that encampment would not be there."

"Yeah." Things skipped through my mind. Stunts, tricks, strategies. As though I'd been born to come up with them by the hundred. "We'll leave them alone tonight. We'll form up and offer battle in the morning but let them come to us. Where are those city maps? I got a notion."

We talked for hours while the chaos of a camp still settling raged around us. After dark I sent men out to rig a few tricks and plant stakes on which the legions could form and guide their advance. I said, "We shouldn't bother ourselves too much. I don't think they'll fight us unless we get in close to the walls. Get some sleep. We'll see what happens in the morning."

Many pairs of eyes looked at me all at once, then, in cadence, shifted to Lady. A swarm of smiles came and went. Then everyone went away behind their smiles, leaving us alone.

Big Bucket and those guys don't fool around. They had gone into the hills and diverted one of the irrigation canals to bring water to the camp. I figured it in my head. To give every man in the mob one cup we needed about 2,500 gallons. With the animals run it to 3,500. But man and beast need more than a cup to get by. I don't know what the flow was on the canal but not a lot of water was getting wasted.

Not much manpower was going to waste, either. The boys from Opal had dug some holding ponds. One they set aside for bathing. Being the boss wazoo I crowded the line.

Still soggy, I made sure Mogaba had done all the things I didn't really have to check. Sentries out. Barricade manned. Night orders posted. One-Eye working Frogface on scouting missions instead of loafing. What have you.

I was stalling.

This was The Night.

I ran out of busybodying so finally went to my tent. I got out my map of Stormgard, studied it again, then got to work transcribing these Annals. They have grown more spare than I like but that has been the price of keeping up. Maybe Murgen will get me to let go . . . I did three pages and some lines and began to relax, thinking she would not come after all, but then she came in.

She had bathed, too. Her hair was damp. A ghost of lavender or lilac or something hung around her. She was a little pale and a little shaky and not quite able to meet my eye, at a loss what to do or say now that she was here. She buttoned the tent flap.

I closed this book. It went into a brass-bound chest. I closed my ink and cleaned my pen. I could think of nothing to say, either.

The whole shy routine was dumb. We had been playing around like this, and getting older, for over a year. Hell. We were grown-up people. I was old enough to be a grandfather. Might even be one, for all I knew. And she was old enough to be everybody's grandmother.

Somebody had to take the bull by the horns. We couldn't go on forever both of us waiting for the other one to make a move.

So why didn't she do something?

You the guy, Croaker.

Yeah.

I killed the candles, went and took her hand. It was not that dark in there. Plenty of firelight leaked through the fabric of the tent.

She shivered like a captive mouse at first, but it did not take her long to reach a point of no turning back. And for goddamned once nothing happened to interrupt.

The old general amazed himself. The woman amazed him even more.

Sometime in the wee hours the exhausted boss general promised, "Tomorrow night again. Within the walls of Stormgard. Maybe in Stormshadow's own bed."

She wanted to know the basis for his confidence. As time labored on she just got more awake and lively. But the old man fell asleep on her.

Chapter Thirty-nine:
STORMGARD (FORMERLY DEJAGORE)

Even I grumbled about the time of day I got everybody up. We all ate hurriedly, my valiant commanders in a clique so they could pester me about my plans. A crow perched on the tent pole at the front of my tent, one eye cocked my way, or maybe Lady's. The bastard was leering, I thought. Really! Weren't we getting enough of that from the others?

I felt great. Lady, though, seemed to be having trouble moving with her usual fluid grace. And everybody knew what that meant, the smirking freaks.

"I don't understand you, Captain," Mogaba protested. "Why won't you lay it all out?"

"What only I know inside my head only I can betray. Just assemble up on the stakes I had put out and offer battle. If they accept, we'll see how it goes. If they don't kick our butts, we'll worry about the next step."

Mogaba's lips tightened into a prune. He did not like me much right then. Thought I didn't trust him. He glanced over to where Cletus and his bunch were trying to assemble shovels and baskets and bags in numbers enough for an army. They had a thousand men out scouring the hill farms for tools and more baskets and buckets and had men sewing bags cut from the canvas coverings from the wagons.

They knew only that I had told them to get ready for some major, massive earthmoving.

Another thousand men were out trying to forage timber. You need a lot of timber to invest a city.

"Patience, my friend. Patience. All will be clear in due time." I chuckled.

One-Eye muttered, "He learned his trade from our old Captain. Don't tell nobody nothing till you find some gink trying to shove a spear up your butt."

They could not get to me this morning. He and Goblin could have had them a fuss as bad as back in Taglios and I'd have just grinned. I used a wad of bread to finish soaking up the grease on my plate. "All right, let's get dressed and go kick some ass."

Two things to be observed about being the only guy in forty thousand to get some the night before. Thirty-nine thousand nine hundred ninety-nine guys are so envious they hate your guts. But you're in such a positive mood it becomes infectious.

And you can always tell them their share is behind those walls over there.

Scouts reported while I was getting into my Widowmaker rig. They said the enemy was coming out of the camp and the city both. And there were a lot of the bastards. At least ten thousand in the camp, and maybe every man from the city who could be armed.

That bunch would not be thrilled to be headed into a fight. And they weren't likely to be experienced.

I arrayed Mogaba's legion on the left, Ochiba's on the right, and put Sindawe's new outfit in the middle. Behind them I put all the former prisoners we'd been able to arm and hoped they did not look too much like a rabble. The front formations looked good in their white, organized and professional and ready.

Intimidation games.

I had each legion arrayed by hundreds, with aisles between the companies. I hoped the other side would not be smart enough to jump on that right away.

Lady grabbed my hand before she mounted up, squeezed. "Tonight in Stormgard."

"Right." I kissed her cheek.

She whispered, "I don't think I can stand to sit on this saddle. I'm sore."

"Curse of being a woman."

I mounted up.

Two big black crows dropped onto my shoulders immediately, their sudden weight startling me. Everybody gawked. I scanned the hills but saw no sign of my walking stump. But we were making some kind of headway here. This was the second time everybody else saw the crows.

I donned my helmet. One-Eye stoked the fires of illusion. I assumed my post in front of Mogaba's legion. Lady moved out in front of Ochiba's bunch. Murgen planted the standard in front of Sindawe's legion, ten paces in front of everyone else.

I was tempted to charge right then. The other side was having a fire drill trying to get organized. But I gave them a while. From the looks of them most of the ones out of Stormgard did not want to be there. Let them look at us, all in neat array, all in white, all ready to carve them up. Let them think about how nice it would be to get back inside those incredible walls.

I signalled Murgen. He trotted forward, galloped along the face of the enemy showing the standard. Arrows flew and missed. He shouted mockeries. They were not terrified into running for it.

My two crows flapped after him, and were joined by thousands more who came from the gods knew where. The brotherhood of death, winging it over the doomed. Nice touch, old stump. But not enough to make anybody run away.

My two crows returned to my shoulders. I felt like a monument. I hoped crows had better manners than pigeons.

Murgen did not get enough of a rise first pass so he rode back the other direction, yelling louder.

I noted a disturbance in the enemy formation, moving forward. Someone or something seated in the lotus position, all in black, floating five feet off the ground, drifted to a halt a dozen yards in front of the other army. Shadowmaster? Had to be. I got a creepy feeling just looking at it. Me there in my spiffy but fake outfit.

Murgen's taunts got somebody's goat. A handful of horsemen, then a bunch, lit out after him. He turned in the saddle and shouted at them. There was no way they could catch him, of course. Not when he was on that horse.

I grumbled. The indiscipline was not as general as I wanted.

Murgen dawdled, letting them come closer and closer —then took off when they were only a dozen yards away. They chased him right into the maze of tripwires I'd had woven into the grass during the night.

Men and horses sprawled. More horses tripped on animals already down. My archers lofted arrows that fell straight down and slaughtered most of the men and horses.

I drew my sword, which smoked and smoldered, and signalled the advance. The drums beat the slow cadence. The men in the front rank slashed the tripwires, finished the wounded. Otto and Hagop, on the flanks, had trumpets sounded but did not charge. Not yet.

My boys could march in a straight line. On that nice flat ground they kept their dress all across their front. That had to be an impressive sight from across the way, where they still had guys who hadn't found their places in ranks.

We passed the first of the several low mounds that spotted the plain. The artillery was supposed to get up on that one and mass fire wherever it seemed appropriate. I hoped Cletus and the boys had sense enough to harass the Shadowmaster.

That critter was the big unknown quantity here.

I hoped Shifter was around somewhere. This whole

thing could go to hell if he wasn't and that bastard over there cut loose.

Two hundred yards away. Their archers lofted poorly aimed shafts at Lady and me. I halted, gave another signal. The legions halted, too. Very good. The Nar were paying attention.

Gods, there were a lot of them over there.

And that Shadowmaster, just floating there, maybe waiting for me to stick my foot in it. Seemed like I was staring up his nostrils.

But he did not do anything.

The ground shuddered. The enemy ranks stirred. They saw it coming and it was too late for them to do anything.

The elephants thundered up the aisles through the legions, gaining momentum. When those monsters passed me the guys over there were already yelling and looking for somewhere to run.

A salvo of twelve ballistae shafts ripped overhead and spattered around the Shadowmaster. They were well aimed. Four actually struck him. They encountered protective sorceries but battered him around. Very sluggish, the Shadowmaster. Keeping himself alive seemed to be his limit.

A second salvo hit him an instant before the elephants reached his men. The ballistae had been laid even more carefully.

I gave the signal that sent my front four thousand men, and the cavalry, howling forward.

The remainder of the men formed a normal front, then advanced.

The carnage was incredible.

We drove them back and back and back, but there were so damned many of them we never really broke them. When they did flee the majority made it into the camp. None got back into Stormgard. The city had closed its gates on them. They dragged their Shadowmaster champion with them. I would not have bothered. He had been useless as tits on a boar hog.

Of course, one of the second flight of ballistae shafts had gotten through his protection. I suppose that distracted him.

His ineffectuality had to be Shifter's doing.

They left maybe five thousand men behind. The warlord side of me was disappointed. I'd hoped to do more damage. I was not going to storm the camp to do it, though. I backed the men off, set men to police up our casualties, placed cavalry to meet anyone coming out of camp or city, then got on with business.

I planted my right wing yards from the road we had followed down to Stormgard, just out of bowshot of the barbican at the gate it entered. My line ran at right angles to the road. I let the men relax.

My levee builders got to work putting their training to use. On the far side of the road they began digging a trench. It started a bowshot from the wall and ran to the foot of the hills. It would be wide and deep and would shield my flank.

The workers carried the earth to the road and began building a ramp. Others began building mantlets to protect the ramp builders as they approached the wall.

That many men can move a lot of earth. The defenders saw we would have a ramp right up to the wall in just a few days. They were not pleased. But they had no means to stop us.

Men scurried like ants. The former prisoners had scores to even and went at it like they wanted blood by sundown.

By mid-afternoon they were taking the city end of the trench downward, deep, and toward the wall, not hiding the fact that they were mining, aiming to go under as well as over. And they had begun breaking ground for a trench on my left flank as well.

In three days my army would be protected by a pair of deep trenches that would funnel my attack up the ramp and over the wall. There would be no stopping us.

They had to do something in there.

I hoped to do something to them before they thought of something to do to me.

Late afternoon. The sky began clouding over. Lightning frolicked behind the hills to the south. Not a good sign. A storm would be tougher on my guys than on theirs.

Even so, despite the cold wind and scattered sprinkles moving in, the builders only broke for a spartan supper before setting out lanterns and building bonfires so they could continue after dark. I posted pickets so there would be no surprises, began rotating my troops out of position for food and rest.

Some day. All I'd had to do was sit in one place and look elegant and give orders I'd already worked out in my head.

And think about what last night had meant, in its highly anticlimactic fashion.

It had been a night of nights of nights, but it had not lived up to the anticipation. Had even been, in a well-we've-finally-gotten-around-to-it way, something of a disappointment.

Not that I would trade it in or take it back. Never.

Someday, when I'm old and retired and have nothing better to do than philosophize, I'm going to sit down for a year and figure out why it's always better in the anticipation than in the consummation.

I sent Frogface flitting around checking the enemy's mood. That was black. They wanted no more fighting after duking it out with elephants.

Stormgard's walls were not heavily patrolled. Most of the male population had marched out in the morning and not made it back. But Frogface reported no great distress around the central citadel, where another Shadowmaster was in residence. In fact, he thought he sensed confidence in the eventual outcome.

The storm marched north. And it was a bitch kitty. I gathered my captains. "We got a mean storm coming. Might make what we're going to try tricky, but we're

going to do it anyway. Be even less expected. Goblin.
One-Eye. Get the dust off your old reliable snooze spell."

They eyed me suspiciously. Goblin muttered, "Here it
comes. Some damnfool reason for not getting any sleep
again tonight."

One-Eye told him, "I'm going to use that spell on him
one of these first days." Louder, "Right, Croaker. What's
up?"

"Us. Up and over those walls and open the gate after
you put the sentries to sleep."

Even Lady was surprised. "You're going to waste all
that work on that ramp?"

"I never intended to use it. I wanted them convinced I
was committed to a certain course."

Mogaba smiled. I suspected he'd figured it out ahead
of time.

"It won't work," Goblin muttered.

I gave him a look. "The men working the trenches at
the city end are armed. I promised them first crack at
getting even. We get the gates open all we have to do is
lean back and watch."

"Won't work. You're forgetting that Shadowmaster in
there. You think you're going to sneak up on him?"

"Yes. Our guardian angel will make sure."

"Shifter? I'd trust him as far as I can throw a pregnant
elephant."

"I say anything about trusting him? He wants us for a
stalking horse for some scheme. He's got to keep us
healthy. Right?"

"Your mind is going, Croaker," One-Eye said. "You
been hanging around Lady too long."

She kept a blank face on. That might not have been a
compliment.

"Mogaba, I'll need a dozen of the Nar. After Goblin
and One-Eye put the sentries to sleep Frogface will climb
the wall with a rope and anchor it. Your boys will go up
and take the barbican from the rear and open the gate."

He nodded. "How soon?"

"Anytime. One-Eye. Send Frogface scouting. I want to know what that Shadowmaster is doing. If he's watching us we won't go."

We moved an hour later. It went like operations go in textbooks. Like it was ordained by the gods. In another hour every one of the freed prisoners, except those we had enrolled in the legions, was inside the city. They reached the citadel and broke in before resistance developed.

They raged through Stormgard, ignoring the rain and thunder and lightning, venting a lot of rage, probably mostly in directions askew.

Me in my Widowmaker suit stalked through the open gates fifteen minutes after the mob rush. Lifetaker rode beside me. The locals cowered away from us, though some seemed to be welcoming their liberators. Halfway to the citadel Lady said, "You even fooled me this time. When you said tonight in Stormgard. . . ."

A gust and ferocious fusillade of rain silenced her. Lightning cut loose in a sudden vicious duel. By the flashes I witnessed the passage of a pair of panthers that I would have missed otherwise. Chills not of the rain crawled my spine. I had seen that bigger one before, in another embattled city, when I was young.

They were headed toward the citadel, too.

I asked, "What are they up to?" My confidence was less than complete. There were no crows out in this storm. I realized I had come to count them my good luck.

"I don't know."

"Better check it." I increased my pace.

There were a lot of dead men around the entrance to the citadel. Most were my laborers. Sounds of fighting still echoed inside. Grinning guards saluted me clumsily. I asked, "Where's the Shadowmaster?"

"I hear she's in the big tower. Up high. Her men are fighting like crazy. But she isn't helping them."

Thunder and lightning went mad for a full minute. Bolts smashed at the city. Had the god of thunders gone crazy? But for the torrential rainfall a hundred fires might have started.

I pitied the legions, out there on guard. Maybe Mogaba would bring them in out of it.

The storm died into an almost normal rain after that last insane fit, with only a few lightweight flashes.

I looked up the one tower that loomed over the rest of the citadel—and, *déjà vu,* in a flash spied a cat shape scaling its face.

"Damn me!"

The thunder had left me unable to hear the horses coming. I looked back. One-Eye, Goblin, and Murgen, still flaunting the Company standard. One-Eye was staring up at the tower. His face was not pleasant to behold.

He was flashing on the same memory. "Forvalaka, Croaker."

"Shifter."

"I know. I'm wondering if it was him last time."

"What're you talking about?" Lady asked.

I said, "Murgen, let's plant that standard up where the world can see it when the sun comes up."

"Right."

We stalked into the citadel, Lady trying to find out what had passed between me and One-Eye. I developed a hearing problem. One-Eye took the lead. We climbed dark stairs where the footing was treacherous because of blood and bodies. There was no more fighting going on above us.

Ominous.

The last fighters of both sides were in a chamber a couple stories from the top. All dead. "Sorcery here," Goblin muttered.

"We go up," One-Eye snapped.

"I know."

Total agreement between them. For once.

I drew my sword. There was no flame in it, and no color to my costume now. Goblin and One-Eye had other things on their minds.

We caught up with Shifter and the Shadowmaster in the parapet of the tower. Shifter had assumed human form. He had the Shadowmaster at bay. It was a tiny thing in black, almost impossible to take seriously as a danger. There was no sign of Shifter's sidekick. I told Goblin, "There's one missing. Keep an eye out."

"Got you." He knew what was going on. He was as serious as ever I've seen him.

Shifter started moving in on the Shadowmaster. It had nowhere to retreat. I gestured Lady to move out to his right. I went left. I'm not sure what One-Eye was doing.

I glanced toward the camp south of the city. The rain had stopped while we were inside the tower. The camp was plainly visible by its own lights. I got the impression they knew something was wrong over here but they were not about to come find out what.

They were nice and close. Put artillery on the wall and life could get miserable for them.

The Shadowmaster backed up against the merlons edging the parapet, apparently able to do nothing. Why were they impotent? This one was who? Stormshadow?

Shifter was close enough to touch, now. One hand darted out and ripped the black robing off the Shadowmaster.

I gawked. I heard Lady's gasp from fifteen feet away.

One-Eye said it. "I'll go to hell. Stormbringer! But she's supposed to be dead."

Stormbringer. Another of the original Ten Who Were Taken. Another one who was supposed to have perished in the Battle at Charm, after murdering the Hanged Man and . . . and Shifter!

Aha! I said to me, said I. Aha! A settlement of scores. Shifter knew all the time. Shifter had been out to get Stormbringer from the start.

And where one mysteriously surviving Taken was in business for herself, might there not be more? Like about three more?

"What the hell? They all still around but the Hanged Man, Limper, and Soulcatcher?" I'd seen those three go down myself.

Lady stood there shaking her head.

Were even those three gone? I had killed Limper myself once, and he had come back. . . .

Chills got me again.

When they were Shadowmasters they were anonymous creeps who had only standard-issue cause to do me grief. But the Taken . . . Some of them had very special and personal cause to hate the Company.

This moment of revelation had turned it into a whole different kind of war.

I have no idea what passed between Shifter and Bringer, but it left the air crackling with electric hatred.

Stormbringer seemed powerless. Why? A few minutes ago she had been bringing in that monster of a storm to whip on us. Shifter was no greater power than she. Unless, somehow, he had come upon that bane of all the Taken, a True Name.

I looked at Lady.

She knew it. She knew all their True Names. She had not lost her knowledge when she had lost her powers.

Power. I had not thought about what I'd had here, almost under my thumb, all this time. What she knew was worth the ransoms of a hundred princes. The secrets locked in her head could enslave or deliver empires.

If you knew she had them.

Some folks knew.

She had a lot more guts than I'd realized, coming out of the Tower and empire with me.

I had to do some rethinking and strategic reorientation. These Shadowmasters, Shifter, the Howler, they all knew what I'd just realized. She was damned lucky she hadn't been snatched already and squeezed dry.

Shifter laid his huge ugly hands on Stormbringer. And only then did she begin to resist. With sudden, startling violence she did something that hurled Shifter all the way across the parapet. He lay there for a moment, eyes glassy.

Bringer made a break.

I came around with a swordstroke I brought in from the moon, right into her belly. It did not mark her but it stopped her in her tracks. Lady hacked at her overhand. She rolled away from the stroke. I whacked her again. But she got up and started heading out again. And her fingers were dancing. Sparks played between them.

Oh, shit.

One-Eye tripped her. Lady and I hacked at her again, without much effect. Then Murgen let her have it with the spearhead on the lance that bore the Company standard.

She howled like one of the damned.

What the hell?

She started moving again. But now Shifter was back. He had taken the form of the forvalaka, the black were-leopard almost impossible to kill or injure. He jumped on Stormbringer and started tearing her apart.

She gave damned near as good as she got. We backed away, stayed away, gave them room.

I don't know what Shifter did or when. Or if he did anything at all. One-Eye might have imagined it all. But sometime during the thing the little black man sidled up and whispered, "He did it, Croaker. It was him that killed Tom-Tom."

That was a long time ago. I had almost no feelings about it anymore. But One-Eye had not forgotten nor forgiven. That was his brother. . . .

"What you going to do?"

"I don't know. Something. I got to do something."

"What'll that do to the rest of us? We won't have an angel anymore."

"Ain't gonna have one anyway, Croaker. He's done got what he wanted right there. Shifter or no Shifter you're on your own soon as he finishes her off."

He was right. And chances were damned good Shifter would stop being Lady's faithful old dog, too. If there was any getting him, this was the time.

The combatants went on for maybe fifteen minutes, shredding each other. I got the impression things were not going as easy as Shifter had hoped. Bringer was putting up a damned good fight.

But he won. Sort of. She stopped resisting. He lay panting, unable to move. She'd locked her limbs around him. He bled from a hundred small wounds. He cursed softly, and I thought I heard him damning someone for helping her, heard him threatening to get someone next.

"You got any special use for him now?" I asked Lady. "I don't know how much you knew. I don't care now. But you better think about what he's going to have on his mind now he don't need you and me for a stalking horse anymore."

She shook her head slowly.

Something slid over the edge of the parapet behind her. Another, smaller forvalaka. I thought we were in big trouble, but Shifter's apprentice made a tactical error. She began to shift forms. She finished just in time to shriek "No!" at One-Eye.

One-Eye had made him a club out of something, and with two quick and heroic swings he bashed Stormbringer and Shapeshifter into complete unconsciousness. They had weakened one another that much.

Shifter's companion flew at him.

Murgen tripped her by tangling her feet with the head of the lance he carried. He cut her. Blood got all over the standard. She screamed like she was trapped in Hell's agony.

I recognized her, then. She had done a lot of yelling the last time I'd seen her, so long ago.

Sometime during the excitement a whole herd of crows had gathered on the merlons, out of the way. They started laughing.

Everybody jumped on the woman before she could do

anything. Goblin did some kind of swift magical bind
that left her unable to do anything but wiggle her eyes.

One-Eye looked at me and said, "You got any suture
with you, Croaker? I got a needle but I don't think I got
enough thread."

What? "Some." I always carried some medical odds
and ends.

"Gimme."

I gave him.

He whacked Shifter and Bringer again. "Just to make
sure they're out. They don't got no special powers when
they're out."

He squatted down and started sewing their mouths
shut. He finished Shifter, said, "Get him stripped.
Whack him if he stirs."

What the hell?

It got gruesome, then more gruesome. "What the hell
you doing?" I demanded.

The crows were having a party.

"Sewing all the holes shut. So the devils don't get out."

"What?" Maybe it made sense to him. It didn't to me.

"Old trick for getting rid of evil witch doctors back
home." When he finished with the orifices he sewed
fingers and toes together. "Put them in a sack with a
hundred pounds of rocks and throw them in the river."

Lady said, "You'll have to burn them. And grind
what's left into powder and scatter the powder on the
wind."

One-Eye looked at her for ten seconds. "You mean I
done all this work for nothing?"

"No. It'll help. You don't want them getting excited
while you're roasting them."

I gave her a startled look. That was not like her. I
turned to Murgen. "You want to get that standard up?"

One-Eye stirred Shifter's apprentice with a toe. "What
about this one? Think I should take care of her, too?"

"She hasn't done anything." I squatted beside her. "I
remember you now, darling. It took me a while because

we didn't see that much of you in Juniper. You weren't very nice to my buddy Marron Shed." I looked at Lady. "What were you figuring on making out of her?"

She did not answer.

"Be that way. We'll talk later." I looked at the apprentice. "Lisa Daela Bowalk. You hear me name your name, the way these others did?" Crows chuckled to one another. "I'm going to give you a break. That you probably don't deserve. Murgen, find some place to lock this one up. We'll turn her loose when we're ready to move out. Goblin, you help One-Eye with whatever he's got to do." I looked at the Company standard, blood-stained once again, flying defiantly again. "You"—pointing at One-Eye—"take care of it right. Unless you want two more of them after us the way Limper was."

He gulped air. "Yeah."

"Lady, I told you. Tonight in Stormgard. Let's go find someplace."

Something was wrong with me. I felt mildly depressed, vaguely let down, once again victim of an anticlimax, of a hollow victory. Why? Two great wickednesses were about to be removed from the face of the earth. Luck had marched with the Company once more. We had added more impossible triumphs to our roll of victories.

We were two hundred miles nearer our destination than we'd had any right to hope. There was no obvious reason to expect much trouble from those troops locked up in that camp south of the city. Their Shadowmaster captain was wounded. The people of Stormgard, for the most part, were accepting us as liberators.

What was to be bothered about?

Chapter Forty:
DEJAGORE (FORMERLY STORMGARD)

Tonight in Stormgard.

Tonight in Stormgard was something, though somehow tainted with that lack of satisfaction that haunted me increasingly. I slept well past dawn. A bugle wakened me. The first thing I saw when I cracked my lids was a big black bastard of a crow eyeballing Lady and me. I threw something at it.

Another bugle call. I stumbled to a window. Then streaked to another. "Lady. Get up. We got trouble."

Trouble snaked out of the southern hills in the form of another enemy army. Mogaba had our boys getting into formation already. Over on the south wall Cletus and his brothers had the artillery harassing the encampment, but their engines could not keep that mob from getting ready for a fight. The people of the city poured from their houses, headed for the walls to watch.

Crows were everywhere.

Lady took a look, snapped, "Let's get dressed," and started helping me with my costume. I helped with hers.

I said of mine, "This thing is starting to smell."

"You may not have to wear it much longer."

"Eh?"

"That bunch coming out of the hills has to be just

292

about everybody they've got left under arms. Break them and the war is over."

"Sure. Except for three Shadowmasters who might not see it that way."

I stepped to the window, shaded my eyes. I thought I could detect a black dot floating among the soldiers. "We don't have anybody on our side now. Maybe I shouldn't have been so hasty with Shifter."

"You did the right thing. He'd fulfilled his agenda. He might even have joined the others against us. He had no grudge against them."

"Did you know who they were?"

"I never suspected. Honest. Not till a day or two ago. Then it seemed too unlikely to mention."

"Let's get at it."

She kissed me, and it was a kiss with oomph behind it. We'd come a long way. . . . She put her helmet on and turned into the grim dark thing called Lifetaker. I did my magic trick and turned into Widowmaker. The scurrying rats who people Stormgard—I guessed we should change the name back when the dust settled—stared at us in fear and awe as we strode through the streets.

Mogaba met us. He'd brought our horses. We mounted up. I asked, "How bad does it look?"

"Can't tell yet. With two battles under our belts and two victories I'd say we're the more tempered force. But there'll be a lot of them and I don't think you have any more tricks up your sleeves."

"You're right about that. This is the last thing I expected. If this Shadowmaster uses his power . . ."

"Don't mention it to the men. They've been warned we might encounter unusual circumstances. They've been told to ignore them and get on with their jobs. You want to use the elephants again?"

"Everything. Every damned thing we've got. This one could be the whole war. Win it, we've got them off Taglios's back and we've opened the road all the way south. They won't have an army left to field."

He grunted. The same went for us.

We got out onto the field. In moments I had messengers flying everywhere, most of them trying to dig my armed laborers out of the city. We were going to need every sword.

Mogaba had sent the cavalry off to scout and harass already. Good man, Mogaba.

The crows seemed to be having a great time watching the show take shape.

The Shadowmaster out there was in no hurry. He got his men out of the hills and into formation despite my cavalry, then had his horsemen chase mine off. Otto and Hagop might have whipped them, but I'd sent instructions not to try. They just came back, leading the enemy, pelting him with arrows from their saddle bows. I wanted them to rest their animals before the main event. We did not have enough remounts to carry a proper cavalry campaign.

I detailed a few men to assemble the former prisoners as they showed and send them off to get in the way of anybody who sallied from the camp. With weapons captured yesterday and during the night more than half were now armed. They were not trained and were not skilled, but they were determined.

I sent word for Cletus and his brothers to move the artillery over where he could give us support and could bombard the encampment gate.

I looked across at the new army. "Mogaba. Any ideas?" At a guess there were fifteen thousand of them. They looked at least as competent as those we'd met at the Ghoja ford. Limited, but not amateurs.

"No."

"Don't look like they're in a hurry to get at it."

"Would you be?"

"Not if I had a Shadowmaster. And had hopes we'd come to them. Anybody else got any ideas?"

Goblin shook his head. One-Eye said, "The Shadowmasters are the key. You take them out or you don't got a chance."

"Teach your grandmother to suck eggs. Messenger. Come here." I had one idea. I sent him to draft one of the Nar and have him head into town, round up a thousand armed prisoners, and go to the city's west gate. When the fighting started he was to hit the camp from behind.

It was something.

Lady said, "One-Eye is right." I think it pained her to have to say that. "And the one to concentrate on is the healthy one. This is a time for illusion." She outlined an idea.

Ten minutes later I ordered the cavalry forward, to nip at the enemy and try to draw their cavalry out, to see what the Shadowmaster would or would not do himself.

I really wished I could count on the prisoners to hold off the men in that camp.

In the half hour it took the Shadowmaster to lose patience with being harassed, One-Eye and Goblin put together the grand illusion of their careers.

They began by re-creating the ghost of the Company they had used in that forest up north, where we captured the bandits, I think both for sentimental reasons and because it was easier to do something they had done before. They brought them out in front of the army, behind me and Lady and the standard. Then I ordered the elephants brought forward and spread them on a broad front, each supported by ten of our best and most bloodthirsty soldiers. It looked like we had a horde of the beasts because their numbers had been tripled by illusion. I assumed the Shadowmaster would see through the illusions. But so what? His men would not, and it was them I wanted to panic. By the time they knew the truth it would be too late.

Cross your fingers, Croaker.

"Ready?" I asked.

"Ready," Lady said.

The cavalry withdrew, and just in time. The Shadowmaster had begun to express his ire. I gripped Lady's hand a moment. We leaned together and whispered those three words that everybody gets embarrassed saying in public. Silly old fart me, I felt weird saying them to an audience of one. Elegies for youth lost, when I could say them to anyone and mean it with all my heart and soul for an hour.

"All right, Murgen. Let's do it." Lady and I raised our flaming swords. The legions began to chant, "Taglios! Taglios!" And my phantom brigade began its advance.

Showmanship. All those elephants would have scared the crap out of me if I'd been over on the other side.

Where the hell did I ever get the idea a general was supposed to lead from the front? Fewer than a thousand of us going to whip up on fifteen thousand of them? . . .

Arrows came to greet us. They did no harm to the illusions. They slid off the real elephants. They bounced off Murgen, Goblin, One-Eye, Lady, and me because we were sheltered by protective spells. Hopefully, our opponents would be unsettled by our invulnerability.

I signalled for an increase in speed. The enemy front began to shudder in anticipation of the impact of all those elephants. Formations started to dissolve.

About time for the Shadowmaster to do something.

I slowed down. The elephants rumbled past, trumpeting, gaining speed, and in a moment all swerving to rush straight at the Shadowmaster.

A hell of an investment just to take out one guy.

He realized the object of the assault while the elephants were still a hundred yards from him. They were going to converge and trample right over him.

He cut loose with every spell he had ready. For ten seconds it seemed like the skies were collapsing and the earth being racked. Elephants and parts of elephants flew around like children's toys.

The whole enemy front was in disarray now. I heard the signals ordering the cavalry forward again, ordering the infantry to advance.

The surviving elephants rolled over the spot where the Shadowmaster floated.

A trunk seized him and tossed him thirty feet into the

air, flailing and tumbling. He fell between massive grey flanks, screamed, flew upward again, possibly under his own power. A flock of arrows darted at him as the soldiers following the elephants used him for target practice. Some got through to him. He kept spinning off spells like a fireworks show, but they seemed purely reflex.

I laughed and closed in. We had the bastard and all his children. My record as a general was going to stay unblemished.

Murgen was there when the Shadowmaster flipped into the sky for the third time. He skewered the sonofabitch with his lance when he came down.

The Shadowmaster screamed. Gods, did he scream. He flailed around like a bug impaled on a needle. His weight carried him down the shaft of the lance till he hung up on the crosspiece that supports the standard.

Murgen struggled to keep the lance upright and get out of the press. Our boys were his worst enemies. Everybody with a bow kept sniping away at the Shadowmaster.

I spurred my mount forward, got beside Murgen and helped him carry our trophy away.

That bastard wasn't spinning off any spells now.

The advancing legions roared their Taglios chant twice as loud.

Otto and Hagop smashed into the confusion in front of Mogaba's legion. There wasn't quite as much confusion as I'd hoped. The enemy soldiers had realized they'd been snookered, though they had not yet gotten into formation again.

They absorbed the elephant charge and the cavalry charge both, taking heavy casualties, but they seemed to have given up the idea of running. Hagop and Otto pulled away before the legions arrived, but the elephants continued to be mixed in with the foe. Just as well. They were beyond control. They had been pricked by enough darts and spearheads and swords to go mad with pain. They no longer cared who they stomped.

I yelled at Murgen, "Let's get this over on that mound where everybody can see that we got him." One of the mounds that dot the plain was about a hundred yards away.

We struggled through the oncoming infantry, climbed the mound, faced the fighting. It took both of us to keep the standard upright, what with all the kicking and screaming and carrying on the Shadowmaster was doing.

It was a good move tactically, carrying him up there. His boys could see they'd lost their big weapon at a time when they were getting their asses kicked already, and mine could see they didn't have to worry about him anymore. They went to work figuring on getting it over with in time for lunch break. Hagop and Otto took the bit in their mouth and circled around the enemy right to get at them from behind.

I cursed them. I did not want them so far away. But the thing was beyond control now.

Strategically, our move was not the best. The boys in the encampment got a whiff of onrushing disaster and decided they'd damned well better do *something*.

Out they came in a mob, their own gimp Shadowmaster floating in front, slipping and sliding around drunkenly but getting off a couple of killer spells that rattled the armed prisoners.

Cletus and his brothers opened fire from the wall and pounded Shadowmaster number two around, cut him a little, and got him so pissed he stopped everything and turned on them with a spell that blew them and all their engines right off the wall. Then he led his mob on out, looking to cause the rest of us just as much grief.

His bunch never did get into a formation, and neither did the prisoners, really, so that turned into a sort of barroom brawl with swords real quick.

The boys at the west gate slid out and hit the camp from behind and got over the wall easily. They went to work on the wounded and camp guards and whoever else got in their way, but their success did not affect the bigger show. The men from the camp just kept after the rest of us.

I had to do something.

"Let's get this thing planted somehow," I told Murgen. I looked out across the chaos before I dismounted. I could not see Lady anywhere. My heart crawled into my throat.

The earth of that mound was soft and moist. Grunting and straining, the two of us were able to force the butt of the lance in deep enough that it would stand by itself, rocking whenever the Shadowmaster had a wriggling, screaming fit.

The attack from the flank made progress against the prisoners. Some of the fainthearted ran for the nearest city gate, joining fellows who had not bothered to come out. Ochiba tried to extend and rotate part of his line to face the onslaught, with limited success. Sindawe's less disciplined outfit had begun to disintegrate in their eagerness to hasten the demise of the enemies they faced. They were unaware of the threat from the right. Only Mogaba had maintained discipline and unit integrity. If I'd had half a brain, I'd have flip-flopped his legion with Ochiba's before we started this. Out where he was now he wasn't much use. Killing off the entire enemy right wing, sure, but not keeping everything else from falling apart.

I had a bad feeling it was going sour.

"I don't know what to do, Murgen."

"I don't think there's anything you *can* do now, Croaker. Except cross your fingers and play it out."

Fireworks spewed over in Ochiba's area. For a while they were so ferocious I thought they might halt the coming collapse there. Goblin and One-Eye were on the job. But the crippled Shadowmaster managed to quiet them down.

What could I throw at him? What could I do? Nothing. I didn't have anything else to send in.

I did not want to watch.

A solitary crow settled onto the writhing Shadow-master impaled on the standard lance. It looked at him, at me, at the fighting, and made a sound like an amused chuckle. Then it began pecking at the Shadowmaster's mask, trying to get at his eyes.

I ignored the bird.

Men began to scurry past. They were from Sindawe's legion, mostly prisoners who had been enrolled the past few days. I yelled at them and cursed them and called them cowards and ordered them to turn around and form up. Mostly, they did.

Hagop and Otto attacked the men facing Ochiba, probably hoping to ease the pressure so he could go ahead and deal with the threat from the camp. But the attack from behind impelled the enemy forward. While Otto and Hagop's bunch were having a great time the men they were butchering cracked Ochiba's line and ran into the armed prisoners from the side.

Ochiba's legion tried to hold, even so, but they looked like they were in bad trouble. Sindawe's men thought they were about to run and decided to beat them in a footrace. Or something. They collapsed.

Mogaba had begun rotating his axis of attack to support Sindawe from the flank. But when he finished there was nothing to support.

In moments his legion was the only island of order in a sea of chaos. The enemy were no more organized than my people were. The thing was a grand mess, the world's largest brawl.

More of my people ran for the city gates. Some just ran. I stood there under the standard, cussing and yelling and waving my sword and shedding a couple of quarts of tears. And, gods help me, some of the fools heard and listened and started trying to form up with the men I'd organized already, facing around, pushing back into it in tight little detachments.

Guts. From the beginning they had told me those Taglians had guts.

More and more, me and Murgen built us a human wall around the standard. More and more, the enemy concentrated on Mogaba, whose legion refused to break. The Shadowmasters' men heaped their dead around him. He did not see us, it seemed. Despite all resistance he moved toward the city.

I guess Murgen and I got three thousand men together before fate decided it was time to take another bite.

A big mob of the enemy rushed us. I assumed my pose, with my sword up, beside the standard. I did not have much show left me. If Goblin and One-Eye were alive at all they were too busy covering their own asses.

It looked like we would drive them off easily. Our line was locked together solidly. They were just a howling mob.

Then the arrow came out of nowhere and hit me square in the chest and knocked me right off my horse.

Chapter Forty-one:
LADY

It wasn't always best to be old and wise in the ways of battlefields, Lady thought. She saw what was coming, clearly, long before anybody else did. Briefly, after Murgen skewered the Shadowmaster, she had hopes it would turn, but the advent of the troops from the encampment caused a shift in momentum that could not be reversed.

Croaker should not have attacked. He should have waited as long as it took, made them come to him, not been so concerned about the Shadowmasters. If he had allowed the new army from the south to come forward and get in the way of the men from the encampment, he could have then hurled his elephants in without risk to his right. But it was too late to weep about might-have-beens. It was time to try rooting out a miracle.

One Shadowmaster was out and the other was crippled. If only she had a tenth, even a hundredth, of the power she had lost. If only she'd had time to nurture and channel the little bit that had begun coming back to her.

If only. If only. All life was if only.

Where was that damned imp of One-Eye's? It could turn this around. There was nobody on the other side to keep it from going through those men like a scythe, at least for long enough.

But Frogface was nowhere to be seen. One-Eye and

Goblin were working as a team, doing their little bit to stem the tide. Frogface was not with them. They seemed too busy to be curious about that.

The imp's absence was too important to be accident or oversight. *Why*? at this critical juncture?

No time. No time to brood about it and slither down through all the shadows and try to find the meaning of the imp's presences and absences, which had been bothering her so long. Only time to realize, with certainty, that the creature had been planted upon One-Eye and wasn't his to command at all.

By whom?

Not the Shadowmasters. The Shadowmasters would have used the imp directly. Not Shifter. He'd had no need. Not the Howler. He would have gotten his revenge.

What else was loose in the world?

A crow flapped past. It cawed in a way that made her think it was laughing.

Croaker and his crows. He had been muttering about crows for a year. And then they had started turning up around him any time anything big happened.

She glanced at the mound where Croaker and Murgen had set the standard. Croaker had a pair of crows perched on his shoulders. A flock circled above him. He made a dramatic figure there in his Widowmaker disguise, with the doombirds wheeling around him, waving his fiery sword, trying to rally his crumbling legions.

While the mind pursued one clatch of enemies the body dealt with another. She wielded her weapons with a dancer's grace and the deadliness of a demigoddess. At first there had been an exhilaration, realizing she was approaching a state she had not achieved in ages, except by the path of its tantric cousin, last night. And then she went over into the perfect calm, the mystic separation of Self and flesh that actually melded into a greater, more illuminated and deadly whole.

There was no fear in that state, nor any other emotion. It was like being in the deepest meditation, where the

Self wandered a field of glimmering insights, yet the flesh performed its deadly tasks with a precision and perfection that left the dead mounded about her and her terrible mount.

The enemy wrestled with one another to stay away from her. Her allies fought to get into the safety of the vacuum surrounding her. Though the right wing had begun to collapse, one stubborn rock formed.

The Self reflected on memories of illuminations won during the night from a pair of bodies, sweating, straining together, on her absolute amazement during and after. Her life had been one of absolute self-control. Yet time and again the flesh had gone beyond any hope of control. At her age.

And she looked at Croaker again, now harried by his enemies.

And the shadow crept into the killing perfection and showed her why she had denied herself for so long.

She thought of loss.

And loss mattered.

Mattering intruded upon the Self, distracting it. It wanted to take control of the flesh, to force things to transpire according to its desires.

She started forcing her way toward Croaker, the knot of men around her moving with her. But the enemy could sense that she was no longer the terrible thing she had been, that she was now vulnerable. They pressed in. One by one, her companions fell.

Then she saw the arrow strike Croaker and drop him at the foot of the standard. She shrieked and spurred her mount over friend and foe alike.

Her pain, and her rage, only carried her into a mass of enemies who attacked from every direction. She cut some, but others dragged her off her rearing steed and harried the beast away. She fought with skill and desperation against poorly trained opponents, but the ineptness of her enemies was not enough. She heaped bodies, but they drove her down to her knees. . . .

A wave of chaos swept over that fight within the battle, men fleeing, men pursuing, and when it passed all that could be seen of her was one arm protruding from a pile of corpses.

Chapter Forty-two:
THAT STUMP

Lying mostly on my back, clinging to the haft of the lance
with my left hand, the standard flapping and the
Shadowmaster flopping overhead. I don't think the
arrow hit anything vital. But the sonofabitch went
through my breastplate and me, too. I think there are a
couple inches sticking out in back.

What the hell happened to the spells protecting me?
I never been hit this bad before.

Coupla crows up with the Shadowmaster. Amusing
themselves, trying to get his eyes. Four or five prowling
around down here, not bothering me. Act like they're
standing guard.

Bunch showed up a while ago, when some enemy
troops came after the standard. Piled all over them till
they went away.

Ah, that damned arrow hurts! Can I get a hand around
there and break the shaft? Pull the sucker back after
the head is gone?

Better not. The shaft might be keeping the bleeding
from getting too bad inside. Seen that happen.

What's going on? Can't move enough to look around.
Hurts too much. All I can see from here is the plain
covered with bodies. Elephants, horses, some men in
white, a lot more not. I think we took a lot of them with
us. I think if the formations had just held up we'd have
kicked their asses.

Can't hear. Total silence. Me? What was that? Silence of stone? Where did I hear that?

Tired. So damned tired. Want to lay down and sleep. Can't. The arrow. Probably be too weak soon, though. Thirsty. But not thirsty like with a belly wound, thank the gods. Never wanted to die with a gut wound. Ha. Never wanted to die.

Keep thinking about sepsis. What if the bowman put garlic or feces on his arrowheads? Blood poisoning. Gangrene. Smell like you're six days dead when you're still breathing. Can't amputate my chest.

Shame and guilt. Brought the Company to this. Didn't want to be the last Captain. Guess none of them did. Shouldn't have fought today. Sure shouldn't have charged. Thought the illusions and elephants would be enough, though. Came close, too.

Know what I should have done, now. Stayed up in the hills where they couldn't see me and let them come to me. Could have sneaked around and used the old Company trickery on them there. Show the standard in one direction and attack from another. But I had to come down here after them.

Feel like a fool lying here in my underwear and a breastplate. Wonder if it did any damn good for Murgen to put that Widowmaker suit on and go try to turn the tide? Mogaba will have his cajones for abandoning the standard.

But I'm here. Still holding the sucker up.

Maybe somebody will come before I pass out. Getting so even somebody from the other side would look good. Damned arrow. Finish it off. Get it over.

Something moving. . . . Just my damned horse. Having lunch. Turning grass into horse hockey. Just another day in the life for him. Go fetch me a bucket of beer, you bastard. You're supposed to be so damned intelligent, why can't you get a dying man a last beer?

How can the world be so damned quiet and bright and cheerful-looking when so many men just died here? Look at that mess. Right down there, fifty dead guys in a patch of wildflowers. Going to smell the stink for forty miles in a couple days.

How come this is taking so long? Am I going to be one of those guys who makes a career out of croaking?

Something out there. Something moving. Way out. Crows circling. . . . My old friend the stump, crossing the plain of the dead on a holiday stroll. Stepping light, though. In a good mood. What was that before? Not yet time? Crows? This critter Death? I been looking my own death in the eye all the way down here?

Carrying something. Yeah, a box. About a foot by a foot by a foot. Remember noticing that before but not paying much attention. Never heard of Death carrying a box. Usually a sword or a scythe.

Whatever the hell it is, it's here to see me. Headed straight for me. Hang in there, Croaker. Maybe there's new hope for the dead.

Geek up on the lance getting all bent out of shape. I don't think he's happy about developments.

Getting closer now. Definitely no walking stump. A people, or something walking on two legs, very short. Funny. Always looked bigger from a distance. Close enough now we ought to be eyeball to eyeball, if I could see any eyes inside that hood. It's like there's nothing in there at all.

Kneeling. Empty hood, yes, inches away. Damned box right beside me.

Voice like a very slight breath of a breeze in spring willows, soft, gentle, and merry. "*Now* it's time, Croaker." Half a titter, half a chuckle. A glance up at the critter skewered on the lance. "And it's time for you too, you old bastard."

Completely different voice. Not just a different tone or a different inflexion, but an entirely different voice.

I guess all the other dead ones being alive set me up for it. I recognized her instantly. Almost as if something inside me had been expecting her. I gasped, "You! That can't be!" I tried to get up. "Soulcatcher!" I don't know

what the hell I thought I was going to do. Run away?
How? Where to?

The pain ripped through me. I sagged.

"Yes, my love. Me. You went away without finishing
it." Laughter that was a young girl's giggle. "I have
waited a long time, Croaker. But she finally exchanged
the magic words with you. Now I avenge myself by
taking from her what is more precious than life itself."
Again the giggle, like she was talking about some simple
practical joke with no malice in it.

I had no strength to argue.

She made a lifting gesture with one gloved hand.
"Come along, my sweet."

I floated up off the ground. A crow landed on my chest
and stared off in the direction I began to move, as though
it were in charge of navigation.

There was a good side. The pain faded.

I did not see the lance and its burden move, but sensed
that it too was in motion. My captor led the way,
floating, too. We moved very fast.

We must have been a sight for anyone watching.

Darkness nibbled around the edge of consciousness. I
fought it, fearing it was the final darkness. I lost.

Chapter Forty-three:
OVERLOOK

Mad laughter rolled out of that high crystal room on top of that tower at Overlook. Somebody was tickled silly about the way things were going up north.

"That's three of them down, half a job done. And the hard half at that. Get the other three and it's all mine."

More insane mirth.

The Shadowmaster gazed out at the brilliant expanse of whiteness. "Is it time to release you from your prison, my beauties of the night? Time to let you run free in the world again? No, no. Not just this moment. Not till this island of safety is invulnerable."

Chapter Forty-four:
GLITTERING STONE

The plain is filled with the silence of stone. Nothing lives there. But in the deep hours of the night shadows flutter among the pillars and perch atop the columns with darkness wrapped about them like cloaks of concealment.

Such nights are not for the unwary stranger. Such nights the silence of stone is sometimes broken by screams. Then the shadows feast, though never do they sate the raging hunger.

For the shadows the hunt is ever poorer. Sometimes months pass before an unwise adventurer stumbles into the place of glittering stone. The hunger worsens with the years and the shadows eye the forbidden lands beyond. But they cannot go, and they cannot starve to death, much as they might wish to die. They cannot die, for they are the undead, bound by the silence of stone.

It is immortality of a sort.

THE BEST IN SCIENCE FICTION

THE BEST IN HORROR

- [ ] 52720-8 ASH WEDNESDAY by Chet Williamson $3.95
- [ ] 52721-6 Canada $4.95

- [ ] 52644-9 FAMILIAR SPIRIT by Lisa Tuttle $3.95
- [ ] 52645-7 Canada $4.95

- [ ] 52586-8 THE KILL RIFF by David J. Schow $4.50
- [ ] 52587-6 Canada $5.50

- [ ] 51557-9 WEBS by Scott Baker $3.95
- [ ] 51558-7 Canada $4.95

- [ ] 52581-7 THE DRACULA TAPE by Fred Saberhagen $3.95
- [ ] 52582-5 Canada $4.95

- [ ] 52104-8 BURNING WATER by Mercedes Lackey $3.95
- [ ] 52105-6 Canada $4.95

- [ ] 51673-7 THE MANSE by Lisa Cantrell $3.95
- [ ] 51674-5 Canada $4.95

- [ ] 52555-8 SILVER SCREAM ed. by David J. Schow $3.95
- [ ] 52556-6 Canada $4.95

- [ ] 51579-6 SINS OF THE FLESH by Don Davis and Jay Davis $4.50
- [ ] 51580-X Canada $5.50

- [ ] 51751-2 BLACK AMBROSIA by Elizabeth Engstrom $3.95
- [ ] 51752-0 Canada $4.95

- [ ] 52505-1 NEXT, AFTER LUCIFER by Daniel Rhodes $3.95
- [ ] 52506-X Canada $4.95

Buy them at your local bookstore or use this handy coupon:
Clip and mail this page with your order.

Publishers Book and Audio Mailing Service
P.O. Box 120159, Staten Island, NY 10312-0004

Please send me the book(s) I have checked above. I am enclosing $_____
(please add $1.25 for the first book, and $.25 for each additional book to
cover postage and handling. Send check or money order only—no CODs.)

Name _____

Address _____

City _____ State/Zip _____

Please allow six weeks for delivery. Prices subject to change without notice.

THE TOR DOUBLES

Two complete short science fiction novels in one volume!